THE HIGH CALLING

BOOKS BY GILBERT MORRIS

THE HOUSE OF WINSLOW SERIES

The Honorable Imposter
The Captive Bride
The Indentured Heart
The Gentle Rebel
The Saintly Buccaneer
The Holy Warrior
The Reluctant Bridegroom
The Last Confederate
The Dixie Widow
The Wounded Yankee
The Union Belle
The Final Adversary
The Crossed Sabres
The Valiant Gunman
The Gallant Outlaw
The Jeweled Spur
The Yukon Queen
The Rough Rider
The Iron Lady

The Silver Star
The Shadow Portrait
The White Hunter
The Flying Cavalier
The Glorious Prodigal
The Amazon Quest
The Golden Angel
The Heavenly Fugitive
The Fiery Ring
The Pilgrim Song
The Beloved Enemy
The Shining Badge
The Royal Handmaid
The Silent Harp
The Virtuous Woman
The Gypsy Moon
The Unlikely Allies
The High Calling

CHENEY DUVALL, M.D.[1]

1. The Stars for a Light
2. Shadow of the Mountains
3. A City Not Forsaken
4. Toward the Sunrising
5. Secret Place of Thunder
6. In the Twilight, in the Evening
7. Island of the Innocent
8. Driven With the Wind

CHENEY AND SHILOH: THE INHERITANCE[1]

1. Where Two Seas Met
2. The Moon by Night
3. There Is a Season

THE SPIRIT OF APPALACHIA[2]

1. Over the Misty Mountains
2. Beyond the Quiet Hills
3. Among the King's Soldiers
4. Beneath the Mockingbird's Wings
5. Around the River's Bend

LIONS OF JUDAH

1. Heart of a Lion
2. No Woman So Fair
3. The Gate of Heaven
4. Till Shiloh Comes
5. By Way of the Wilderness

[1]with Lynn Morris   [2]with Aaron McCarver

GILBERT MORRIS

the HIGH CALLING

BETHANYHOUSE
Minneapolis, Minnesota

Published by Bethany House Publishers
11400 Hampshire Avenue South
Bloomington, Minnesota 55438

Bethany House Publishers is a division of
Baker Publishing Group, Grand Rapids, Michigan.

Printed in the United States of America

Library of Congress Cataloging-in-Publication Data

Morris, Gilbert.
  The high calling / Gilbert Morris.
    p.   cm. — (The House of Winslow ; 1940)
    Summary: "Kat Winslow is volunteering as a missionary. But her calling is interrupted by two scorned suitors. Perhaps her high calling is to one of these men instead?"—Provided by publisher.
    ISBN 0-7642-2825-0 (pbk.)
    1. Winslow family (Fictitious characters)—Fiction. 2. Women missionaries—Fiction. I. Title.

  PS3563.O8742H54   2006
  813'.54—dc22
                                                    2005028046

To Leonard Owen—

The Good Book says, "There is a friend that sticketh closer than a brother." I haven't had too many friends like that, but I'm proud to have you, Len. Thanks for being my friend!

GILBERT MORRIS spent ten years as a pastor before becoming Professor of English at Ouachita Baptist University in Arkansas and earning a Ph.D. at the University of Arkansas. A prolific writer, he has had over 25 scholarly articles and 200 poems published in various periodicals and over the past years has had more than 180 novels published. His family includes three grown children, and he and his wife live in Gulf Shores, Alabama.

CONTENTS

PART FOUR
September–October 1940

THE HOUSE OF WINSLOW

★ ★ ★ ★

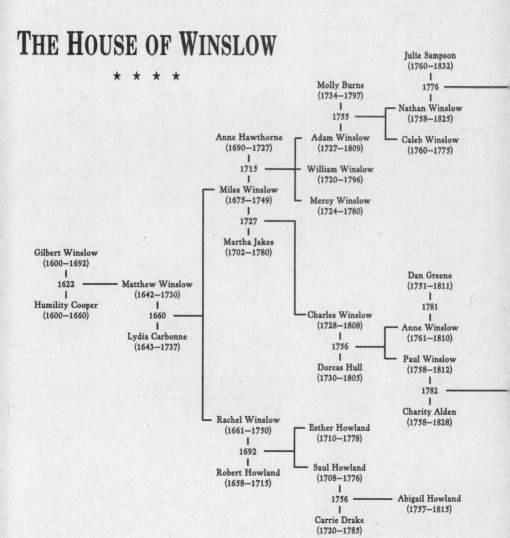

Gilbert Winslow
(1600–1692)
|
1622 ——— Matthew Winslow
(1642–1730)
|
Humility Cooper   1660
(1600–1660) |
Lydia Carbonne
(1643–1737)

Miles Winslow
(1675–1749)
|
1727

Anne Hawthorne
(1690–1727)
|
1715

Martha Jakes
(1702–1780)

Adam Winslow
(1727–1809)
|
1755

William Winslow
(1720–1796)

Mercy Winslow
(1724–1780)

Molly Burns
(1734–1797)

Julie Sampson
(1760–1832)
|
1776 ———

Nathan Winslow
(1758–1825)

Caleb Winslow
(1760–1775)

Charles Winslow
(1728–1808)
|
1756

Dorcas Hull
(1730–1805)

Dan Greene
(1751–1811)
|
1781

Anne Winslow
(1761–1810)

Paul Winslow
(1758–1812)
|
1782 ———

Charity Alden
(1758–1828)

Rachel Winslow
(1661–1750)
|
1692

Robert Howland
(1658–1715)

Esther Howland
(1710–1778)

Saul Howland
(1708–1776)
|
1756 ——— Abigail Howland
(1757–1815)

Carrie Drake
(1720–1785)

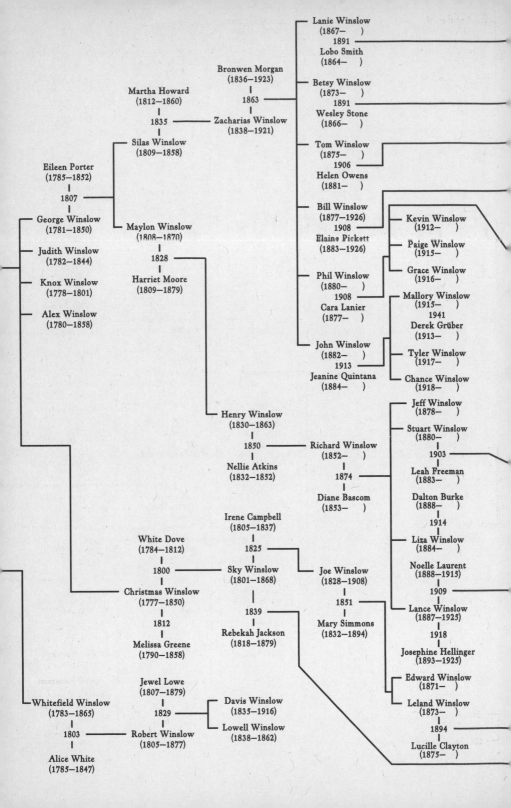

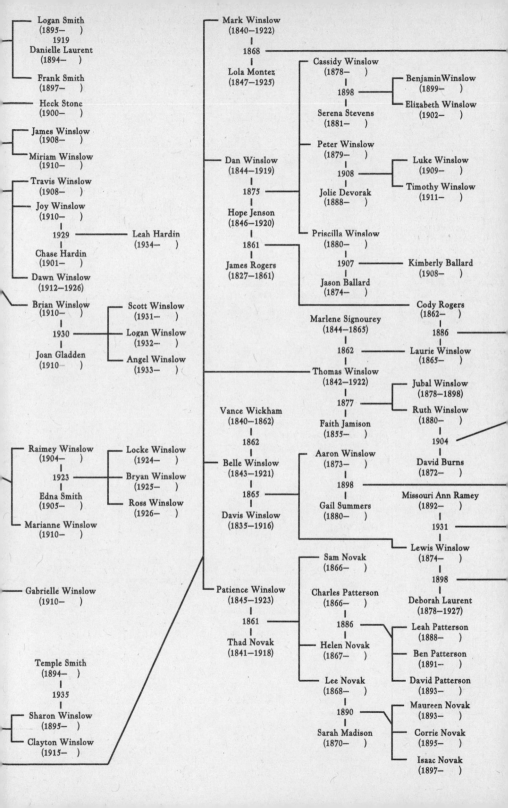

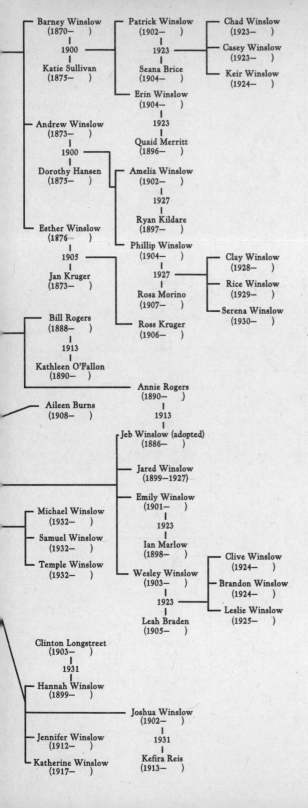

PART ONE

June–August 1937

★ ★ ★

CHAPTER ONE

OUT OF THE PAST

★ ★ ★

"Michael, you stop that!"

Katherine Winslow was deluged with a pail full of soapy bath water that struck her square in the face. She wiped her eyes, then grabbed one of the three youngsters who were laughing and wrestling in the tub. "Michael, you deserve a spanking for that!"

"I ain't Michael. I'm *Temple*."

"I should've known it was you. Now you three rinse yourselves off and don't you dare throw any more water on me!"

Temple grinned at her impudently. "You're gonna have to take a bath anyway before we leave for the fair, ain't ya? I was just helpin'."

Kat bit her lip to keep from laughing. She could not help but think how her five-year-old half brothers were so different in behavior while physically as alike as three peas in a pod. The triplets had been a trial for her father, who was somewhat old to be raising young children. If it had not been for the steadiness of their mother, Missouri Ann, the boys would no doubt have perished.

"Why did you think it was me?" Michael demanded.

"I don't know. I just called out the first name I could think of."

"Well, I'm the oldest, and I ain't mean like Temple is." Michael was indeed the oldest of the three boys, being some ten minutes older than Samuel—who was approximately an hour older than Temple. Michael always maintained that his seniority enabled him to make the decisions. Samuel, the quietest of the three, rarely argued with this, but Temple, a rebel through and through, would argue with a signpost.

Picking up the pail that had just been emptied on her, Kat turned the water on and began rinsing the boys off. When they were all relatively free of soap, she ordered them out of the tub, handing them each a towel. "Now, dry yourselves off." As she watched, a smile tugged at her lips. There was something inherently amusing in three redheaded, blue-eyed boys looking so much alike. She had helped raise them and knew firsthand what a great effort that was.

The bathroom door opened and a large woman with black hair accented by one broad silver streak and snapping black eyes came in. "Aren't these young'uns dressed yet?"

"Aw, Ma, it's Michael's fault! He had so much dirt it took this long to get him clean."

Somehow Missouri Ann Winslow had no trouble telling her three sons apart. "You would blame it on your brother, Temple. Now you hush up and get into these clothes."

Missouri Ann turned to her stepdaughter with a smile. "You look like you got in the tub with 'em, daughter."

"I might as well, Mom." Kat laughed and ran her hand over her sopping hair. She shook her head and smiled ruefully. "It's like giving a bath to three yearlings—only not as easy."

"You go on and get dressed. I'll take care of these rascals."

"All right, but get them out of here so I can take my own bath."

Missouri Ann glanced back at her stepdaughter as she herded the boys out. "You sure aren't going to get much of a vacation here this summer. You'll be itching to go back to that college right soon. You won't be getting much rest, but you've already been a heaven-sent blessing to me!"

"This is such a nice change of pace after studying so hard all year, and you know how I enjoy the boys."

After Missouri Ann had shut the door, Kat quickly drained and refilled the tub. She undressed and climbed in, soaking in the luxurious quiet and thinking of how close she had grown to her stepmother. Her own mother had died when she was ten, and when her father had married Missouri Ann Ramey, many had said the marriage would fail. Lewis was much older than his wife, and she was almost his exact opposite in temperament. She was an outspoken Christian who witnessed to everyone she met and had visions and dreams, which to everyone's surprise, except the family, seemed to come true.

Kat lay down flat in the tub and lifted her legs in the air, toes pointed at the ceiling. She had been looking forward to the Georgia State Fair for weeks and could hardly believe the day had finally arrived. *I hope Hercules wins that blue ribbon tomorrow. He deserves it. He's the most beautiful Black Angus in the state.* She quickly finished her bath. She removed the stopper and watched the water as it swirled in a miniature whirlpool, something that always fascinated her.

She got out and dried off and then made her way to her bedroom. She took her time getting into her pale blue cotton dress she had laid out. It had a scalloped white collar, three-quarter-length sleeves, and a high waist cinched in by a white belt. As she fixed her hair and put on her makeup, her mind was on the fair, which was always the high point of the Winslows' summer. "Lord, I'd appreciate it if you'd let Hercules win that blue ribbon!" she prayed aloud and then grinned at herself in the mirror. She completed her ensemble with a pair of white patent-leather shoes and a cloche hat with the brim turned up.

★ ★ ★

Clint Longstreet, Kat's brother-in-law and the family's farmhand, tugged at the harness on the massive Black Angus steer, but it was like trying to move a mountain. "Come on, you ornery critter!" he muttered between gritted teeth. "Get in this here trailer before I build a fire under you!"

"Why, Clint, I'm surprised! You can't even load a bull onto a trailer."

Clint turned to see Kat, who had come up behind him. He had watched her change from a scrawny tomboy into a tall beauty. She was five-foot-ten, with a mass of tawny hair and large, clear gray-green eyes that dominated her features. Her wide mouth, high cheekbones, and squarish face were strong rather than exceptionally feminine.

"You look good enough to go to church, Kat. Shame to waste that new outfit on nothin' but a state fair."

"I'll wear it to church Sunday. Here, let me get Hercules into that trailer."

Stepping back, Clint watched as Kat stepped up beside the massive steer. The beast tried to lick her face, but she jerked her head away and laughed. "No, you can't do that, Hercules. Now come along, boy. Up into the trailer . . ."

Hercules was as docile as a kitten with Kat, who had raised him from the time he was able to stagger around as a newborn calf. Clint admired Kat tremendously. She was a fine athlete who enjoyed playing softball, basketball, and many other sports—including football. Once she had argued with Clint that she ought to go out for the high school football team, but he had told her father about her plan, and her father had talked her out of that!

She moved easily, and Hercules followed her up into the trailer. She stood with the animal for a moment, one arm around his neck and the other hand getting a thorough licking. "You're going to win that blue ribbon tomorrow. You hear me?" Turning, she came down off the ramp. "He's going to win, Clint."

From where they stood on the porch, Lewis and Missouri Ann Winslow could easily hear her words. Lewis was not a large man and did not look his sixty-three years. His hair, once brown, was now pure silver, but his dark brown eyes were as clear as ever. He had lost his first wife in 1927 and never thought to marry again—but Missouri Ann had burst into his life almost with the violence of a hurricane. Now he put his arm around her and hugged her. "You know, Missouri, I think tomorrow's going to be a hard day for Kat."

"Why would you think that?"

"I don't think it's hit her yet that Hercules is going to be made into steaks. She's made a pet out of him. I told her not to do it, but you know how she is—stubborn as a blue nose mule."

Missouri Ann put her arm around Lewis and held him. She was slightly taller than he and heavier built, but that had never been a problem for either of them. "She'll grieve herself a spell, but I reckon she'll handle it."

"You've done a good job with her, honey."

"Why, she didn't take much raisin'. You know she talks all the time now 'bout finding out God's will for her life. I think that's wonderful."

"That's your doing. She got her Bible training from the right place. Missouri Ann Winslow's Bible College."

She smiled at his teasing. "Well, she's a fine young woman, and God's going to use her."

Lewis's eyes were on his daughter. He thought about what a difference Missouri Ann had made coming into his life when he had almost given up. "You know, I think my favorite verse of Scripture is the one in Proverbs that says, 'Whoso findeth a wife findeth a good thing.'" He leaned over and kissed her, which surprised her. He was affectionate enough in private but usually was somewhat restrained in public.

"Well, I've got a verse that's not in the Good Book but it ought to be—'She that findeth a husband findeth a real good thing.'"

"Come on, wife. Let's load up the kids and get into the car. Maybe I'll win you a Kewpie doll at the shooting gallery."

★ ★ ★

The smell of hot dogs and mustard and fresh brewed cider was in the air as Kat wandered past the booths that offered the food. The air was alive with laughter and shouting as the fun seekers had come to Macon for the Georgia State Fair. Her dad had helped her unload Hercules at the agriculture building, and she now had the rest of the day to enjoy the fair. The livestock judging wouldn't start until tomorrow. As she wandered among the rides, she looked up at the Ferris wheel, remembering the first time her father had taken her on one. She had been terrified by the height and still remembered how he had put his arms around her and held her tightly, promising her she would be okay.

Now as she looked up, a whim swept over her. She had not ridden the Ferris wheel for several years, for she was still not completely free of her fear of large machinery. Nevertheless, she stepped up and paid her fare, and just before the attendant put the bar down, a voice said, "Mind if I share your seat?"

Looking up, Kat saw a short, muscular young man with a sunburned face and a pair of impudent blue eyes, grinning at her. "There are plenty of other seats," she said.

"But none with such a pretty girl on them. Come on, have a heart."

Ordinarily Kat would have refused, but something about the fellow's air pleased her. He had a fresh-looking face and freckles galore. "All right, but you stay on your own side."

"My name's Dave Tompkins."

"That's a nice name," Kat said but did not give her own. The bar snapped in front of them, and the seat swung as they went upward.

"I didn't get your name."

"People just call me Kat."

"Cat? That's your name?"

"A nickname."

Kat hung on to the bar as the Ferris wheel swept into the full cycle. As it rose, she glanced out, enjoying the panorama of the fair. They were higher now than all the other rides, and she heard people laughing and screaming as they were turned upside down and swung in circles. Far off was the agricultural building, where the livestock judging would take place. Farther off were the tree-covered hills, which actually looked soft from this distance.

Dave Tompkins made a valiant effort to get Kat to talk about herself, but when the ride ended, he knew no more about the tall young woman than when he had gotten on. "Better give me your telephone number," he said urgently. "I might need to call you."

"Thank you very much, but I don't think so." Kat laughed at his expression and said, "You'll find some girl to give you her number. Good-bye, Dave."

He seemed a nice enough fellow, but she was not particularly interested in dating at the moment. She left the young man staring after her with disappointment etched on his features and forgot about him almost at once. Kat continued on her circuit of the rides and the games of chance, then happened to pass by two young women who were gazing up at a large poster. Curiosity caused her to pause, and as she looked up at the poster, a grin turned up the corners of her lips.

"He's a dream, ain't he?" The speaker was a rather tall, gangly girl who was wearing a bright red dress that made her sallow skin look terrible. She poked the girl beside her with her elbow and said, "What do you think, Roxy?"

"Well, I'll tell you what I think." She leaned to whisper something in her tall friend's ear, which caused the girl to laugh stridently.

"Me too," she said.

The girl called Roxy was wearing a tight dress that set off her full figure admirably. Her hair was more carefully done than her friend's, but there was a boldness in her dark eyes. "His name's Brodie Lee," she told Kat. "I seen him do his stunt flying yesterday."

"He ain't as pretty as that picture, is he?" the other girl asked.

"Why, yes he is!" Roxy said. "He's better lookin' than Robert Taylor. You know what? I'm gonna see if I can get him to take me out."

"Bet'cha can't!"

"You hide and watch me!" Roxy told her friend with confidence. "Come on. It's almost time for the stunt flying to start. I'll be right there when he gets out of that there airplane!"

★ ★ ★

Brodie Lee's hands moved on the stick, and his feet worked the pedals almost as if he were playing a pipe organ. The biplane flipped upside down, and he shoved the throttle forward. Even though the ground was nothing but a blur under him, he always knew exactly where he was at all times. He watched the ground grow closer and felt the shoulder strap cutting into his shoulders as he skimmed along. Most men would have wondered if the safety belt was going to hold, but Brodie never gave a thought to things like that.

Somehow skimming across the fields upside down with the blades of the propeller dangerously close to the grass filled him with a keen pleasure. He was aware that several things could go wrong that could kill him instantly, but that was something that happened to other fellows—not to Brodie Lee!

His upside-down view of the field revealed telephone wires strung between poles just ahead, and instead of flipping the plane over, he simply went under them.

"That ought to give 'em something to holler about," he proclaimed and laughed loudly. Then he flipped the plane over, banked it sharply, and steered back toward the field, which was lined with spectators. "You got your money's worth that time, I reckon," he said as he brought the plane in for a perfect landing. He got out and leaped to the ground.

His mechanic was striding toward him, his face like a thundercloud.

"Don't say it, Fred!" Brodie started.

"I will too say it! You've got no business goin' under them wires! You're gonna kill your fool self!"

"Not a chance. I was born to be hanged. Better check her out, Fred. She might need a little tunin' up."

Leaving the plane and the unhappy man, Brodie strolled toward the crowd and was soon surrounded by the curious and the admiring. One of them proved to be a reporter with a camera who insisted on taking several pictures while Brodie answered questions.

The questions were familiar enough, and Brodie had answered them many times. As he gave his usual answers, his eyes went over the crowd and stopped when they fell on a well-shaped girl whose dark eyes were fixed on him. She had a slight smile on her lips, and as their eyes met, something seemed to pass between them.

Brodie answered another question and then said, "That's all for now, folks. There'll be another performance tomorrow—same time. I'll do something real special for you. It'd be nice if you'd come back."

The crowd slowly broke up as the dark-eyed girl came forward.

"Could I have your autograph?" she asked.

"You have a piece of paper and a pen?"

"No, but I reckon we can get one someplace."

This was invitation enough for Brodie. He had learned to read young women exceptionally well and grinned broadly. "All right. But first I've gotta go back and check over the plane. What's your name?"

"Roxy Gentry."

"All right, Roxy. Why don't you go powder your nose or

something and meet me back here in, oh, say half an hour."

"I'll be waiting." She turned and walked away, her hips swaying provocatively.

"There's always one at every show," he told himself. "I wonder why that is."

Brodie turned to go, but as he did, he noticed a tall young woman who had been standing off to one side. *Another one*, he thought, *but this one looks even better*. He went over toward her.

"Hello," she greeted. "That was quite a show."

"Thanks. My mechanic thought I was crazy to fly under that wire, but I wanted to give you pretty ladies a good show."

"That was something, all right."

Brodie made one of those instant decisions for which he was famous. He mentally cast Roxy aside and said, "How about you and I go have a bite to eat?"

"We can't do that."

He moved closer to her and saw that her complexion was the smoothest he'd ever seen. A summer darkness shaded it, and there was a freshness about her. "Why not?"

"Roxy will be back."

"Oh, well, she'll find somebody else soon enough." He liked the way this woman's eyes met his directly.

He was surprised when the woman smiled broadly and then shook her head. "You haven't changed, Brodie. Still trading off one woman for another."

He searched his memory frantically, but he could not remember ever meeting this woman. "I wouldn't do a thing like that," he protested weakly.

"Glad to hear you've changed your ways. Now you'd better wait for Roxy."

If anything pleased Brodie Lee, it was a challenge. He saw that this woman was different in every way from Roxy. There was a liveliness about her that he liked instantly. Besides, she was prettier than Roxy. She had class!

"What's your name?"

"You don't remember?"

"I know I ought to. When was it we met?"

At that moment Roxy, who had turned around and seen what was happening, came back at once. "You through with your airplane?" she asked brightly and took his arm in a possessive manner. She glared at the tall young woman and then tugged at him. "Let's go."

"Better hang on to him, Roxy," the tall girl said with a smile. "He's slippery."

"Why would you say a thing like that?" Brodie said. He was desperately trying to remember where he had seen this young woman, but nothing came.

"If you lose him, you can always identify him by his birthmark, Roxy."

"His birthmark!" Roxy glared at her. "Where's that?"

"Oh, it's on his back—just above his waist on the right side. It's shaped like a fish. You can't miss it."

"And how do you know that?" Roxy snapped.

Brodie's jaw had dropped open, and for once in his life he could not think of a single thing to say. Obviously this woman did know that intimate fact about his anatomy!

"You ought to be ashamed to know a thing like that!" Roxy declared. "Come on, Brodie!"

"We're old friends," Kat said. She laughed at Brodie's expression as Roxy hauled him away. "Bye-bye, Brodie," she called. "Good to see you again!"

★ ★ ★

It was late afternoon before Kat made her way toward the agricultural building to check on Hercules. A man stepped in front of her and she stopped abruptly. "Well, it's Mr. Brodie Lee, the famous aviator."

Brodie wore a puzzled look. "Hey, I've been looking all over the fair for you."

"What did you do with Roxy?"

"Never mind her. How did you know about my birthmark? Where did we meet?"

"You can't even remember an old friend who would know a thing like that? You must have a real bad memory."

Kat turned to leave, but Brodie grabbed her arm. "Wait a minute. We've gotta settle this."

"Is this here bozo annoying you, Kat?"

Brodie whirled to see a lanky man dressed in overalls and wearing a white broad-brimmed straw hat. Brodie suddenly let out a yelp. "Clint Longstreet, you son of a gun!" He grabbed the other man by the hand, and Kat stood back and watched the two beat themselves on the shoulders.

"How in the blue-eyed world did you find Kat in all this commotion?"

"Oh, he didn't have any trouble finding me," Kat said. "The trouble is he didn't know me when he found me. By the way, Brodie, how did you and Roxy make out?"

Brodie flushed and shook his head. Clint was amused to note that Brodie looked tremendously embarrassed. Clint had always been fond of the younger man. The two had become fishing and hunting partners after Clint had moved to Georgia with the Winslow family. Despite their ten-year age difference, they had always enjoyed each other's company. "What's wrong with you, Brodie? You act like you just swallowed a cocklebur."

Kat was finding the whole situation vastly amusing. "He's ashamed because I caught him dumping a girl—the same way he dumped me once."

"I never did any such thing!" Brodie protested.

"Yes you did. You just don't remember."

"What are you up to these days, Brodie?" Clint asked.

"I've been doing some crop dusting up in our old stomping grounds. I do some stunt flyin' on the side, which is why I'm down here in Macon for the fair."

"Next time you've got a couple hours to spare, you should drop by the farm. Maybe we can go huntin' or fishin'."

"I'd like that."

"Well, I've got to get back to the hotel and help Hannah with the girls," Clint said. He and Hannah had two girls who were the pride and joy of his life.

As Clint moved away, Brodie said, "I never dumped you, Kat!"

"Yes you did. You were going to take me fishing over at Eleven Point River, but you stood me up."

"Oh, that . . . well, I-I think I got sick or somethin'."

"No," Kat said coolly. "You got Margie Hunt. You left me in the lurch and took *her* instead. I waited for you all day, but you never came."

Brodie shuffled his feet and ran his hand through his thick red hair. "I don't seem to remember that."

"I do. Margie told all of us girls about it. She told *everything* the next day at softball practice."

Brodie was a voluble young man never lacking in words. But Kat's gray-green eyes somehow made him feel tongue-tied. "Well, I was a pretty thoughtless fellow in those days."

"And still are—as Roxy would probably say."

"Will you forget about Roxy!" he declared, throwing his hands wide apart. "Kat, I'm really sorry. I don't even remember that day, but it was the wrong thing to do. I do remember how much fun we had going fishin' and huntin' with Clint and Josh."

"It's all right. I got my feelings hurt, but I was only a freshman, and Margie was a senior—and a cheerleader."

"I wonder what ever happened to her."

"She moved away two years ago with her husband. He's in the army."

"Look," he said. "I'll have to make this up to you. How about I take you up for a flight?"

"No. I'm afraid of heights. Besides, I never let the same man break my heart twice." Her words might have been harsh, but her smile was warm. "Don't worry about it. It's all right."

"Come on, you've got to give me a chance. How about we go out tonight? Just get a meal and talk about old times."

Kat hesitated, then smiled. "All right, Brodie. That would be nice."

★ ★ ★

"I enjoyed the movie," Kat said as Brodie brought the car to a stop in front of the Royal Hotel. "Good night."

"Wait a minute! Don't say good-night yet."

Kat felt his hand on her arm and smiled at him. "I think it's time we call it a night. Surely there couldn't be anything else left to say."

It had indeed been a full night. Brodie had taken her to see the latest Humphrey Bogart film that everyone had been talking about. After the movie, they had driven around in the car Brodie had borrowed from his mechanic and talked about old times. Brodie had apologized several times throughout the evening for not recognizing Kat at first, but he had explained that she had undergone quite a transformation from her younger years.

Brodie, four years older than Kat, had grown up on a farm not far from the Winslows. After graduating from high school, he had left for the oil fields of Oklahoma, which broke the hearts of several young women. He took flying lessons while he worked in the oil industry and eventually became a crop duster. That led to an interest in being a stunt pilot, and before long he was performing all over the States.

He leaned back against the seat. "You know, I've thought so many times about the good times we had—you and Josh and Clint and me."

"Those were good days. I had the worst crush on you that anybody could ever imagine."

"I never knew it."

"Why, it would have been strange if you had. But I got over it. Girls get over things like that."

"You remember the time we went coon huntin', the four of us, and you fell in the river? I had to pull you out."

"Yes. I nearly froze to death. That must have been in the middle of winter."

The two recalled other adventures they'd had along the river, and then Brodie changed the subject. "You've never married, huh?"

"No. Not yet. I'm only twenty, remember?" she teased.

"Ever been engaged?"

"No. Not that either."

"Why is that? I would think you'd have lots of guys interested in you."

Kat thought for a moment. She was always truthful, speaking exactly what she thought. "You were the only one I ever loved."

Her honesty shook Brodie, and he reached out and touched her cheek. "I never knew that."

"Why, I was fourteen with a bad complexion—and you were the star quarterback of the football team. Oh, how I hated all those girls you went with!"

He suddenly reached out and pulled her toward him. She did not resist, but after a brief kiss, she pushed him back. He tried to kiss her again, but she said quickly, "I'm not Roxy. You should know that, Brodie."

He released her at once. "I don't know you. All I can think of is that little girl, that scrawny kid. But she's gone and here you are." He studied her for a moment and then asked, "What are you going to do with yourself? What's your dream?"

"What's yours?"

"I asked you first."

"I want to do whatever God has planned for me."

He suddenly felt uncomfortable. "Well, that's a right good dream."

"What about you, Brodie?"

"Guess I just want to be the best flier in the whole world."

"But that won't last. Things like that have to end. What then?"

He shook his head. "I never think that far ahead."

"I've got to go in." Kat smiled and squeezed his shoulder. "I had a nice time tonight."

"I'll see you tomorrow."

"You'd better find Roxy. You'll have no luck with me."

"Roxy? Not a chance." He got out quickly and walked her to the door. She smiled at him and then went into the hotel without saying more. As Brodie walked back to the car, he was surprised at his own feelings. He had known many women, but he'd never met one like her before. *She sure did grow up nice!*

CHAPTER TWO

STATE FAIR

★ ★ ★

As Kat led Hercules through the wide doors that opened into the arena, she wanted to turn and run. The feeling was so strong she had to grit her teeth and force herself to look at the stands that surrounded the large arena. She had been here twice before but always as a spectator. Now the colors of the crowd made a kaleidoscope before her that seemed to whirl, and she closed her eyes while taking two steps. When she opened them again she had a grip on herself, and she whispered, "Hercules, don't let them bother you. They're just people."

Indeed, they were just people, but there were a great many of them! The arena was full of thousands of faceless people. Kat focused on the section where her family sat—and there they were, all but her sister Jenny, who was away at medical school. Her father, anchoring one end of the row, was waving frantically at her. Two of the triplets sat between him and Missouri Ann, with the third on her lap as she smiled broadly at Kat. Clint and his wife, Hannah, sat on either side of their two children.

Kat's only brother, Joshua, sat with his wife, Kefira. He

let out a yell that Kat could easily identify—the one he always gave when he was hot on the trail of a coon. The sound rose above the crowd and made the judges turn and frown. Kat was glad they would not know which of the contestants had such fervent support.

Around the ring they went, Hercules and Kat being fourth in a line of steers led by their owners. She held her head high and smiled at the crowd, although now that the moment had come, she wasn't sure she had much hope of winning. She had lovingly raised Hercules from the time he was a spindly-legged newborn until now, three years later, he was the epitome of what a Black Angus bull should be. He moved ponderously beside her, muscles waving like water under his black hide. She put her hand on his silky neck and whispered, "Even if we don't win, you're still the best, Herc." She felt the working of the mighty muscles, and Hercules nodded up and down as if he understood what she was saying.

An aide helped the contestants line up, and Kat stood in her place, offering a morsel of apple to Hercules. She glanced up at her family in the stands and then down the line at the judge who had started scrutinizing the animals on her left. Kat looked closely at the three other bulls that came before Hercules, trying to see their faults, but they suddenly seemed to have none.

She studied the face of the judge, a man with sandy hair and a sour expression that looked as though he had just bitten into a lemon. He moved slowly around each animal, running his hand along its back and sides, pulling the mouth open to look at the teeth. Kat had never seen such a thorough judge, and her heart sank. Surely there would be some fault in Hercules that she was too prejudiced to see.

Finally the man stood before her, and Kat met his icy blue eyes. Judges usually smiled and said something encouraging to the contestants concerning their entry, but this man's lips were sealed up tight. Without a word, he scrutinized Hercules, who ignored him totally. Kat held her breath, preparing for a long and thorough examination, but after the judge had circled Hercules once and run his hand along the animal's back, he turned and went on to the next entry.

Kat sighed with disappointment. *He didn't even look closely at him.* She put her hand on Hercules' neck and fed him another slice of apple. "Don't you mind, Herc," she whispered so faintly no one could hear. "He just doesn't know what he's doing." A keen sense of humiliation kept her from looking up at the stands, and although she was not usually given to tears, they rose involuntarily to her eyes. She blinked hard to get rid of them, still keeping her eyes from the stands. All this time and trouble she had gone to, only to be cast aside without a second look! Kat was surprised to realize she was actually angry—so much so that she almost wanted to strangle that cold-eyed judge!

The time seemed to stretch on forever as the judge moved down the line, and Kat noticed that he spent a considerable amount of time with each entry. She stood stiffly, fighting off the tears and wishing she could simply walk away and escape the focus of all the spectators. Finally she looked up and saw a tall man standing alone at the edge of the ring. His eyes were fastened on her. He had a thin, wedge-shaped face that appeared almost aristocratic. His light brown hair was brushed carefully back from his face and had a slight curl in it, she noticed. Then she saw in his expression what she felt was pity. Unable to bear this, she lowered her head and stared down at the ground in front of her.

Finally, after what seemed like an eternity, she was aware that something was happening. Lifting her head cautiously, she turned to her right and saw that the sour-faced judge was walking down the entire line of animals. She straightened and lifted her head and faced him proudly. *He's not going to see how hurt I am!* When he was right in front of her, he turned abruptly, and as he did, a smattering of applause broke out, which Kat could not understand. Then the judge's thin lips turned up at the edges, and he stepped forward.

"You have the finest animal I have ever seen in thirty

years of judging, Miss Winslow."

Kat could not believe her ears, nor did she realize what he was handing to her. She took it almost blindly, then recognized that it was a blue ribbon!

She couldn't stop the tears then, and she felt the judge pat her shoulder and say, "Congratulations. You've done a fine job."

"Thank you," she whispered, blinking back the tears and looking around as the arena filled with applause. She stood quietly while the judge presented the second- and third-place awards but then could wait no longer. She turned and threw her arms around the neck of the huge steer. "Oh, Hercules, you did it!" she cried. "You're the best in the world!"

Then before she knew it, her father was hugging her, followed by Missouri Ann and the rest of her family. Hannah's girls were pulling at her, and a photographer blinded her with a flashbulb.

"You're going to be a pretty sight squalling like that," Clint whispered. But he slipped his arm around her and handed her a handkerchief. "Wipe your face, and we'll make them get a better shot."

Kat wiped her face with the handkerchief, and then she turned and faced the photographer, holding her head high. The photographer waved her family off to one side and took another shot as she beamed into the flash, her hand possessively on Hercules' muscular neck.

★ ★ ★

Kat clutched the blue ribbon in her left hand and led Hercules out of the ring as her family left to go save a table in the cafeteria. "I'll be there in just a few minutes," she called.

As she led the animal into the stall in the cattle building, she heard someone call her name.

"Miss Winslow?"

Kat turned and there stood the tall man with the aristocratic air she had seen in the ring.

"My name is Parker Braden," he said with a British accent. "I wonder if I . . . I'm sorry. I didn't realize you were distressed."

Tears had risen to her eyes as she had led Hercules out of the ring—and now she suddenly realized with horror that they were running down her cheeks. She had a great distaste for women who cried, especially those who cried in public. But somehow the victory after her humiliation had caught her at a bad moment.

"I . . . say, can I do anything?"

"N-no, thank you." Kat groped for a handkerchief but then remembered it was in her purse, which Missouri Ann was keeping for her. The man reached into the breast pocket of his coat and pulled out a handkerchief. "Perhaps this will help."

"Thank you." Kat took the handkerchief, noticing the *B* embroidered in the corner of the fine material. She turned slightly away from the man and wiped her face.

"Please, keep it," he said as she tried to hand it back. "You may need it later." He had a very nice smile, and now that she saw him up close, she was impressed with his appearance. He was wearing a snowy white shirt with a suit that was not of the typical cut, pale gray with a razor pleat in the front of the trousers, and an unusual tie.

"I don't think I'll need it anymore. I don't usually cry in public," she said defensively.

"Well, a victory sometimes does that to us even more than a defeat."

"It does, doesn't it?" she said, wondering how an aristocratic, wealthy man like this would know anything about defeat. She suddenly felt the urge to explain her tears. "It's just that I raised Hercules here from a calf. As a matter of fact, I helped bring him into the world and now—" She suddenly screwed up her face and shook her head. "It just came to me as I was leading him out of the arena . . . that part of my life is over, and I'm afraid he's going to be . . ."

Mr. Braden seemingly grasped all that Kat was saying at

that instant. "I know exactly how you feel," he told her. "When we lose an animal we love it gets to us, doesn't it? Last year I lost a dog that I raised from a pup." He shook his head faintly with wonder in his eyes. "I cried like a baby for a week. I think there'd be something wrong with us if we didn't feel like that."

"Do you really think so?"

"Most certainly! I can't feel very much for people who don't love animals. I suppose that's very prejudiced of me."

Kat had gained control of herself for the moment. "You're not from here—from America—are you, Mr. Braden?"

"No, I'm not. Everyone knows that as soon as I open my mouth, of course." He smiled then and shook his head. "I'm from England. Outside of London, actually. As a matter of fact, I would like to speak with you if you have time."

"With me?" Kat wondered if this was an attempt to pick her up. He didn't look like that sort, but one couldn't tell about foreigners.

"Yes. One reason I'm in this country is to study different breeds of American cattle. My family owns a cattle farm back home. We're interested in acquiring some new breeds." He looked at Hercules and said, "I know practically nothing about the Black Angus, but they are such beautiful animals. I thought you might be willing to tell me a little about the breed."

"Why, I'd be glad to."

"Excellent! Perhaps we could go someplace and celebrate your victory over a spot of tea while you educate me."

"I'm going to meet my family for dinner right now, but I could meet you in the cafeteria later on—say, seven o'clock?"

"That would be fine."

"But I doubt if we can find tea—unless it's iced tea."

"Perhaps some of your American soda pop. I find it fascinating."

"We have plenty of that."

"I'll see you at seven o'clock, then."

Kat made her way out of the stables and found herself wondering what it would be like if a rich stranger like this bought Hercules for a stud. The thought pleased her, for she had never been able to face the thought of her pet being led off to the slaughterhouse. She was not unaware of the facts of life, for she had been around such things all of her life, but she had let herself get too fond of this particular animal and now began to wish fervently that Parker Braden might be persuaded to buy him and give him a good home in far-off England.

★　★　★

Kat carefully applied some new lipstick, pressed her lips together, and then leaned closer to check her reflection in the mirror. She was sitting at her dressing table and suddenly looked down at the diary that lay open before her. The date was June 11, 1937, and her eyes followed the lines she had written the night before.

> . . . and so Parker is coming to have dinner with us tonight. Actually it'll be the third date we've had, not counting the night we went out at the fair. I never met a man I liked so much!

Kat closed the diary and put it into the dressing table drawer. She stared at herself in the mirror and shook her head. "You're acting like a fifteen-year-old on her first date."

She was a little disturbed over the excitement she felt at the evening that was to come. She had gone out with Parker only the previous evening. He had taken her to the nicest restaurant in town, and she had enjoyed his company immensely. She had found herself inviting him to join them for a family meal the following night, and he had agreed at once.

Moving in front of the mirror, Kat studied the new dress she had bought for a special occasion and had never worn. The fitted black bodice was cinched in with a green belt,

38

which gave way to an accordion-pleated dark green taffeta skirt that had wide horizontal stripes of alternating green and black. She slipped on her black suede pumps. *I'm always trying to look shorter,* she thought, *but I don't have to do that with Parker. He must be at least six foot one.*

She turned around, loving the way the skirt flowed outward. She did not typically indulge in expensive clothing. Indeed, this was the most expensive dress she had ever bought, but she was glad she had it. She had thoroughly enjoyed Parker's company the night before and wanted to look nice for him.

She heard a car pull up in front of the house and ran to look out the open window. "Brodie, what are you doing here?" she yelled. He was wearing a light blue shirt open at the neck, blue jeans, and a pair of half boots. A gray Stetson with a low crown completed his costume.

He looked up and grinned. "Come on down, sweetie. I've got a big night planned for us."

"Go away, Brodie. I've got other plans."

He shook his head. "With that limey?"

"Yes, if you must know. He's coming for dinner. Now go away."

"I'm a little hungry myself, you know."

"Well, you can't eat here."

But he simply ignored her and moved toward the house.

"He can't stay for dinner!" Kat said and frowned. "I'll have Dad make that clear to him."

★ ★ ★

"Mom, why in the world did you invite Brodie to supper?" Kat was in the kitchen helping Missouri Ann prepare the meal.

She shrugged her shoulders. "He won't eat much."

"I don't want him here tonight. Why in the world did you let him stay?"

"I've always liked Brodie."

"He could always get around you, Mom."

"I don't know why you'd say that," Missouri Ann said. "Anyway, it's good to see him back in these parts. Now, you be nice to him, you hear?"

Missouri Ann went out toward the porch to call the triplets in to wash up, but she returned immediately. "I think Mr. Braden is here," she told Kat. "I didn't open the door because I thought maybe you should greet him first."

Kat went through the living room, where Brodie was talking to her dad, and opened the front door. "Hi, Parker. Come on in."

"Hello, Katherine. You look lovely tonight."

"Thank you," she said, feeling a bit embarrassed that Brodie had heard the compliment. She introduced Parker to her father and Brodie.

Brodie stood up to shake Parker's hand and then slipped his arm around Kat's waist. "Kat and I grew up together, Parker. But I was a little too old for her, you know. So I left and let her grow up. But we're dating steady now."

"You . . . you stop that kind of talk, Brodie Lee!" She pushed him away and composed herself. "You'll have to ignore Brodie. He's hung around me as long as I can remember. I've tried to discourage him, but he doesn't have any manners, as you can see."

Parker just laughed and said, "I can see you two are old friends."

"Have a seat, Parker," Lewis said. "Kat tells me your family's in cattle farming."

"That's right, Mr. Winslow. We have a few acres of our estate at Benleigh dedicated to livestock. It's one of several enterprises we're involved in."

"Tell me about your livestock. . . ."

★ ★ ★

Parker Braden was enjoying his meal tremendously. The food was excellent, as succulent a roast as he had ever tasted, and the vegetables were quite unusual—fried squash, fried okra, corn on the cob, crunchy cucumbers. And he loved the fresh-baked bread that gave off a heavenly odor and practically melted in his mouth.

He was finding the family delightful. He was enjoying watching the antics of the three identical boys all seated around the end of the table. They were giggling and kicking one another under the table, and at times they seemed to know what the others were thinking without a word passing between them.

He had found Lewis Winslow to be a keen-minded man and had discovered that at one time he'd had a great deal of money but had lost it all in the stock market crash in 1929. Now, however, the man seemed content, as did the rest of the family.

Before dinner, Lewis had shown Parker pictures of all of Lewis's children by his first wife, explaining where they were and how many children they had. Parker found himself liking Lewis Winslow very much. Lewis himself had not mentioned it, but Missouri Ann told him that Lewis had won the Medal of Honor in the Spanish-American War.

As they ate, Lewis related the story of his courtship of Missouri Ann in a humorous way. "You see, Mr. Braden, I was out hunting, and I fell and broke my leg. This woman found me and took me home with her. She set my leg, and as soon as I was able to listen, she told me that God had sent me to be her husband and that we were going to have beautiful children."

Parker laughed outright at this. "What a smashing way to begin a courtship!"

"Oh, there's more to it than that, Mr. Braden," Missouri Ann said quickly. "I knew that God had sent him my way, but Lewis hadn't heard from God about me yet. So it took a while for him to come around, and when he did, I made him come a-courtin' me proper-like, don't you see?"

"A very nice way to get a husband," Parker said with a smile. "Usually it's much more difficult to find the right spouse—man or woman."

Suddenly Missouri turned and looked at Parker intently. "Do you English people believe God does things like that?"

Parker was not taken aback, for Katherine had warned him that her stepmother was very direct. "Some do, I believe."

"Well, *I* believe it," Brodie said. He had made himself part of the family, talking much more than Parker, and now he winked across the table at Kat. "Why, I never even thought of gettin' married myself, because I knew God was gettin' me a bride all ready. Never was interested in another woman. Always knew I'd come back and marry you, Kat."

"You liar!" Kat laughed, unable to help herself. "You dated every girl in school alphabetically and never even looked at me a single time."

"Oh, I was just giving you time to fatten up a little. You were pretty scrawny then, you know. And I knew you'd get rid of your complexion problems later."

"Brodie Lee, you hush up!" Missouri Ann spoke up. "You're makin' fun of the ways of God."

"No I ain't!" he protested.

"Yes you are! What you need is to get saved, Brodie Lee! Washed in the blood and filled with the Holy Ghost!"

"You might be right about that, Mrs. Winslow. I probably will one of these days."

"You don't need to put it off the way things are goin' in the world."

Lewis turned sober at once. "What about this fellow Hitler over in Germany, Mr. Braden?"

"Just Parker will be fine. It's bad news, I'm afraid. He and Mussolini have teamed up together. You can't believe a word that Hitler says. He promises he won't take any more territory, but he's a liar straight out of the pit. He's got to be stopped."

The talk went on about the European situation, which was sounding graver by the day. Finally Parker looked at Lewis and asked, "What do you think America will do if there is a war?"

"It's hard to say. My country's slow to fight. If we're

attacked, we'll fight, of course."

"Hitler would never do that. He's evil, but he has too much sense to attack America—at least not until he's conquered Europe. Then you can look for him to be knocking on your doorstep," Parker said grimly.

Brodie said, "I heard on the radio that he's got the biggest air force in the world."

"That's true, I'm afraid. Germany was forbidden to build military aircraft after the Great War, but Hitler got around it by calling aircraft by other names. He built planes and called them *transports*, but they're actually bombers. German fliers in Spain are now bombing the Loyalists. They call themselves the Condor Legion. They've got the best combat training in the world."

"Did I hear Kat say that your family is in the airplane business?" Brodie asked, his eyes intent.

"Yes, that's right."

"I thought your family was in cattle farming," Lewis said.

"We are, but that's only one of our businesses. My father also owns an aircraft factory," Parker explained. "We don't build the whole aircraft, just parts. But the orders have doubled recently. I think our government has finally realized that there's no way we can avoid this war. Sooner or later those barbaric Huns will be coming over the Channel to invade England."

"Tell me about those fighter planes you're building over there," Brodie said. "I've heard a little about them."

"Listen," Kat interrupted, "if you're going to talk about the war, you men go into the parlor while Mom and I clean up the dishes."

Lewis laughed. "When she speaks like that, we have no choice but to obey. Come to the parlor, men!"

★ ★ ★

Kat was seething inside. "Isn't Brodie *ever* going to leave?" she asked Missouri Ann as she went into the kitchen to get more coffee.

Missouri Ann turned from the sink, a smile on her lips. "Reckon as how I'll have to help you." One of the triplets was tugging on her skirt asking for a drink, and she handed him a glass of water. "You go and take your fellow for a walk, Kat."

"Brodie will want to go with us."

"No he won't. I'll sit on him."

Kat laughed. She knew that when Missouri Ann Winslow said something, it would come to pass. She went back into the parlor, where Brodie was firing questions about airplanes to Parker, who answered them patiently.

"Parker, I'd like to show you one of the new calves," Kat said. "I know you've been curious about what the stock looks like."

"Say, I'll go with you," Brodie said. "I've been aimin' to see that calf myself." He started to rise, but Missouri Ann grabbed him by the back of the collar, pulled him back on the couch, and then plunked down beside him. "You just sit right there, Brodie. I want to hear about this fancy airplane you fly upside down. Tell me all about it."

She turned to wink at Kat, who immediately left the room with Parker by her side.

As they stepped outside, Parker said, "That fellow Lee is a rather persistent chap, isn't he?"

"Oh yes. It's quite surprising, actually. I hadn't seen him for years until he showed up at the fair."

"He's quite a pilot. We need fellows like him in England, or rather, we will if the war keeps escalating."

"Brodie has always liked to do daring things. If there's a war, he'll probably find it."

They walked along under the full moon until they got to the barn. Kat showed him the calf, and Parker got down to examine it, commenting on how sturdy it seemed.

As they left the barn, Kat said, "Let's not go back inside. How would you like to see where we used to go fishing?"

"I'd love to see it."

Kat led him across the field behind the house and through the woods, stopping at the river, which looked silver by the light of the moon. "It was right there," she said. "I was such a tomboy when I was a kid. Before we moved here, we lived right in the heart of New York City, and I used to beg my dad to take me fishing in Central Park. I was always digging for worms in our gardens."

"It's hard for me to imagine you on your knees digging for worms."

"I still love to go fishing. There's nothing quite like fresh fried fish, straight from the river."

The two walked along the river, and Kat said, "Tell me about your family."

"Well, there's just my parents. I'm an only child. I would have had a younger sister, but she died at birth. And then there's Aunt Edith, who lives with us."

Kat sat down on a fallen tree and motioned Parker to sit beside her.

"Aunt Edith exists for one purpose," Parker continued. "She lives to marry me off."

"Why would she do that?"

"She's very strong on family. She wants to keep the title until it passes on down to infinity to the end of the world, I suppose."

"The title? You have a title?"

Parker seemed uncomfortable. "Well, as a matter of fact, there is a title involved. It doesn't mean too much, though."

"So . . . what is it?"

"My father is a baron—Lord Braden. When he dies, I'll have the title."

"I'm terribly impressed. I've never spoken to the son of a baron before."

"It's not that important. It's a pretty lowly title, in fact. I'm just an ordinary manager of an airplane factory who raises cattle on the side. Please don't make a fuss over the title."

"You manage your father's factory? You didn't tell me that."

"Some people get all caught up in jobs and titles. That's why I didn't tell you before. I just wanted you to treat me like a normal person."

Kat tried to pry more out of him, but he resisted, steering the conversation back to her family.

"I rather like your stepmother's way of finding a husband," he said.

"It's a wonderful story, isn't it?"

"It is. I've never heard another quite like it. Do you plan to use the same technique?"

"In a way I do."

Startled, Parker turned and studied her face. It was hard to see her eyes in the moonlight, but he noticed the richness of her expressive, clean-edged lips. He could not help also noticing the lovely turn of her throat and the perfect fit of her dress. The moonlight ran over the curve of her shoulders, and her face was a mirror that changed as her feelings changed. She wasn't smiling, but the the hint of one was tugging at the corners of her mouth.

Parker Braden felt himself stirred by her in a way that startled him. She was tall and shapely, and as young as she was, her eyes mirrored some sort of wisdom. She gazed at him silently, and he knew that a woman's silence could mean many things. He was not sure what it meant in her, but it pulled at him like a mystery. He only knew at that moment that she was a young woman with a great deal of vitality and imagination and beauty.

"And that surprises you," she finally said, "that I'm waiting for God to send me a husband."

"Actually it does. It's a wonderful story about your stepmother and your father, but do you think that sort of thing can happen to anyone?"

"I'm not sure, but I've set my heart on following whatever it is God has for me."

The heavy air of summer moved against Parker with a sweet and winey odor. The silver disk overhead diluted the darkness and suddenly he felt the immensity of the skies, but he ignored it, for he was fascinated by Katherine Winslow. "So you will wait until God brings a man into your life, and then you'll marry him?"

"It's more than that, Parker," she whispered. Her lips were soft and vulnerable as she spoke, and her skin was like alabaster in the pale light that bathed them. "I know that God has something for me to do. I sense that He has a high calling for me, and I intend to find out what it is."

Parker was moved by her speech. "I say, that's a wonderful aspiration." He reached out and took her hand. He raised it to his lips and kissed it but didn't release it. "I've never met a woman like you."

Kat was startled by the gesture, and her face grew warm. "Nobody has ever kissed my hand before."

He smiled. "I kissed the queen's hand once, but yours is much better."

"Wait a minute. Don't work your wiles on me." She pulled her hand back, but they both laughed.

"I'm afraid we should be heading back," he said, rising from the log and pulling Kat to her feet. "I want to hear more about this high calling of yours, but it's getting late. I'll surrender to Mr. Lee tonight. He seems to be set for a long evening. But would you let me come back tomorrow?"

"That would be nice."

"Perhaps we should arrange a secret meeting place. If we don't, I have a feeling that Mr. Brodie Lee will be there waiting for us."

Kat laughed and shook her head, her tawny hair falling free over her shoulders. "Yes, we'll run away and hide from Brodie."

She tilted her chin up in contemplation. "Say," she said, "I have an idea. Are you up for an adventure?"

"Um, yes . . . I guess so."

"I'll talk to Clint in the morning and see if he'll join us. We'll give you a real taste of the United States, Georgia style!"

The two started back toward the house. They were met by Sergeant, the large bluish-gray dog that sniffed them thoroughly as he investigated them. When Kat patted his head, he followed the pair back to the house.

CHAPTER THREE

"NEVER TRUST A LIMEY ON A COON HUNT!"

★　★　★

Lewis leaned across the fence, Parker towering beside him, admiring the herd of black cattle grazing in the field. The sight of the sleek animals always gave Lewis a sense of great satisfaction. He had never forgiven himself for losing everything he had possessed in the stock market, but somehow with the help of Clint Longstreet, he had made this farm into a paying proposition. At times he still marveled at how it had all come about, for he had known nothing about farming when they moved to Georgia. Clint, however, had been a great help, and the family had managed to build up the herd over the past eight years.

"They're such beautiful animals," Parker remarked. "You must be very proud of them."

"I guess I am, but it's really Clint who deserves the credit. And Missouri Ann. She never lost hope." Lewis turned a quizzical glance on the tall Englishman. "You ever thought about getting yourself a wife, Parker?"

"I suppose every man thinks about that."

"But no prospects?"

He laughed, but the sound was not particularly humorous. "Plenty of prospects. There is no shortage of marriageable women in England."

"Or here either, for that matter."

"I thought when I first came here that Brodie Lee had an understanding with Katherine."

"Brodie? Not him! He plays the field. He's a good man, though, and a great pilot from what I hear."

"I saw his show at the exhibition. He could do marvelous things with that airplane of his. But there's nothing going on between him and Katherine?"

"Why, no. She hadn't even seen him for years. He left right after he graduated. Always been footloose."

The conversation soon turned to the conflicts in Europe and the various aircraft that were now being used. "It was terrible about the Hindenburg disaster, wasn't it?" Lewis asked. He referred to the airship that had burst into flames a month ago, killing thirty-six people. It had been coming in for a landing in New Jersey when something had ignited the hydrogen gas as it was settling down toward earth.

"An awful tragedy."

"Do you think the Nazis will use dirigibles in a war?"

"Oh no. They tried that in the Great War," Parker said with a shrug. "They were vulnerable even then. They wouldn't last long now. But Hitler's got plenty up his sleeve besides that. The world seems to be coming apart, doesn't it? There's Stalin killing people by the hundreds, everybody who's in his way. Russia's like a truck that's lost its brakes on a steep incline."

"Hitler's a maniac, all right," Lewis agreed, nodding moodily. "He has the mind of a murderer. The only difference is he has the authority to kill thousands instead of just a few. You're worried about your home, aren't you, Parker?"

"Yes, I'm afraid I am. It's only a matter of time until we're going to look up and see German planes coming at us from France."

"But France wouldn't fight against England."

"No, but she can't stand against Germany. I think Hitler will take her easily. This war will be lightning fast, and it'll be won or lost by air power. The French can't understand that, and our own people are just beginning to."

The two men turned and walked slowly back toward the house. "I hear you've agreed to go on that coon hunt with Clint and Kat tonight," Lewis remarked.

"Yes. It sounds like a bit of fun."

Lewis laughed. "Have you ever hunted foxes? I hear Englishmen do that."

"Oh yes. It's a little different from a coon hunt, though. You're on horseback."

"What do you do with them when you catch them? You don't eat them, do you?"

"No, of course not. As a matter of fact, Oscar Wilde once described a fox hunt as the unspeakable in pursuit of the inedible. Just another of our foolish British habits. We have a lot of them."

"Well, if you like to run through the woods in the middle of the night, a coon hunt will be just the thing for you."

"I'm looking forward to it. It will be most entertaining, I'm sure."

★ ★ ★

"I don't reckon you can hunt in them fancy threads," Clint said with a grin. "You'd better come along with me."

Parker followed Clint into the house and up the stairs. When he turned into one of the bedrooms, Clint said, "I keep some of my old clothes up here. It's handier than havin' them over at my place, even though it's just down the road." He pulled some overalls off a hook, then a garish green-and-red shirt.

"I say, that shirt would frighten a coon to death, wouldn't it?"

"I reckon it's not exactly what you'd wear to meet the queen, but it'll do for tonight." He opened the closet door and pulled out a pair of well-worn work shoes. "You can try these on for fit too."

Clint left the room while Parker tried on the shirt and overalls. He put on the brogans too, which turned out to be just a bit large for him, but he managed to tie them on securely. He stood up and opened the door. "It feels like these overalls are falling off! There's no belt."

"You'll get used to it. I've worn them most of my life. Here, you can wear this cap."

Parker took the billed cap that said *FORD* across the front and snugged it onto his head. "How do I look?"

"Like a limey tryin' to look like an American." Clint grinned. "Let's show the rest of the party how you look."

They filed downstairs, where they found Kat waiting for them. She was wearing well-worn blue jeans, a light blue shirt, and heavy half boots. She laughed aloud at Parker.

"Do I look that ridiculous?"

"Yes, you do, but the raccoons won't notice. Are you sure you want to do this, Parker?"

"Certainly! One should investigate the customs of the aborigines in whatever country one visits."

Clint stared at him. "What did you just say?"

"Never mind, Clint. Let's go get some coons," Kat said.

★ ★ ★

Kat turned to Parker, who was puffing along in the dark woods beside her. He had a scratch on his right cheek and was hanging on to a sapling as they made their way up a steep slope. "Do you want to rest, Parker?"

"No!"

"Don't be so proud. That's the way you men are."

"I hate to be bested by a woman."

"Well, sometime I'll go to England and go with you on a fox hunt. I'll probably fall off the horse and you can feel superior again."

Parker released the sapling and smiled down at Kat. "I

wish you *would* come to England. There's so much there I'd like to show you."

She started to make a witty remark but saw the seriousness on his face. "Why would I go to England?"

"To see me, of course. Maybe to teach us all more about American cattle."

She hesitated. "I'd like that, but I'm sure it would cost a great deal."

"It *is* rather expensive. You'd have to go on a ship. I wouldn't trust one of those airplanes."

Suddenly Kat lifted her head. "Listen, the dogs have treed."

"They've done *what*?"

"They treed a coon."

"How can you possibly tell that?"

"By the way they're barking."

"It's a mystery to me. They still sound the same."

"You have to grow up with the sound to tell the difference. Come on, let's see what they've treed."

The two hurried through the woods and came to where Clint was shining a flashlight up into a tree. "We got one," he said. "We've got to get him down now."

"How does one do that?" Parker asked.

"Well, I could shoot him, but I can't see him. Somebody's got to go up and shake him down."

"I'll do that," Kat said.

"Oh no, let me," Parker offered.

"Not exactly in your line, Parker," Clint said, dubiously scratching his jaw. "Let me do it."

"No, I'll do it," Parker insisted. "I can climb a tree well enough, I think. Besides, I wouldn't know what to do with the scoundrel if one of you were up there shaking him out."

Clint laughed. "All right. Up you go. Knock him out of the tree, and the dogs will hold him until I can put him to sleep."

"I hate this part of it," Kat said. "Let's just let him go."

"No. Missouri Ann said to bring home a coon. She's gonna feed it to Parker tomorrow."

Parker made a face and then leaped up, caught a branch, and pulled himself up. Once he was standing on the first branch, it was much easier. He kept climbing upward, pulling himself along, but he could not see anything that moved. "I can't see him!" he yelled.

"He's up there over on this side," Clint yelled. "I just saw his eyes glow."

Parker climbed up higher and then suddenly saw a form out on one of the branches. "Here he is, but how do I get him out of the tree?"

"Go out on the branch. He'll probably jump when you get closer."

"All right." Holding tightly to an overhead limb, Parker moved out along the branch. The farther he went, the more insecure he felt, as the branch gave slightly under his feet. "I can see him, but I'm not sure he's going to jump."

"Jump up and down on the branch. Get it to bouncing. He'll have to go then," Kat called back.

"All right. I'll try it." Parker held tightly to the branch as he began carefully jumping on it. Suddenly he yelled, "There! He's coming down!"

As Parker scurried back toward the trunk, he heard the dogs yowling, but above their noise he heard Clint shouting something in a panic-stricken voice. "What is it?" Parker yelled as he shinnied down the tree and jumped to the ground. Kat was yelling and circling around Clint, who was rolling wildly around on the ground with the animal.

"What should I do?" Parker yelled.

He got no answer, but suddenly the animal took off running, and Clint rolled up to a sitting position. Kat beamed the flashlight on his face, and Parker was shocked to see Clint's clothing ripped and a bleeding scratch on one side of his face.

"You crazy limey! Don't you know a wildcat from a coon!"

"A wildcat? Was that what it was?"

Clint got to his feet, his face registering disgust. He pulled out a handkerchief and pressed it to his cheek. "Yes, it was a wildcat. Why didn't you tell me?"

Suddenly Kat began laughing. She had a great laugh, and Clint glared at her at first, but then could not help joining her. "Well, I've always said never trust a limey on a coon hunt."

"Let's build a fire and give the dogs a break," Kat said.

"All right," Clint agreed.

"You'd better let me put some antiseptic on that cut," she told Clint. "That wildcat's claws might be infectious."

"All right, but if there's anybody else going up a tree tonight, it'll be me. Not you, Parker."

★   ★   ★

Kat and Parker sat together beside the fire, listening to the distant barking of the dogs. Clint had taken them out on another run. The moon lay far down in the sky, turned butter yellow by the haze in the air. Parker gazed at the tiny crystal spots in the sky while inhaling the sweet smells of the forest.

He was sitting so close he could feel Kat's arm pressed against his and could smell the faint scent of perfume.

"I can't get over the fact that your father is a baron," she said.

He shook his head. "I've told you that really doesn't mean much."

"But it must mean *something*."

"Not really anymore. There was a time when it had some importance, but movie actors are getting titles now just for making a movie! Don't give it another thought."

"But I bet your family is proud of the title."

"Well, Aunt Edith is. I suppose my parents are too. They see some sort of glory in the title passing down from grandfather to father to son."

"But won't it please you when the title is yours?"

"I really don't think about it much. I'm more concerned with the situation in Europe turning into a full-blown war.

When a man goes up against the enemy, it doesn't matter whether he has a title or not. The only question is, can he stand under fire? In the heat of battle, a plumber has as much courage as a baron or a duke, when it comes right down to it."

"Do you live in a castle?"

"Castle! Bless you, no! Who would want to live in one of those things?"

Kat turned to him, her face expressive. "They seem so romantic."

"Not when you're freezing! The only heat comes from enormous fireplaces, but that goes right up the chimneys. And they're moldy and damp. No, the house we live in is no castle. And it's only two hundred years old."

"*Only* two hundred! Why, that's as old as my country!"

"Yes, but things are different in England. It's a nice house, and we've had bathrooms put in. That was a help."

"I'd love to see it."

"It's a bit of a white elephant, really. It costs a fortune to keep it going. That's where most of the profit from the factory goes—to keep the house in decent shape. We should have sold it years ago."

The two sat quietly listening to the dogs, the night's darkness pressing in upon them. Suddenly a falling star made a brilliant white scratch across the ebony skies.

"Did you make a wish?" Parker asked quietly.

"I always do."

"I don't suppose you would tell me what it was."

"No. It wouldn't come true if I did."

They fell silent, watching for more shooting stars.

"I was just thinking," Kat said. "You don't seem like the type of man who will stay single. I think you'll marry someday."

"I suppose so. My family has shoved every suitable girl at me for several years now."

"Suitable? What does that mean?"

Parker shrugged his shoulders. "Money . . . family."

"Is that all?"

"Pretty much. Not very romantic, is it?"

"No, it's not. Have you ever been in love?"

"No. Not ever."

"Me neither. Except with Brodie, of course. But I was awfully young then." Kat got to her feet. "I'm going to look for some more wood. The fire's going down." She laughed as he got to his feet. "You English have such good manners."

"That's one of the few things we have left. England's gone downhill in the past fifty years, but we're still ever so polite!"

The two gathered more dry sticks and tossed them onto the fire, watching the sparks shoot up. They both reached for the same stick and their hands brushed. Giggling, they ended up throwing it onto the fire together.

Parker caught her eyes with his own. Kat's expression seemed to grow alert with some old memory. Her gaze intensified as he reached out and took her by the forearms, and he saw her full lips swell into a smile. He could not know exactly what she was thinking, but he knew what her face was doing to him. Leaning closer, he whispered, "You're a temptation to a man."

Kat did not resist as he drew her into a kiss. As he held her close he felt the quickening of her heartbeat and the pressure of her lips as she responded to his desires. But then she pulled away, and he released her at once.

"I'm sorry. I shouldn't have taken advantage."

"You didn't, Parker. It takes two to kiss." Her breath was coming faster than normal, and she struggled to find the words she wanted. "I-I'm not suitable for you, Parker."

"At the moment," he said quietly, "I don't care."

"We're not made for each other," she said more firmly now.

"You don't really believe that, do you, that people are made for each other?"

"I'm not sure, but I do know one thing."

"What's that?" he asked, already knowing what she would say.

"I believe God has something for me to do—and I don't

think it's being Lady Braden. That's too easy."

"Not as easy as you might think, my dear."

Kat looked at Parker inquisitively. He was foreign to her in a way that was more than a matter of nationality. She sensed that he was deeply troubled, but she also did not want to hurt him, for he seemed to have a basic goodness in him. "It was my fault," she said. "I'm sorry."

"There's no fault to it. When a man and woman come together, sometimes that's exactly what's supposed to happen. I accept your reasoning that God wants you to do something, but you yourself say you don't know what it is."

Kat could not answer, for he had spoken the truth. With some relief she heard the crashing of brush a short distance away and said quickly, "There's Clint coming back."

"Yes. Well, we'll talk about this again."

She shook her head. "There's really nothing to talk about, Parker."

"I think there is," he said quietly, then turned and watched as Clint and the dogs came blundering out of the darkness in a rush.

CHAPTER FOUR

KAT GETS AN OFFER

★ ★ ★

Organ music swelled from the dome-shaped radio with the orange dial, followed by the distant barking of a dog. An excited announcer came on, saying, "Ovaltine presents *Little Orphan Annie!*" Immediately a group of singers began:

Who's that little chatterbox?
The one with pretty auburn locks?
Cute little she
It's Little Orphan Annie!

Missouri looked up with irritation. "You boys turn that radio down. You're going to deafen me."

"Oh, Ma, we've gotta hear *Little Orphan Annie,*" Temple protested. The three boys were gathered around the radio, their faces almost pressed against it. Missouri and Kat could hardly stand the unbearable volume.

"You heard what I said. Turn it down! Come on, Kat, let's go get those peas shelled for supper. I can't stand that program anyway."

The two women left the parlor, and the three boys, with their ears glued to the radio, listened as Little Orphan Annie set out to rescue someone.

"I just don't see why those boys like that program. I can't hardly stand that radio most of the time."

Kat smiled at Missouri. "Well, I've noticed you never miss *Stella Dallas*, Mom."

Missouri glanced sharply at Kat, then roughly pulled the sack of peas and plumped it down on the kitchen table in front of her. "I don't care anything about that either."

The daily drama had been taking the country by storm with its syrupy story line and music. The announcer always reminded listeners they were about to hear "the true-to-life story of mother love and sacrifice in which Stella Dallas saw her own beloved daughter, Laurel, marry into wealth and society and, realizing the difference in their taste and worlds, went out of Laurel's life."

Actually, Missouri Ann read no novels, had never been to a theater in her life, and was secretly ashamed of herself for listening to such "a mess," as she called the soap operas. Lewis had never let her forget that he had come in upon her once when she was listening to the show and crying over the plight of Stella and her daughter. Now she pulled out a bunch of snap peas, ran her finger along one, and let the peas drum into a bowl. "That old radio oughta be thrown out anyhow. There's nothin' on it worth listening to."

"Oh, I don't know," Kat said as she took a seat and grabbed a handful of peapods. "I think that new program is funny. You know—Edgar Bergen and Charlie McCarthy."

Missouri Ann shook her head in disgust. "Imagine! Listenin' to a dummy talk on the radio! What's this country coming to?"

The two women made good progress on the peas as Kat told Missouri about an unusual duck she had seen on the river the day before. After a time, Missouri noticed that Kat had fallen silent. She looked up and said, "What ails you, girl? You look plumb down in the mouth."

"Oh, nothing."

"I know better'n that. I reckon you're thinkin' about that English fella. Have you had any more calls from him?"

Parker had left several days earlier to go look at other

cattle in Texas. "He called yesterday and he said he'd probably call again today."

"I don't know what you two talk about—him bein' from
across the water and all."

"He's very easy to talk to, Mom."

"Well, he sure has been persistent."

Kat smiled briefly. "Yes, he has."

"You're not serious about him, are you?"

Kat's troubled look grew more pronounced. She slowly
shelled a peapod and then looked up, meeting Missouri
Ann's eyes. "I like him a lot, but I could never marry him—
even if he asked." She shelled another pod and then shook
her head, adding, "Which he won't."

"Why not?"

"Because of his family. They're nobility. They would
never accept me."

Missouri Ann shot her an indignant look. "Wouldn't
accept you, my foot! They'd be lucky to have a girl like you
in their family!"

"It's different over there. There are dukes and barons—
and the family line means a lot."

"Well, I can't see how the Winslow family wouldn't be
good enough for 'em! As a matter of fact, if you remember
your family history, Gilbert Winslow came over from
England in the first place."

"That was a long time ago. Things are different now."

Missouri continued to say what she thought about anyone who would look down upon Katherine Winslow and
finally shook her head. "You know I've spent plenty of time
on my knees asking God what He wants you to do."

"Have you got an answer yet?" Kat trusted Missouri
Ann's prayers more than she did her own. She was well
aware, as was all the family, that this woman was closer to
God than anyone else they knew.

"I don't have anything pinned down yet, but God won't
let himself be pinned down. I know one thing. He's got
something for you to do."

"You know," Kat said, "I've been thinking maybe I

should get a nursing degree. As you know, I've just been taking general courses in college up to now, but what if God called me to go to Africa and do medical work? That would be something, wouldn't it?"

"Do you think God might be calling you to that?"

"No, not specifically."

"Well," Missouri said firmly, "a body can't just call himself to be a missionary. We had a preacher that talked about missionaries going to the heathen. He always said, 'Some got called and sent—and some just up and went.' And those that just up and went," she pronounced firmly, "got themselves into a mess! No, daughter, I reckon you'll just have to keep on waiting."

"I'm afraid of taking a wrong path. If I—" Kat broke off and looked up at the ceiling. Missouri Ann did the same, and Kat exclaimed, "That's an airplane!"

"It sure is! And it sounds like it's gonna fly right in the front door!"

The two women jumped up and ran out the front door, nearly stumbling over the triplets, who had preceded them. They all stood in the yard looking up.

A bright red biplane was twisting and gyrating in the air in a most alarming fashion. Then it straightened out and headed directly for the house.

"He's gonna land right on us!" Missouri cried out in alarm. "You boys run to the porch!"

"It's all right, Ma. It's Brodie," Kat called out. She laughed as Brodie turned the plane sideways and waved at her. She waved back and saw him turn the plane upside down and then pull it into a wide loop.

"That crazy fool's gonna kill himself!" Missouri cried.

But Brodie pulled the plane out of the loop and landed it expertly on the field behind the house. The two women and three boys scurried to the back of the house to make sure he was okay. He climbed out before the propeller had even stopped turning.

The boys ran to meet him, climbing all over him and begging him to take them up in the plane. Brodie was laughing and teasing them, but he told them, "Your ma wouldn't let you do that until you're at least a year older." He put the boys down and pulled his helmet off. "Hello, sweetheart. You surprised to see me?"

"I'm never surprised to see you, Brodie," Kat said, smiling broadly. This man brought such life and vitality with him—as if an aura of excitement surrounded him. He was the most vital person she knew, and when he took her hand, she let him kiss her on the cheek.

"You taste good," he said. "But I hope you've got something to eat. I'm starved."

"Come on in the house," Missouri Ann said. "I reckon we can scrape up something. You boys leave Brodie alone now." She hauled the three boys off into the house, and when the screen door slammed, Kat asked, "What are you doing here?"

"I've come to see my best girl." He came toward her, obviously intending to embrace her. She tried to dodge, but he was too fast. He grabbed her around the waist and spun her in a circle, her feet clear off the ground. Kat was squealing and protesting, and then he set her down and kissed her firmly. "After I get something to eat, I wanna take you for a ride."

"I'm not going up with you in that thing!"

"Yes you are. You need to live a little, Kat. But first I need something to eat."

★　★　★

Kat had put on blue jeans after Brodie had warned her solemnly it would be immodest climbing into an open airplane in a skirt. "You might shock my sensibility. You know how sensitive I am."

"I know all about that," she said with a laugh. He gave her a helmet and helped her strap it on. "Now, you get in there, young lady, and I'll show you somethin' you've never seen before."

"Brodie, I told you I don't want you doing any tricks. None of your acrobatics. You promise?"

"Well, if that's what you want, but I do wanna show you what the world looks like from up there."

With some trepidation, Kat climbed into the front seat. Brodie tightened her safety belt and put his hand on her shoulder. "Now, you just sit right there."

"I think I'm making a big mistake."

"No you're not." He climbed into the back seat. "Here we go now."

Kat sat tensely in the airplane. She had never been in any sort of plane before, and everything about it seemed uncomfortably flimsy. As the engine revved up, the roar of it almost deafened her. The plane started forward, bumping over the ground, and Kat kept her teeth tightly clenched. Suddenly the nose tilted up, and the ground seemed to drop, as if the plane were still and the earth were moving away. Breathless, she felt a moment of panic.

"Hang on, sweetheart," Brodie shouted, "we're gonna grab a piece of sky!"

The plane continued to climb and soon banked to one side. "There's your farm," Brodie said. "How does it look from up here?"

"Look! You can see the river from here!" she shouted back over the wind.

Brodie banked steeply to the other side. "Look right down there," he yelled. "That's where we saw the bear that time when we were kids. You remember?"

"Yes. Clint shot it and it's a rug in his house now."

High above the landscape she knew so well on the ground, the new sights delighted her. At her request, Brodie slowed the plane down until it scarcely seemed to move. She saw where the old church house had stood until it burned down, leaving only the chimney still pointing up to the sky. She traced the roads and the cars as they made their way toward town.

Finally they passed over Summerdale, the small town not far from the farm. It all looked like a living map. "Look," she said. "I can see the men playing checkers in the town square." The group of old men gathered there every day to chew tobacco and play checkers and tell lies about their younger days.

"Let's give 'em a thrill," Brodie yelled and, without waiting, plunged the plane into a steep dive. Kat braced her feet and begged him to stop, but they headed right toward the town square. One of the men jumped up and knocked the table away, and the others scattered like quail.

"Brodie!" she screamed, and at the last moment he pulled the plane up. He was laughing with delight, and she tried to shame him, but instead she began laughing with him. "They'll hang you for this."

"No they won't. I just wanted to give 'em somethin' to talk about. I'm gonna fly along the river now."

★ ★ ★

"Oh, that was such fun, Brodie!" Kat exclaimed as he helped her out of the plane.

He pulled off his helmet and ran his fingers through his red hair, which shone brilliantly in the sunlight. Squinting against the brightness, he laughed. "Were you scared?"

"Not after the first few minutes."

"Come on, let's go to town and I'll buy you a chocolate milk shake. Then we'll try to stir up some excitement."

"I really need to get back to the house."

"No you don't. You need to entertain me. Come on. Let's ask Clint if we can take his truck."

Kat protested but soon found herself seated beside Brodie headed for town, thinking about the old days when she'd been infatuated with this man. *I've got to be careful,* she thought. *I can't let that happen again. He wouldn't be a good husband for a woman who is looking for God's will.*

★ ★ ★

"Why, Parker," Missouri Ann said as she opened the screen door. "Come on in."

"I should have called before I came."

"No need of that. Come on back to the kitchen."

"Is Kat home?"

"No, she went to town with Brodie. She's gone plumb crazy over that flying machine of his."

"I didn't know she was interested in flying."

She motioned Parker to a seat at the kitchen table and then pulled a pie out of the upper compartment of the wood stove. "This is fresh peach pie. You eat that in England?"

"Something like it."

"Well, see if this suits your likin'." Missouri Ann picked up the coffeepot that always remained on the stove, even in the hottest part of summer. "Would you like some coffee?"

"Why yes, thank you. That'll be fine." Parker tasted the pie and exclaimed, "My, this is wonderful!"

"Well, it's middlin', I reckon." Pouring them both a cup of coffee, Missouri Ann sat down and picked up the conversation. "Brodie came by about a week ago, and he took Kat up in that plane. It would scare me to death, but she enjoyed it. He's been here every day since. They've been flyin' all over the county. He wants to teach her how to fly, but I told her pa to set his foot down about that. It's not natural for a woman to be doin' a thing like that."

Parker laughed. "I don't know about that. One of the most famous fliers ever was Amelia Earhart." His face sobered. "I met her once. She's a fine lady."

"They haven't heard from her since she disappeared out there over the ocean, have they?"

"No, I think everyone's pretty much given up hope."

"What do you reckon happened?"

"It's pretty dangerous flying over the ocean. If you go down, your chances of surviving or ever being found are pretty small. But that won't stop people from flying."

Parker ate the pie and lingered over his coffee, thinking about how different this simple kitchen was from the one where the meals were prepared in his own home. This large room was probably the most used room in the house, as the family tended to gather there while Missouri Ann or Kat cooked. A black wood stove dominated one end, and a rectangular table with cane-bottom chairs anchored the center. The walls were covered with pictures chosen by Missouri, and some of the drawings done by the triplets decorated one area. A calendar with a large picture of an angel guarding two children about to fall into a creek was prominent, and he saw that each day was neatly crossed off.

He thought about the ornate kitchens that were operated by servants in his own home. The family never gathered there, and Parker felt a sudden twinge, for there was a hominess about the Winslow house that appealed to him greatly.

"What all have you been doin' since you've been gone?" Missouri Ann asked.

"I've been looking over cattle down in Texas." He shook his head. "Texas is so big. Anywhere you go you can see for miles—farther than anyplace I've ever been. And it's so dry—the rivers are nothing but dust right now." Parker continued to tell about his travels, and finally he fell silent.

"I reckon Brodie and Kat will be back pretty soon," Missouri Ann said.

"Is he serious about her, Mrs. Winslow?"

"First of all, I don't feel comfortable being called Mrs. Winslow. Why don't you just call me Missouri Ann? And to answer your question, I don't think he is. Of course, Brodie is a lot of fun. He was raised in these parts. His family didn't amount to much, but Brodie's different. He's got lots of ambition. I reckon it's pointed in the wrong direction, though."

"Aviation is a good profession for some." Parker shrugged. "He's skilled at what he does."

Missouri Ann understood why Parker was asking for her opinion of the relationship between Kat and Brodie. She hesitated, then said, "I don't think Kat's really interested in Brodie. He's a Sunday man. Not much good for everyday work. Women like him, though. They've always chased after him, even when he was just a yonker."

She took a sip of her coffee and looked at Parker with a grin. "I ask most everybody I meet how they stand with the Lord, and I can't make any exceptions, even if you are a baron."

Parker smiled. "I've been wondering when I would get your sermon. I felt a little sad because you didn't preach to me as Kat says you do to everyone."

"Well, I always like to know where a body stands."

"I've always believed in God," he said simply. "And I remember going to what you would call a revival when I was just ten years old. It was an outdoor meeting that I went to with a friend of mine, and the minister preached like no one I'd ever heard before. All of our ministers are such scholarly men, and as a boy I was very bored by their sermons. But this man had something special about him. I didn't know what it was. It was as though he were speaking directly to me."

Missouri Ann leaned forward and nodded. "He had the Spirit of God. That's what he had. What happened?"

"He preached about the death of Jesus, and I found myself crying. As I think back on it, it might have been pretty embarrassing for a lad of my age, but I didn't care. He finally asked everyone who wanted to follow Jesus to come forward, and I did. There were only three of us, and he prayed with each one of us. I'll never forget it, Missouri. It's just as clear in my mind as if it happened today. Since then I've tried to follow the Lord and be obedient to Him."

"Well, that's mighty good, Parker. I'm pleased to hear you're a man of God."

Parker stared into his coffee cup as if he expected to find some answer there. When he looked up there was a troubled light in his eyes. "I'm afraid there's going to be a war in my country. I think most men of vision see that. All of us will be called upon to fight." He hesitated and twisted the cup around nervously. "I may be called on to kill men. I don't know if I can do it. I don't know if I *should* do it."

Missouri Ann suddenly felt a great affection for this fine young man. He was different from the men who grew up in this area, refined as he was in his speech and manners, and there was a goodness and firmness and honesty in him that she appreciated. "A man has got to do what God tells him to, and a man that won't fight for his folks is no man at all. No Christian enjoys having to shoot other people, but it's happened in our own country and in yours too, I reckon."

Missouri Ann got up and brought back her worn black Bible. She began to read to him, moving from the Old Testament to the New, barely glancing at the words. It was as if she had memorized the entire book! Parker had never met an individual who knew the Bible as this woman did.

"I reckon as how you can be sure of one thing," she said. "Whatever happens, I'll be praying for you, young man."

"That's good of you, Missouri. I need it." He rose then, saying, "Is your husband around? I'd like to ask him some more questions about his livestock."

"No, I'm afraid he's not. He should be back in a couple hours."

"I'll come back later, then."

"That'll be fine. Come back anytime."

She walked out to the car with Parker and watched as he drove off, then shook her head. "That's one fine gentleman. His country is headed right into trouble and he knows it, but he's trustin' the Lord." She turned back toward the house and spoke to the chickens that had gathered there. "Get out of the way, you fool chickens! Get back in your pen where you belong!"

★　★　★

When Kat entered the house with Brodie a while later, Missouri Ann noticed that her daughter was flushed and excited. She was laughing, and words tumbled out of her as she told her stepmother about their latest flight.

Missouri Ann shook her head. "I wish to goodness you'd stop goin' up in that contraption. You better be careful with my girl here, Brodie."

"You can believe I am careful, Missouri Ann."

"Parker stopped by while you were gone," Missouri told Kat. "He was sorry to miss you."

"Is he coming back?" Kat asked quickly.

"Yes. He's coming back later this afternoon to talk to your dad."

Brodie shifted his weight. "I wish that Englishman would go home. He's trying to steal my girl."

"No he's not," Kat said. "He's looking for cattle. And besides, I'm not your girl."

Brodie made a face, squeezing his eyes together. "But you will be before long. I ain't educated like he is, but I reckon I know about men. He don't look at you like a man interested in Black Angus cattle."

"Oh, don't be foolish, Brodie!"

"I'm not foolish. I guess I know when a man is interested in a woman. I'll see you later." He turned and left the room abruptly.

"Brodie's workin' up a bad case on you, daughter. I hope you're not encouraging him."

"Oh no, we're just having a good time."

"That's not the impression I get from him."

Kat stared at Missouri and then changed the subject. "I need to go change clothes. I got some oil on me. We were working on the engine."

She went upstairs to her room, changed her clothes, and then sat down to read her Bible. She found she could not concentrate, though, for thoughts of Parker Braden kept coming back to her. She was disturbed that she was thinking of him so much of the time. She began to pray, but again her thoughts were jumbled, and she found herself thinking back to Parker's embrace. She had been kissed before, but something about this man was different.

Frustrated with her lack of concentration, she went over to the window and surveyed the farm. She noticed that

Clint was mending a fence, so she went outside to help, hopeful that the physical labor would clear her mind.

★ ★ ★

When Kat came back to the house, she noticed Parker's car in the driveway and smiled. She went inside and found him talking with her father in the parlor.

He got up at once and greeted her. "I've missed you," he said with a smile.

"I've missed you too."

"Big news, Kat," Lewis said. "Parker's going to buy the beginnings of a herd from us."

"What about Hercules? Are you going to buy him, Parker?"

"Oh yes. And you don't have to worry about his being made into beef steaks. He'll be a stud."

Her eyes danced, and she hugged him. "Oh, that's wonderful! I've been so worried about him."

"Well, you don't have to worry anymore. He'll have an easy life." Quickly he added, "Why don't you and I go out to the pasture and we can talk about which of the cows I need to take back with me. Then perhaps you'd like to go into town with me afterward."

"That would be wonderful! Just let me go wash my hands. I'll be right back."

Lewis watched his daughter leave and shook his head. "I'm glad you're buying that bull. She loves him like he was a cat or dog or something."

"I'm glad for her. She's very sentimental, isn't she?"

"About animals she is." Lewis grinned. "If she loves a husband like she loves that steer, she ought to have a good marriage."

★ ★ ★

Kat and Parker were lingering over their meal at the Colonial Grill—Summerdale's fanciest restaurant—when the waitress came over and refilled their coffee cups. "Will there be anything else?"

"No. I think we're fine," Parker said. He waited until she left and then leaned across the table toward Kat. "I'll miss American cooking when I get home."

"Isn't English cooking good?"

"I don't think it's as good as yours. The cooks just put everything together and let it simmer. It's not seasoned like yours. I may have to change their minds."

Kat basked in the warmth and security of his smile. She had been pleased beyond words at the news that Hercules was going to lead a long and happy life, and she had been excited to talk with Parker about which of the cows to take with him. She knew them all by name, as well as their every flaw and virtue.

Parker interrupted her thoughts. "I've got something to ask you, Katherine."

"I've been curious about why you always call me Katherine. Everyone else calls me Kat."

"You don't mind, do you? I think Katherine is such a beautiful name."

"Actually, I like it," she said. "Especially the way you say it. What did you want to ask me?"

"I'd like you to make the trip with me to take the cattle back to England."

Kat stared at him. "Why, I can't do that!"

"I don't see why not. You've got some time before your fall classes start." He leaned forward and put his hand over hers. "I'd also like you to meet my family. And it would be helpful to have you with the animals to get them settled, you know." He laughed and shook his head. "I'm being devious. I really want to be with you. It would be a nice trip. The ship wouldn't be fancy at all—just a cattle ship—but we could have fun and have lots of time together. You've never been on a ship like that, have you?"

"Oh no—never!"

"It's so relaxing. The world feels far away, and we could talk. I could find out all about what you did as a little girl, and you could pry into my boyhood secrets."

Kat was stunned by the enormity of his offer. She had never entertained any such idea. He was looking at her with an expression that told her how much he wanted her to come. She tried to think of reasons to refuse, but before she had time to answer, she heard footsteps and turned to see Brodie advancing toward their table. His hat was pushed back, and his face was flushed. *He's been drinking*, Kat thought, angry that he had spoiled the pleasure of the moment.

"Well, limey, I see you brought my girl to town for me."

"Brodie, go away," Kat snapped. She had discovered that Brodie did not often drink, but he had a reputation for making trouble and becoming aggressive when he did.

Brodie ignored her and stood glaring down at the Englishman. "I reckon you think you can come over here and take our women anytime you take a notion."

"I had no such thought," Parker said quietly.

"You and your fancy talk and fancy clothes! I don't care what you say—you ain't takin' my girl!"

"I don't think this is the place to discuss it," Parker said. He was aware that everyone in the place had turned to watch them. "Perhaps we could talk somewhere else."

"Right here's good enough for me."

Kat was alarmed, and she tried to interrupt Brodie, but he persisted.

"I'm afraid I'll have to ask you to leave," Parker said quietly. "Your behavior is not that of a gentleman."

"I'll *gentleman* you!" Brodie yelled. He grabbed Parker by the jacket and hauled him to his feet. He swung wildly and Parker blocked the blow, but Brodie was an accomplished fighter. Even drunk, he had the skills developed over years of fighting. His next swipe caught Parker high on the temple, and Parker went down into his chair, dragging the tablecloth with him.

He jumped back up and tried to protect himself, but Brodie waded in swinging.

Kat could not believe what was happening, and she cried for help. The manager of the restaurant was already running toward them, and a couple of men dining nearby had jumped up to grab Brodie and subdue him.

"Brodie, you stop at once!" Kat cried out. "Are you crazy?"

Brodie struggled to shake the men off who were holding him tight, but then he blinked his eyes and quieted when he saw the blood running down the Englishman's face. "I-I'm sorry . . . I don't know what got into me."

"Get out of here! Go away!" Kat cried, her face pale and her lips trembling. "I'm ashamed of you, Brodie Lee. Now leave!"

The manager intervened, "You're not going anywhere, young man. We've called the police and they'll be here any minute."

Brodie gave Kat an anguished look and allowed himself to be led to the foyer to wait for the police.

Kat went to Parker at once. "I'm so sorry, Parker. He was drunk."

"Yes. I noticed that." His mouth was bruised and his eyebrow was bleeding.

"Come on. We'll have to go clean you up."

"It's not that bad," he protested as he straightened up the table and chairs and apologized to the other guests, feeling mortified more than injured.

After paying for their dinner and making more apologies to the restaurant manager, they went outside to speak to the police, who wanted to know if they wished to press charges. Parker merely suggested that they lock him up overnight to let him sober up, figuring that a night in jail and a stiff fine for disturbing the peace might be enough to teach Brodie a lesson.

"I'm sorry about all this," Kat said as they walked to Parker's car. "Brodie's not like that except when he's drinking. And he doesn't do that often. He's had a hard life."

Parker pulled a handkerchief from his pocket and held it over his eyebrow. "Actually," he said slowly, "I don't blame him. He's in love with you, Katherine."

"No he isn't."

"I think he is," Parker said as he started the car.

She tried to ignore his statement. "When we get home, I'll put something on that cut."

The two said little on the way to the house, but when he stopped the car Parker said, "I won't go in. This isn't a bad cut, and I'd rather not have to explain to your parents."

"I understand. It was such a good evening until Brodie came."

Parker got out of the car and walked around to open her door. When she got out, he said, "I hope you'll think about making the trip to England with me."

She had forgotten about the trip in the confusion. Now she still didn't know how to answer him. "I'll . . . I'll pray about it, Parker."

He grinned ruefully. "Well, there's no way a man can argue with that. I'll pray about it too. I think it would be a wonderful thing for us."

She saw him lean toward her, and she took his light kiss. He smiled and said good night, then got into the car and drove off.

Kat went into the house and found the boys already in bed, but her father and Missouri Ann were waiting for her.

"Did you work things out with Parker?" Lewis asked. "About the cattle, I mean?"

"He wants me to go to England with him, Dad, to help with the cattle."

Lewis shot a quick glance at Missouri Ann. "Are you going to do it?"

"I don't know. I need to think about it and pray about it."

"Would you like to be Lady Braden someday?" her father asked.

Kat stared at her parents. "No. The title would mean nothing to me." She turned and hurried upstairs.

"She's troubled about this, Missouri."

"Yes, she is. I'm thinkin' she's in love with that Englishman."

"I hope not. I would hate to have my daughter living so far away."

"She wants to do God's will, Lewis," she said. "We'll have to pray that she finds it."

CHAPTER FIVE

YELLOW LIGHT, RED LIGHT

★ ★ ★

The story on the front page of the newspaper fascinated Kat—as it did almost everyone in the western world. For weeks now she had been reading of the scandal concerning the former king of England, who had romanced and finally married an American divorcée. Last December, for the first time in English history a king had stepped down from the throne "for the sake of the woman I love," as the article quoted.

As she read the story curiously, Kat wondered what Parker thought of all this and decided to ask him. He had been persistent in his pleas for her to return to England with him, and she had been in agony over her indecision.

Tossing the newspaper down, she rose to go check on the bread she was baking. Her parents and the boys had left for the day, so the house was unusually quiet. As she turned to go down the hall toward the kitchen, however, she heard a car pulling up in the driveway, and she went to the door. It was Brodie. Her lips tightened and she greeted him coolly.

"Hello, Kat. Can I come in?"

"I suppose so." She reluctantly opened the door.

He followed her into the kitchen. Bending over the stove, she tested the bread with a broom straw. Seeing it was still not done, she closed the door and turned to find Brodie twisting his hat in his hands.

He blurted out, "Hey, Kat, I came to say I'm sorry—you know, for what happened the other night."

"You should be."

"Well, I really am. It was the first time I'd had a drink in six months. I don't know what got into me."

"You shouldn't drink, Brodie. It makes you into something you're not."

"I know that. I won't do it again."

"You'll have to apologize to Parker."

"Sure," he said quickly and stood a little straighter. "I'll do that as soon as I find him. But I didn't want you to be mad at me."

"I *am* upset with you. The story is all over town, and everywhere else in the county, for that matter."

Brodie gnawed his lower lip, looking subdued, and despite her anger, she felt compassion for him. She knew all about his abusive stepfather and how he'd been forced to leave home to get away from him. Kat sighed and said, "Sit down, Brodie."

"Sure. Could I have some coffee?"

Kat poured him a cup, then poured one for herself. She sat down, and he began to speak easily, as if to put the incident behind him. "Maybe we could go out tonight," he finally said, hope in his eyes.

"Not tonight, Brodie."

His face fell, and he got to his feet. "I'm real sorry," he said. "You won't see that side of me again."

He looked so woebegone—almost the same way the triplets looked when they had gotten into trouble—that her heart melted. "It's all right, Brodie. I'm not angry anymore."

"You're not? Good! Do you want to go up in the plane with me?"

"Maybe tomorrow. I need to cook supper for tonight."

"All right. How 'bout if I land out back in the field about eight o'clock in the morning?"

"All right. You'd better go now. I've got a lot to do."

She sighed as Brodie left. "He'd be such a good man if he could just settle down," she said to herself, shaking her head.

★ ★ ★

When Parker answered the knock on his door at the Summerdale Motel the next day, he was surprised to see Brodie Lee standing there.

"Hello, Parker. Can I talk to you?"

"Of course," he said, opening the door wide. "What's on your mind?"

Brodie stepped in and stood uncertainly in the middle of the room, but then found the courage to speak. "Well, I made a sap out of myself at the restaurant the other night. I just came by to . . . to tell you I'm really sorry. You should have shot me."

Parker laughed. "It wasn't that bad."

"Yes it was. I should have known better than to get drunk. I think I've had enough of that to last me a lifetime." He put his hand out and gave Parker a twisted grin. "I'm sorry."

"It's all right, Brodie." Parker took his hand and felt the power of his grip.

Brodie heaved a sigh of relief. "I'm just one of the roughs, but I do care for Kat."

"She tells me she had quite a crush on you when she was younger."

"I guess so. She was just a kid when I left town, but she's not now."

The two men stood silently weighing each other, and finally Brodie said, "I know you've got everything—money, manners, a title—but I'm not giving up."

"That's fair enough, Brodie."

Parker stared at the closed door after showing Brodie out and felt a strange sense of camaraderie with the young man. *He's got some good in him, poor chap. He hasn't always had it easy.*

★ ★ ★

At the same time Brodie was making his apologies to Parker, Kat was at the church helping organize an outing for the youth group. The pastor, Luke Maxwell, was new in town. He was a tall, lanky man with sharp features and a quick sense of humor. He had come to appreciate Kat's help with the young people as well as with the choir, since she had a beautiful singing voice. He stood chatting with her after the others had left.

"Could I talk with you, Pastor Maxwell?"

"Why, of course. Would you like to come into my office?"

"No. This is all right." They were in the sanctuary, and Kat was nervously twisting her hands together, something Maxwell had never seen her do. Maxwell was a bachelor and had thought several times of asking her out. He had refrained, however, fearing that dating a church member could lead to trouble. "Let's at least sit down," he said. "I'm tired."

Kat sat down beside him in the front pew and glanced anxiously around the sanctuary.

When she didn't immediately tell him what she wanted to talk about, he said, "You've been a godsend to me, Kat."

She nodded.

"You'll be going back to college before long, won't you?"

"I . . . well, yes, I will. But I'm thinking about changing my coursework and studying nursing."

"Excellent idea! There's always a need for good nurses."

Kat looked down at the floor for a moment. When she finally turned to face the pastor, he saw that her eyes were troubled.

"How do you know for sure what God's will is?" she asked.

Maxwell rolled his eyes upward and laughed shortly. "I wish I had a specific answer to that. I've struggled enough in my own life trying to make decisions."

"Have you really? Preachers have that problem too?"

"This one does." He smiled wryly. "I've always envied people who talk of hearing specific messages from God."

"My stepmother's like that. She seems to have a direct line to heaven, but I'm not so fortunate."

"Neither am I. Most of us aren't, Kat. Most of us stumble along trying to please God, trying to find out what His will is. I'd hate for you to know about the times I misread God's will."

She laughed. "Well, I can see I've come to the wrong person to get a specific answer."

Maxwell grinned at her. "In my counseling, I very rarely give people a direct word about which way to take their life. That's a very dangerous thing."

"I suppose it is. But I do need to find out what God wants with me. You see, ever since I was saved, I've always felt that God had a specific work for me to do. Every time we have a visiting missionary, I expect God to tell me, 'Go to Brazil or go to China.' But then the missionary leaves, and I still don't know. It's very frustrating."

Maxwell had already learned quite a bit about some of the members of his church. He and Lewis Winslow were becoming friends, and the two had talked about their families. So Maxwell was not ignorant of the concerns of this young woman who sat beside him. He had also heard about the fight between Brodie and Parker in the restaurant. Cautiously he said, "I think it's very hard for young people to decide what to do with their lives."

"Don't you have any advice at all for me?"

Maxwell was touched at the longing in Kat's voice. She was a strong woman with a beautiful spirit. She had a way of speaking that ran like slow-measured music through his mind, and his thought was, *Whoever gets this woman will have won a prize.* Aloud he said, "I can only tell you my own personal method. But I warn you, it's not foolproof."

"I'd like to hear it."

"When I feel that God wants me to do something and I have not the vaguest idea which path to take, I just choose one with the best judgment I can muster up. And I go down that path until I get a yellow light. You know how it is in traffic. When that yellow light comes on, it means Beware. Something's wrong here. You're going to have to stop."

"And then what?"

"I keep going until I get a red light. Until something tells me very clearly this is wrong. That's when I just throw it all up and go find another way. Not much help, is it?" he asked ruefully.

"It's something at least. Would you pray for me, Pastor Maxwell?"

"I do that already, Kat. I've talked with Missouri Ann. She loves you very much, and she's told me how you feel. That God has a call on your life. Of course God has a call on every life, but yours may be something special."

"I've always thought so, and now I've come to a place where I have to make a decision."

"Well, let's pray first, and then you choose a path and keep going down it, until you see a yellow light."

★ ★ ★

Late one Thursday night, Parker and Kat were sitting outside on the swing. The boys were in bed, and Lewis and Missouri Ann were inside listening to *Fibber McGee and Molly* on the radio.

Parker had been telling Kat about his plans for his trip back to England, and finally he said, "I don't want to press you, Katherine, but time is growing short."

As she turned to face him her nearness set off a shock within Parker. He watched as she stopped smiling. He noticed every slight change of expression, the small comings and goings that reflected her uncertainty, and her spirit brushed against him in a way that no woman's ever had. Her face finally settled into an almost desperate expression, which moved him deeply. Leaning over, he put his arm around her. "I don't want to be a burden to you. I know you're troubled about which direction to take. But I think, in a way, you're worried about finding God's will."

"Yes, I am, Parker. Terribly worried."

"This might be a way to find out, mightn't it?"

"Find out what, Parker?"

He did not answer for a moment, then tried to smile, but found it quite an effort.

"Find out what, Parker?" she asked again.

"You could find out . . . if . . . if I'm a man you might be happy with for the rest of your life."

His voice was summer soft, but his eyes were fixed steadily on hers. As his arm tightened around her, she fumbled for an answer.

"But Parker . . . th-that's impossible!"

"Why is it impossible?"

"Because . . . well, for one thing, your family would never accept me."

"They'll have to if I marry you. You can win over anyone if you put your mind to it, Katherine."

He saw the hint of her will and pride in the corners of her lips and eyes. The fragrance of her clothes and the faint perfume she was wearing came powerfully to him, and he felt the warmth of her personality even as he waited. Her soft fragrance slid through the armor of his self-sufficiency, and he knew that he loved this woman as he could never love another. "Please, Katherine, come with me on this trip. You could help with the cattle and meet my family."

When she did not speak, he added, "Going to England wouldn't mean a final commitment. It would just be an opportunity to spend a lot of time together. And God might speak to you about His plan for your life."

Kat felt she had come to a fork in the road. She must choose one path or the other. She remembered Pastor

Maxwell's discussion about the yellow light and red light. At the moment, nothing would have been easier than to have simply whispered yes, but somehow she did not feel that freedom to speak. She knew Parker was waiting for her answer, and she desperately wished that God would speak clearly and tell her what to say. "You'll have to give me a little time," she finally murmured.

Parker was disappointed, and it showed in his face. "There isn't much time left, Katherine, but I'll wait." His arm was still around her shoulders, and he whispered, "I love you very much. This kind of love that I feel for you comes very rarely, and I know I will never feel it for any other woman."

His words stirred Kat, but something still held her back. She longed to put her arms around him and let him hold her, but she could not. She got up slowly, and he rose to stand beside her. "I-I'll have to think about it."

"All right, my dear," he said. Regret tinged his voice, but he did not urge her further, and she was grateful for his thoughtfulness. She stood irresolutely and then turned and went into the house.

Parker did not move. Disappointment flowed through him, and he wanted to go after her, but he resisted. He simply pulled himself together and slowly followed her inside, putting on a neutral face to meet Lewis and Missouri.

CHAPTER SIX

"FOR THE REST OF OUR LIVES"

★ ★ ★

When Brodie asked Kat to come along on a crop-dusting run, she at first refused. Ever since Parker had asked her to marry him, her mind had been in a state of confusion, and she had little inclination for such adventures. But Brodie had continued to pressure her, and finally she had agreed.

The sun was coming up in the east, sending its pale, fresh light across the small airstrip just outside of town. It flashed against the windowpanes, cutting long, sharp shadows against the dust of the runway and brightening it to a velvet gray carpet.

"I've always liked this time of the day," Brodie said as the two walked toward the plane. "We've got a whole fresh new day ahead of us."

It had been quite dark when they had left the house, with the stars glimmering in the sky, but as they had driven to the field, the black eastern horizon had cracked apart and now long waves of light were rolling out.

"Be chilly for an hour," Brodie said as they approached the plane. "But it's a good time of the day." He helped Kat clamber up into the front seat. She sat there watching the rising flood of clear, brilliant sunshine bathe the earth. As Brodie prepared the plane, she did enjoy the morning's freshness. By the time he crawled into the back cockpit, the coolness was already starting to dissipate, and she knew it would soon be as hot as it had been all July. The engine coughed, and the propeller gave a spasmodic jerk, then a series of staccato explosions, and the muffled roar of the engine broke the stillness of the morning air.

Kat felt a touch on her shoulder and turned quickly. Brodie was standing up in his seat leaning over the cowling, grinning at her. "Maybe when we get up," he shouted, "we'll fly off to Hawaii. I could hold you prisoner there."

Despite the problems that were weighing her down, Brodie could still make her laugh. "Be sure you take me where there's plenty to eat," she shouted back.

Laughing, Brodie settled back into the rear seat and fastened his belt. He put his hands on the throttle and the plane began to move. Kat found herself looking forward to the experience this time. She had often watched the crop dusters, marveling at how they maneuvered their biplanes into position, and now she took a deep breath as the plane left the earth and soared into the sky. She felt the plane bank and the engine pick up momentum, and soon they were skimming over the earth. The land below was divided into fields, making it look almost like a bedspread—squares of green crops and yellow crops broken up with newly plowed black dirt.

"Here we go. That field right there."

Kat looked ahead as the plane dipped. She felt her body lift up out of her seat and the straps cut into her shoulders as the plane dropped. Her heart gave a lurch as Brodie dove toward the earth, but at the last instant he pulled the nose up and they were skimming across a field, the wheels nearly touching the plants. Looking back, she saw a white cloud of insecticide following the plane.

Brodie grinned and waved at her, and she waved back. When she turned back to face forward, her heart gave another lurch, for there directly in front of them was a towering grove of trees. She almost screamed, but at the last instant Brodie pulled the plane up into a steep climb. This time the wheels *did* brush the tops of the trees. She heard the branches scraping along the bottom of the plane, and the propeller even clipped the tip of one of the trees.

Kat made a grab for the sides of the cockpit as the plane lurched violently to the right. She knew without the shoulder strap she might have fallen out, but then the plane straightened up, and she saw the field with the white cloud slowly settling over it. Once again Brodie took the plane down to plant-top level and sailed across the field, releasing the insecticide.

Back and forth across the field Brodie went, and finally he pulled it up and shouted, "That takes care of that one. We'll have to go back pretty soon and refill the hopper, but we've got a little left."

All morning long they moved from field to field, landing frequently to pick up more chemicals. It was hard work, Kat discovered. She had always assumed the job was easy. But as the sun rose higher into the sky and the heat waves shimmered off the field, it became tedious.

She was also shocked at how dangerous the work was. More than once at the end of a field, Brodie was met by banks of rising trees. At the end of one field, there were two groups with a gap no more than ten feet wide. He had simply turned the plane sideways and flown through. When they leveled off again, Kat found a branch stuck in the windshield and gasped at how close they had come to destruction.

She knew it must be difficult for Brodie to keep his full attention on the obstacles. Sometimes telephone wires stretched across their path, and once he simply skimmed under one, making her hold her breath. By noon, she was more than ready to call it quits.

Crawling out of the plane, she said, "That'll be about enough for me, Brodie. It's a bit too hair-raising."

"It's a might touchy, for a fact," he said with a shrug. "Most people think dustin' crops is exciting and sort of glamorous, but mostly it's just plumb dangerous. A friend of mine clipped a wire with his wheels two months ago. Flipped the plane over and it all landed right on top of him. It could happen anytime if you don't keep your mind on your business." He saw the lines of fatigue on Kat's face and said, "I'll take you back to the house."

They got into his car, and as they pulled onto the road, Kat said, "Brodie, this is dangerous. I wish you wouldn't do it. You could get killed."

"Why, people fall on banana peels goin' to church and break their necks. This job is okay if you keep your mind on what you're doin'."

She shook her head, knowing she couldn't really talk him out of it. *The man was born without any nerves*, she thought to herself.

Brodie kept her entertained as they drove. Finally when they reached town, he said, "How 'bout we go get a chocolate milk shake?"

"That sounds good."

The two of them went into the drugstore and were greeted by Otis Hines, the pharmacist. He and Brodie had grown up together, and he waited on them himself. "I'll make you a shake so thick it'll practically stand up without a glass."

Otis's promise was good, and the two had to spoon the mixture out until it melted down a bit.

"What are you going to do with yourself when you're a little older, Brodie? You're not going to dust crops all your life."

"To tell you the truth, this was my last day of crop dusting."

"Really? What are you going to do now?"

"I got me a new job. I'm gonna start flyin' the mail. I decided maybe it's time to settle down a bit, get a good steady job. Probably gets pretty boring, though."

"How come you didn't tell me until today?"

"Aw, you know how I am. Impulsive, you might say. I only decided a couple days ago, and I leave tomorrow."

Kat remembered a feature story she had read recently about the dangers of flying the mail. The death statistics were not favorable for the men who flew the lonely flights through all kinds of weather and over the highest mountains. "I wish you had a safer line of work. I don't think there's anything really safe about flying."

"Bother you if I went up the flue, huh?"

"Of course it would!"

"Well, that's good news." He reached over and took her hand, giving her that infectious grin of his. "You go on and become a nurse like you're talkin' about. Then I'll pile myself up and get hurt real bad. You can nurse me back to health and fall in love with me. Nurses always fall in love with me. They just can't help themselves."

Kat laughed and slapped him playfully on the shoulder. "If I didn't like you, Brodie Lee, I'd give you a piece of my mind!"

Brodie put his finger up in the air and pronounced seriously: " 'Dr. Brodie Lee's guaranteed peace of mind for women with problems. We never close.' That's the sign I'm gonna hang up."

They finished their milk shakes and left the store, still snickering over their silly conversation. Halfway home, Brodie pulled off the road and said, "My feets' burnin' off. Let's go dip 'em in this here creek."

Kat had no objections. They found a shady spot underneath some towering hickory trees and were soon dabbling their feet in the water. It was not cold but was still refreshing.

"We could move on down a ways where it's private and do a little skinny-dipping," he said with a straight face.

"I don't think so."

"I didn't think you would." He shook his head regretfully. "I remember once when you happened along when your brother and I were skinny-dipping. As soon as you figured out we didn't have a stitch on, you ran off. You've always been too modest for your own good."

She laughed. "You're impossible, Brodie."

"Reckon that's the common opinion."

A slight breeze stirred the branches, cooling them off slightly. They watched the minnows darting around in groups, making silver streaks in the clear water. "Now, how d'ya reckon those fellas know to go in the same direction all at the same time?" Brodie mused. "It seems like they got just one brain between 'em. Look—there they go again."

"I never cease to be amazed at God's creations," Kat murmured. "Like how He makes minnows that can think at the same time . . . and birds . . . why, they do the same thing. You've seen flocks of birds flying along, then suddenly every last bird will just turn together—as if they had some kind of signal. I could never believe in a thing like evolution to produce creatures like that."

"Me neither. I reckon some Yankees might have come from apes, but we rebels didn't."

"You read that in a book."

"No I didn't. I made it up."

"Well, *I* read it in a book! And it was a *Confederate* soldier who said, 'I may have come from an ape, but Robert E. Lee, he didn't come from no ape.'"

Brodie laughed. "Well, at least he was right about the Robert E. Lee part. He was one of my kin, you know."

"No, I didn't know," Kat said, "and I think you're just making that up too!" She kicked her feet to splash him good, and they both laughed and lay back on the grassy bank.

After a long silence, Brodie said, "Well, Miss Katherine Winslow, are you going to marry that limey?"

Kat had not mentioned Parker's proposal to anyone except her parents, and she knew they had not mentioned it to Brodie. "What makes you ask that?" she demanded.

"He's the marryin' kind. I could see that right off."

"That doesn't mean I'd be interested in marrying him."

"So you're not going to marry him?"

"Well, I'll have to admit, Brodie, he's asked me to go with him to take the cattle back to England."

"He's lookin' for more than a cattle herder, I reckon."

Reluctantly Kat nodded. "Yes, he is," she admitted.

"Are you going?"

"I don't know. I can't make up my mind."

He sat up and picked up a stone, flipped it into the water, and watched the circles spread to the edges of the creek. Then he turned to her and reached out for her hand.

Kat let him pull her up but faced him warily, not sure if he intended to kiss her or was just watching her. She had to admire Brodie. Physically, he was one of the most attractive men she had ever seen. At six feet tall, he was lanky but very strong. His red hair and green eyes made a startling impression on women, and an intense masculinity seemed to flow out of him.

"I'm not very up on this sort of thing," he said, still holding her hand, "but I think you and me would make a mighty good pair."

For a moment Kat did not realize the import of his statement, and then she blinked with surprise. "Is that a proposal?"

"Yep, it sure is. I've known a few gals in my time, Kat, but never one I wanted to make the long haul with."

Usually Brodie was teasing, but Kat knew he was serious this time. He was watching her carefully, his eyes half hidden behind his lowered lids. There was a relaxed looseness about him, even though his features were solid. His tanned, muscled body suggested a man turned hard by time and effort. Kat hesitated, not wanting to hurt his feelings. Still, she knew there was but one answer she could give him.

"Brodie, you know that I'm a Christian and that you're not. The one thing I would absolutely demand in a husband is that he be a man of God."

Brodie released her hand and looked down, lacing his fingers together. He stared at them for a long time—so long that Kat could hardly bear the silence. She knew she had hurt him, despite her good intentions. He was so tough outwardly, but he had a well-hidden tenderness in him, and she felt her words had struck him like a hard blow.

Finally he let his breath out in a sigh and turned to face her. He covered his feelings well, but she could see the hurt in his eyes. "Well, that rules me out."

"Oh, Brodie, you don't love me! We hardly know each other."

He did not argue but instead picked up his socks and began to pull them on. "I guess we'd better get back."

The two put on their shoes and walked back to the car. As he opened the door for her, Kat said, "I'm sorry if I've hurt you, Brodie."

"I didn't really have much hope, Kat, but I want you to know this: I'll always be there for you."

A lump came to her throat. She wanted to reach out and touch him, but she knew better. "That makes me feel good."

He drove her home but did not offer to get out when they reached her house. "I guess this is good-bye, Kat. I'll be leaving in the morning."

"Brodie, I'll miss you so much."

She saw a hopeful flicker in his eyes, but then his mouth grew tense.

"Take care of yourself, Kat."

She got out of the car, and as soon as she'd shut the door, he waved and took off down the road, leaving a plume of dust behind him.

She watched the car disappear, feeling as if a giant weight had fallen on her. She had come to depend on Brodie's friendship, and now it was over, just like that. Gloomily she went into the house, said hi to the boys, who were listening to the radio, and went directly to her room.

She closed the door and leaned back against it. Feeling desperate, she knelt beside the bed and buried her face in the bedspread. "I'm going to stay here, Lord, until I make up my mind one way or another," she prayed. Realizing her words hadn't come out the way she intended, she cried out, "I didn't mean it like that, Lord. I only want to know what *your* will is for me. Please tell me."

★ ★ ★

"I don't know what's gotten into Kat," Lewis fretted. "She hardly speaks to anybody anymore. Stays in her room all the time. Is she feelin' poorly?"

"No, she's not," Missouri Ann assured him. "She's been seekin' the Lord. She's tryin' to make up her mind about whether to marry Parker."

Lewis looked up quickly. "Do you think she will?"

"She will if she thinks God is telling her to. She's got grit, that girl has! You might as well get used to the idea, Lewis. We may be losing her soon."

★ ★ ★

Parker was gazing at Katherine, who had said very little during the evening. They had shared a fine dinner, expertly cooked, as usual, by Missouri Ann and Katherine. After dinner, he had played with the boys, who were fascinated by his accent and tried to imitate it. Afterward, he had spent some time in the parlor with the entire family, but finally Kat had risen and invited him to accompany her outside.

Parker stood beside her on the porch, looking out on the yard. The sun had settled westward, melting into a shapeless bed as it touched the faraway low-lying mountains. The air was getting cooler, and light northerly breezes touched them gently. Pearly shadows covered distant objects, and the dusty roads had taken on soft silver shadings. The peace that came with evening magnified distant sounds, and for a moment Parker stood there, savoring the moment.

He started to speak, but Kat turned and said in a rush, "I can't go to England with you, Parker." He saw that her lips were trembling, and there was a vulnerability about her he had not seen before. Her wide-spaced eyes seemed bottomless at that moment, and her tawny hair lay rolled heavily on her head. She was wearing a gray dress that deepened the color of her eyes. Her face was drawn with a determined look that told him she had made up her mind.

He admired her beauty but with a deep pang in his

heart, knowing even before she spoke that it would never be for him. "I thought you might at least go with me for a visit," he said quietly. "Where's the harm?"

"I can't go . . . because . . . because I love you, Parker."

He had expected anything but this. He reached for her, but she put out her hands, fending him off. "Marry me, Katherine. I love you and you love me. What more could we ask for?"

"There's more to it than that."

"I don't understand."

"I don't feel that I have God's blessing to marry you. There's something else He has for me. And if I go with you, even just for a visit, I know I won't love you any less. If I stay here, I can at least try to forget you, but if I were with you, sooner or later I'd give in to you."

At that instant Parker Braden admired this woman intensely. She was freely expressing her love for him and at the same time was strong enough to admit that she could not trust herself.

Neither of them knew what to say. It was one of those moments in time that seemed to stretch out endlessly, and finally Kat knew she had to at least try to explain. Her voice was filled with pain as she said, "If I can't believe God has put this in my way and intends for it to happen, what would going with you accomplish? It would only bring pain to both of us."

Parker stood absolutely still. Arguments leaped to his lips, but as he gazed at her face, he knew that her mind was made up. He was flooded with hopelessness and disappointment. "I think you're making a mistake, Katherine—one that will hurt both of us for the rest of our lives."

For a moment Kat thought he would try to hold her and kiss her. She was afraid that if he did so, she would give in, for she truly did love this man.

But Parker did not move toward her, nor did he reach out for her. He spoke so quietly she barely caught his words.

"I'll be going now. I think you've made the wrong choice, but I see I can't change your mind." He turned and walked down the porch steps, his back straight. Kat wanted to cry out to him, but she bit her lip and kept her silence. She watched as he got into the car and drove away into the darkness, knowing she had lost him forever.

★ ★ ★

The next morning Parker came early to load the cattle, and he and Kat kept up the appearance of being amiable while she helped him herd the cattle into the truck. But Kat could hardly bear to look at him. When the job was finished, Parker said good-bye to Lewis, Missouri Ann, and the boys. Finally he stood before Kat.

"Are you sure you won't change your mind and come with me?"

Her throat felt so dry she couldn't answer. She merely shook her head.

"Will you write to me, then?"

"I'll try, Parker," she whispered.

"Good-bye." With this final brief, almost harsh, word, Parker turned and got into the truck. The driver started it up, and Parker waved at the boys and her parents, but he did not turn to look at her. This hurt Kat more than anything else, but she knew it was her own doing.

Missouri Ann approached her as the truck rumbled away. She said nothing but reached out and put her arms around Kat. She continued fighting back the tears, all the time crying silently, *I love him, God! Why can't I have him?*

Finally she pulled away and walked blindly away from the house. She did not want to speak to anyone. As she retreated, she heard Michael ask, "What's wrong with Kat?" She broke into a run before she could hear the answer. She crossed the field and didn't stop running until she was in the woods. When she reached the river, she stopped and stared down into the flowing water, remembering the day she had walked along here with Parker. A frog let out a startled croak and plunked into the water. She sat down on the ground, drawing up her knees and folding her arms around them.

She felt entirely drained as she thought about the days ahead. She pulled a snapshot out of her pocket. Earlier in the summer, she and Parker had borrowed a speedboat from a friend of her father and had taken it out on a nearby lake, laughing like children as he drove it full speed, making sharp careens and turns. The picture she had taken captured his essence, tall and fine featured, his eyes full of laughter.

From somewhere far off a mourning dove began cooing. Kat had always loved that sound, but now it seemed more sad than beautiful, matching her mood. She lowered her head against her arms and began to sob. She wanted to jump up and run after the truck, but she knew that wasn't the right thing to do.

A raccoon with three cubs tumbling after it waddled along the creek, occasionally stopping to look for mussels. The bright eyes beneath the mask eventually found Kat. The animal stopped dead still and stared at her as the cubs continued to frolic. Then, seeing no harm in her, the coon turned back to the water and continued fishing with its delicate, nimble hands.

PART TWO

March–July 1940

★ ★ ★

CHAPTER SEVEN

A WORD FROM GOD

★ ★ ★

As Kat entered the hospital room, the sun slanted down through the single window, falling on a very young boy who lay flat on his back staring up at the ceiling. For an instant Kat hesitated but then put on a bright smile and walked over to the patient. After much indecision and soul-searching, she had finally committed to studying nursing and was now working at the small hospital not far from her home.

"Good morning, Bobby. How are you feeling today?"

"Not too good."

"Well, I think you're going to feel a whole lot better real soon."

Six-year-old Bobby Joe Massey looked very small, his thin body outlined under the sheet. He had been in the small Georgia hospital for nearly three weeks, and Kat had become very attached to him.

"I'll tell you what. Why don't I read to you? Would you like that?"

"Yes, ma'am."

Kat picked up one of the children's books, and as she

did, Eileen Massey walked through the door. "Oh, hello, Mrs. Massey. I was just going to read Bobby a story."

Eileen Massey smiled through eyes that betrayed her tension. "Bobby likes it so much when you read to him. If you're going to be here, do you mind if I run to the cafeteria and get a cup of coffee?"

"You go right ahead. Bobby and I will be fine."

Kat pulled up the chair and began to read the book about a little engine that could do more than it was supposed to. When she was finished, she reached out and took Bobby's hand. "Now, if a little engine can do wonders, the Lord can certainly do wonders for you. You believe that, don't you, Bobby?"

The boy did not answer, and Kat noticed that his lower lip was trembling. She gently pushed back his hair from his forehead. "It's going to be all right."

"I'm scared."

"Of the operation?"

"Yes." He looked at her desperately. "Will you be there?"

Actually Kat would not be on duty the next day, but the boy's look was so pitiful that she smiled and said, "Well, of course I'll be there! Friends like you and I have to stick together. I'll tell you what, why don't we just let Jesus know that we need Him tomorrow. All right?"

"All right."

Kat bowed her head and began to pray. She had prayed much for Bobby, and once when she had left without offering to pray, Bobby had requested it. She prayed for the surgeons, that they would have skill and that Bobby would be made completely well. She concluded by saying, "Lord Jesus, we know you're the Great Healer and Bobby needs you—so I know you're going to be with him, and I thank you for it."

Opening her eyes, Kat saw that Bobby looked almost cheerful. "I'll be here before you go in, and I'll be here when you come out. It won't be long before you're outside playing soccer."

"I don't know how to play."

"Well, I'll teach you." Leaning over, Kat kissed him on the cheek and winked. "You try to cheer your mother up now."

"I will, Miss Kat."

As Kat left the room, Mrs. Massey was coming down the hall. "It means so much, Nurse Winslow, that Bobby's come to trust you," she said.

"Bobby and I have prayed, and I'll be here tomorrow before he goes into surgery. Everything's going to be fine. You just wait and see."

Kat took the woman's thanks and made her way to her station. She picked up her purse, said good-bye to the other nurses, and left the hospital.

As she stepped outside, her hat nearly blew off in the stiff March wind. She hung on to it and scurried down the sidewalk that led toward the parking lot. She had not gone far, however, when she heard her name being called and looked up to see Brodie Lee. He was loping easily toward her, and she suddenly thought how rarely he walked anywhere. He had more energy than any man she had ever known.

He stopped in front of her, grinning crookedly. "I've been waitin' for you."

"When did you get back, Brodie?"

"About two hours ago. I called your house, and your dad told me what time you got off." He took her arm and propelled her along. "Come on. We've got some catchin' up to do. I haven't been around to watch you lately. Tell me what mischief you've been gettin' into."

As Brodie hurried her along toward his car, Kat reflected on their strange relationship. Brodie had been in and out of her life for the past three years. He would fly in, stay for a few days or a week, and then be gone for long periods. He had held several jobs, including flying for the U.S. Postal Service and flying transports. He had even volunteered to help the Loyalists in the civil war in Spain, spending the last part of 1938 there and staying through until the war was over in April of 1939. He hadn't been to the Winslow farm now for several months, and as Kat got into the car, she asked, "Where have you been?"

Brodie started the car and said, "Mostly just hopping around the States, delivering mail again. After that stint in Spain, I decided to stay out of dangerous situations for a while." He gunned the car out of the lot, breaking every speeding law on the books, as always. "There's gonna be a change in my life."

"That's good. What are you going to do?"

"I've decided to get a job sellin' ladies' shoes. Then I'm gonna marry you and sit on the front porch every day after work readin' the paper."

"I can just see that," she said with a laugh. "You can't sit still for ten minutes."

"You just don't know me, Kat. I actually hate activity. I'm a natural-born bum."

"You are not! You're the most active human being I've ever met. You're like an ant in hot ashes."

He denied all this and finally pulled up in front of a diner. "How about if you buy me lunch? I'm pretty well broke."

Kat just laughed and shook her head as the two got out of the car, went into the diner, and seated themselves. When the waitress came, Brodie winked at her and said, "This is our anniversary. We've been married twelve years."

The waitress, a small young woman with snapping black eyes, said, "You must have gotten married when you were ten years old."

"Actually I was twelve and my wife, Gwendolyn here, was eight. She liked older men."

The waitress laughed. "All right. What'll you have?" She took their order and as soon as she left, Brodie started fishing in his pocket but came up empty-handed. "Give me some change, will you? I wanna plug the jukebox."

Kat gave him some change, and he went over and made his selections. By the time he returned to the table, Frank Sinatra was softly crooning "I'll Never Smile Again."

"That's the way I feel the whole time I'm gone," he said.

"I'll never smile again until I see you."

"That's sweet, Brodie."

Jimmie Davis picked up the tempo with "You Are My Sunshine," and Brodie joined in with him, singing slightly off-key. "I like this song," he said, tapping his fingers on the table. "I've been keepin' up with the popular music."

Tommy Dorsey's orchestra was next, playing an older tune, "I'm Getting Sentimental Over You."

Brodie, who appeared to know the words to every popular song ever written, sang along with all of them. When the last song was over, he said, "You know what? I read in a magazine article about a test they did with some chimps at the Philadelphia Zoo. They played a bunch of wild jazz for them and scared the chimps half to death. They ran all over the place hiding under benches. But when they played this recording by Tommy Dorsey, the apes became tranquil and just sat there."

"You made that up."

"I did not! It was in the newspaper, so it must be true. I guess it proves jazz is just a fad, but ballads will never go out of fashion."

"Or it may have proved that the chimps didn't have very good taste."

Brodie grinned at her. He reached over and put his hands over hers and held them until the waitress returned with their order. She put the food down, saying, "Happy anniversary."

"Thanks, sweetheart. I'll wait on you when you get old."

As the waitress left, he said to Kat, "I guess you wanna ask a blessin'."

"Yes, I do." They both bowed their heads, and Kat said a short prayer of thanks. She was worried about Brodie, for she knew he lived a dangerous life and God was not a part of it. As they began to eat, he asked her about her own life. She told him about Bobby and some of the other patients at the hospital.

"And what's next? Are you gonna work at the hospital until you're old and gray?"

Kat bit into the hamburger and chewed it thoroughly. "I've applied to several missions organizations."

"So you won't be staying around here?"

"I don't think so."

Brodie swirled the dark fluid around in his coffee cup and then looked into her eyes. "You still tryin' to read God's mind?"

"I wouldn't put it like that, Brodie. I'm still trying to find out what God wants me to do."

Abruptly he asked, "You still hearing from that limey Braden?"

"Once in a while. I don't know if his wife appreciates it, though. Her twins are two-and-a-half now, you know. And he loves them as if they were his kids too."

"Wow—time sure does fly."

"Isn't that the truth?"

"Is he still making airplanes at his pop's factory?"

"No. He left that position to join the Royal Air Force. He's a wing commander." This caught Brodie's attention, as she had known it would. When his eyes widened, she added, "He shot down five German planes."

"Now, that's really something!" Admiration shaded his tone, and he nodded with appreciation. "I'd like to get in on that action."

"Didn't you get enough fighting in Spain?"

"It wasn't much of a fight. The Germans had all their best planes, and all the Loyalists had was a few rickety crates. It was hard enough just to get them into the air. We had no chance at all of winnin'—not with Germany pouring their men and planes in there. Their Condor Legion was an awesome fightin' force."

He took a big bite of his burger. "You really should consider marryin' me, you know. If we were married—"

"Brodie, it would scare you to death if I said yes. You know it's true. Now let's have some dessert."

★ ★ ★

Kat got out of the car in the hospital parking lot, and Brodie leaned out the window. "Don't forget. Tomorrow night we're doin' the town. Bring plenty of money along. It may be expensive."

Kat smiled and shook her head. He never changed. "All right. I'll see you tomorrow."

She got into her own car and drove home, where she was energetically greeted by Michael, Samuel, and Temple. As usual, they tugged and pulled at her, each vying for her attention. They were nearly eight years old now, and she marveled at how much they had grown. They were all tall, getting their height, no doubt, from their mother.

"You should take us to the movies tonight, Kat," Temple said. "There's a gangster movie on. Lots of people get shot, I bet."

"I'm not taking you to one of those awful movies, Temple."

Samuel, the quietest of the boys, asked, "Will you help me with my homework?"

"I sure will, but you're so smart you don't need much help." She reached over and hugged him, and he hugged her back. He was more affectionate than his brothers, and she could tell he was going to be a fine man.

Michael piped up, "I got an *A* on my arithmetic at school today, just like you said I would."

"In that case, you deserve a reward." She searched into her purse and pulled out a Hershey bar. "There."

"Hey, what about me!" Temple yelled. "I got a *C*."

"A *C* doesn't deserve a candy bar. You get an *A* and we'll see. What about you, Sam?"

"I got a *B*."

"Well, you get half a candy bar, but don't you boys eat them until after supper."

The three ran off yelling, and Kat went to the kitchen, where Missouri Ann was fixing supper.

"That smells good, Mom. What is it?"

"It's chicken potpie and some hot-water pastry, and

we're gonna have rice puddin' for dessert. You look plumb tired."

"I am a bit. Let me go change, and then I'll help you."

"There's no need of that. I was cookin' 'fore you were born. I reckon I can handle one more meal."

"I know you can, but I want to help."

"You help enough workin' at that hospital and then helpin' take care of these rascally boys."

"How's Dad today?"

Missouri Ann turned away from the stove and hesitated for a moment. "He's still not feeling too great today."

"I'm worried about him, Mom."

"Well, there's no sense in worrying. I've been talking to the good Lord, and He's promised me that your pa's gonna be just fine. And when Dr. Jesus says a man is gonna be all right, there's no need to worry."

"I wish I had your faith."

"You're pickin' it up as you go along, just like all the rest of us." She peeked in the oven to check on the potpie. "Oh, there's a letter come for you. I put it on the table over there."

Kat picked up the letter and read the return address, her eyes brightening. "It's from International Missions. I sent them an application, but since they hadn't answered yet, I thought they weren't going to." She read the letter silently for a few moments. "Ma, they're offering me a position with them!"

"Is that so? Does that mean you'll be a missionary?"

"It says here they want me to do medical work in England. They've got mission stations all over the world."

"Don't they have doctors of their own there?"

Kat was reading the letter more closely now. "I'd be working with very poor people off the streets of London. And their nurses also do some work in one of the large London hospitals."

"Do you think you'd like to go there?"

"You know, ever since I applied, I thought this would be the mission organization that would take me. Of course I had no idea where they would send me." She lowered the letter and shook her head. "You know, it's the strangest thing. I suddenly feel that this is exactly what God wants me to do. Oh, Mom, isn't that wonderful!"

"It's the Lord speakin' to you, child. You've been seeking Him about your callin' for three years or more now, and the Scripture says that everyone who seeks finds. Does it say when they want you to go?"

"Almost right away. In a month."

"Reckon you know how much your pa and I will miss you. And the boys. They're gonna plumb perish without you."

"It'll be hard for me too. I've never really been away from home before."

"Well, you won't be alone," Missouri said with a smile.

"Yes. The Lord will be with me." Kat put her arms around the large woman. "I'll miss you."

Missouri returned the embrace. "We'll have to break the news to your pa. He's gonna be awfully sad. Why don't you go up and tell him."

"I'll have to tell the boys too. Maybe I'll take them out to a movie or something tonight and tell them when we get home."

"That Temple. He wants to see one of those awful gangster movies."

"There's another movie on—a cartoon called *Pinocchio*. It's harmless enough, I hear. Maybe I'll take them to see that."

Kat went upstairs and found her father in his room. He had been lying down, but he sat up at once, propping a pillow behind his back. "Well, daughter, you're home."

"How do you feel, Dad?"

"A little better. I don't think I have the flu, and I don't need it."

"I'm glad you're getting better. Dad, I've heard from one of the mission boards that I applied to. They've accepted me."

"That's wonderful! Sit down and tell me all about it."

She sat on a chair near the bed and read parts of the

letter to her father. They talked about the types of conditions she might encounter in her new work and all that she would need to do to get ready to leave.

"I can't tell you how proud I am, Kat. We Winslows have some missionaries over in Africa and other places, and now we'll have one in England. I'll miss you, though. We all will."

She looked out the window for a moment. "I'm a little apprehensive."

"About what?"

"Well, I've never been away from home before—not really. Just on short vacations. But now I'll be far away from everyone I know."

Lewis reached over and took her hand. "You'll do fine," he said warmly, his eyes approving. "You'll be sharing the Gospel with people who need the Lord, and that's what being a missionary is, whether it's in Africa or in England."

★ ★ ★

"I tell you, there ought to be more fellas around like that Rhett Butler," Brodie proclaimed, taking his eyes off the road to turn to Kat. "He had the right idea."

"That was such a good movie! He reminds me a little of you."

"Me!" Brodie grinned. "Well, he's not quite as good-lookin' as me, but we're probably about the same height."

"I don't mean the way you look. Nobody looks like Clark Gable."

Brodie feigned a crest-fallen look. "Why, you sure know how to hurt a fella."

"But you are a lot like Rhett. He joined the Confederacy when the cause was lost, and that's what you did in Spain, isn't it?"

Brodie seemed unable to talk about his own better qualities. "Shucks, I just wanted to go see what all the shootin' was about. Found out too."

"Weren't you ever scared, Brodie? You don't seem to be afraid of anything."

"Oh, I've been scared of lots of things."

"Tell me one."

"You remember a couple years ago when Orson Welles did that program of his?"

"You mean the 'War of the Worlds' broadcast?"

"Yeah, that's the one. Well, I might as well confess. I was over in Georgia doin' some crop dustin', and when I got home that night I was all by myself, having a few beers. My buddies hadn't come in yet. I turned on the radio and heard this announcer. You know how it went. The Martian monsters were setting fire to everythin', pulling up power lines and bridges. Then they were wadin' across the Hudson River. Well, I was just drunk enough to believe it. It scared me pretty good. I thought they were gonna kill us all!"

"What did you do?"

"I went outside and looked north toward New York and waited for the end to come."

"And you were really scared?"

"You might say I was plumb uncomfortable."

"When did you find out it was a hoax?"

"Oh, when the boys come in a little later, I told 'em about it, and they laughed and said it was just a fool radio program."

"I remember that. It scared me too."

"I don't know why it would," Brodie said curiously. "You always say you're ready to go meet the Lord. You shouldn't be afraid of dying."

"I'm not . . . but even if you know you're saved and going to heaven, it's different when you're actually facing it. I guess death frightens everybody because we haven't done it before. There's no way to practice it."

The two continued talking about the radio program until he pulled up in front of the house. As she had known he would, he reached over and tried to kiss her.

"Thanks for taking me to the movie, Brodie." She fidgeted with her purse in her lap. "I've got something to tell you. I've been trying to think of a way to bring it up all night."

"Are you going to preach me another sermon?"

"No. Not this time." She hesitated, then said, "I'll be leaving soon."

He listened as she told him of her plans, and when she had finished, she said, "I really believe this is God's will for me. It's exactly what I've been waiting for."

"So you're going off and leavin' ol' Brodie, huh?"

"You'll get along fine. It's my folks I worry about—and the boys."

He was quiet for a moment, absently running his fingers around the steering wheel. "I'll miss you, Kat."

"I'll miss you too, but I'll write. And you can write me back."

"Well, I ain't much on writin' letters, but don't forget me."

He got out of the car and came around to open her door. He walked to the steps with her, and when she turned to him, he said wistfully, "I feel like an orphan."

"Don't be foolish. You go for months at a time without seeing me and you do just fine."

He reached out and ran his hand over her hair. He said nothing for a time and then leaned forward and kissed her on the cheek. "Good-bye, Kat." He turned and walked back to the car.

As he drove away, Kat was puzzled. *I expected him to try more than that when he said good-bye.* It was not like Brodie Lee to give up on anything as easily as he had this night.

She quietly slipped into the house, knowing everyone would be asleep. When she got to her room, she took her journal out of her drawer and wrote: *March 26, 1940: God has called me to England. At last I know what He wants me to do!*

CHAPTER EIGHT

A MUCH-NEEDED LEAVE

★ ★ ★

The heat had caused towering cumulus clouds to rise from about five thousand to eight or ten thousand feet, and they were still climbing. As Parker Braden glanced down, he saw no enemy, but straight ahead, just behind a mound of clouds piled up like the Alps, he spotted a dozen Heinkel twin-engine bombers. They were going around in a circle, nose to tail, in the defensive position they sometimes took when they had no fighter escort.

Suddenly the radiotelephone crackled and delivered a message that was entirely too garbled to understand. Shaking his head with disgust, Parker scanned the sky for German fighter planes but saw none. It happened this way from time to time, but usually when bombers came over across the Channel they were heavily escorted with Me-109s or the two-engine 110s. Occasionally, however, bombers tried it on their own for some reason Parker had never been able to understand. As a rule a bomber without an escort was dead, and the Germans were well aware of this.

"Enemy straight ahead, Wing Commander," said the mild voice of Bernie Cox, the leader of Blue One.

"I see them, Blue One, and I don't see any fighters."

"All right. Here we go. Pick your target."

Parker glanced over at his wingman in the adjacent aircraft, Tommy Higgins, who had arrived only a week earlier. Parker had groaned when he'd learned that the young man had only fifteen hours' experience flying Spitfires, and he had given him a crash course. Higgins was willing enough but green as grass. "Stay with me, Tommy. Don't go wandering off."

"I read you, Wing Commander." Higgins's voice crackled with excitement, and he pulled his Spitfire in until his wing was only five feet away from Parker's.

Parker nosed his Spit downward and felt a brief moment of pity for the crews of the Heinkels. There had been a time when he had felt exhilarated at such moments, but that was gone now. All that lay before him was the unpleasant job of killing human beings. He felt washed clean of fear as he led the squadron toward the hulking slab-winged bombers. Each one of them had five guns, and although they blazed away continuously, they had little chance of hitting the Spitfires, which fell on them like lightning.

He picked his target and, when he was four hundred yards away, hit the trigger under his thumb. The tracers marked the path as the ammunition raked the Heinkel.

Scratch one Heinkel and four or five lives.

The Germans were tough, and they broke formation when they saw that they had been jumped. All should have gone well, but suddenly Parker saw Tommy Higgins head directly toward two of the Heinkels that were trying to flee. He yelled, "Break off, Higgins! Break off!" But Higgins, if he heard the warning, paid no attention. He had slowed his Spitfire, probably to make his aim better, and the combined guns of both Heinkels blared, hitting him dead on. Black smoke poured out of the small fighter plane, its canopy completely shattered.

Parker flipped his plane over and came up from underneath the Heinkels, aware that Sailor Darley was beside him. The two had no need for speech. They had flown together long enough to know exactly what to do. He used the last of his ammo to destroy the Heinkel and saw that Sailor had wiped out his plane also.

"Regroup," Parker said wearily, not even looking at the Heinkels that were plunging toward the earth below. When Eagle Squadron was back in formation, he commended his men. "Good show. Let's go home now."

As he led the squadron back toward the field, Parker felt the great weariness that had become a part of his life settle on him. Glancing out, he was aware of the beautiful blue sky, the towering white clouds hanging over the earth like fairy-tale castles. The blue sea crawled steadily beneath him, always moving, meeting up with the white cliffs of Dover with their pristine beauty he loved so. As always, the sight touched him.

But hard on the heels of that came the thought of Tommy Higgins, now a bloody corpse sinking beneath the sea in the wreckage of his plane. It had become almost a vigil with Parker to struggle with the twin aspects of his life, the beauty that he saw when he flew and the ugliness of the job that always involved death. His hand tightened on the stick, and for one moment he had the wild impulse to turn and fly away anywhere except to the airfield, where he knew as soon as he landed he would begin getting ready for the next rendezvous with the enemy.

The impulse passed quickly, and he shook his head to clear it. He forced himself to think of beautiful things. He resolutely thought of his two stepchildren, Paul and Heather, and as the Spitfire roared toward the field, the leader of Eagle Squadron was thinking not of Germans or of Me-109s but of sitting on the floor and letting the two-year-olds crawl over him, pulling his hair and squealing as he tickled them. This was the other world that Wing Commander Braden chose to live in whenever the killing was done.

★ ★ ★

As Parker climbed out of the plane and stepped to the ground, he was met by Denny Featherstone, his early crew chief. "Go all right, sir?"

"Fine, Denny. No holes for you to patch up this time."

Featherstone's second-in-command, Keith Poe, had been scurrying around the plane. "Did you have any kills, sir?"

"Yes. We had good luck. Got a whole flight of Heinkels. Six of them. They had no fighter cover. Don't know why. The blighters came alone."

Featherstone and Poe were called "plumbers," as all of the members of the ground crew were. They and ten others serviced the Spitfires and usually grew incensed when the planes took any battle damage.

"Sir," Featherstone said, "me and this lunkhead here are havin' an argument."

"Nothing new about that." Parker's flight suit seemed to be pulling him down. He pulled off his helmet and said, "What is it this time?"

"Well, I say that Hitler is the Antichrist," Featherstone said, glaring at the smaller crewman. "And this muttonhead here says he ain't. Now, I ask you, sir. Who else would be the Antichrist if not Adolf?"

Despite his weariness, Parker smiled. The two men were devout students of biblical end-time prophecy and spent as much time arguing about minor points of Scripture as they did working on the Spitfire. "Who do you think it is, Poe?"

"Well, I'm not exactly sure who it is, but I'm sure who it ain't. It can't be Hitler."

"Why not?" Parker asked curiously.

"Because the Antichrist has to come out of the Middle East somewhere. He sure as shootin' won't be a dirty kraut!"

Featherstone began to protest, but Parker held up his hand and turned away. "Let me know if you decide." He hesitated, then said, "Higgins went for a Burton." By this odd expression, the men understood that Higgins was dead. Parker saw something change in the eyes of the two men and said nothing.

Featherstone gnawed his lower lip and looked down at

his feet. He shuffled them and then looked back up at Parker. "It's a bad thing how quick some of these young fellows go. It was only his second mission."

"Yeah," Poe mumbled, "and he was gonna be an ace. He talked about it all the time."

"Well, he won't be an ace now," Parker said wearily. "Look, I've got a twenty-four-hour leave. This ship's in good shape. I don't see why you fellows shouldn't have some time off too. Go ahead, but be back in twenty-four hours."

Both men brightened up, and Parker turned to leave. Before he was out of earshot they had begun to argue again, this time about the timing of the Great Tribulation. Parker shook his head in wonder. "Well, some men like rugby and others like to argue about the Bible." He could not see that one was any more harmful than the other.

He went to make out his report, and as soon as he had done so, he wrote a letter to Tommy Higgins's family. This task was getting harder all the time. Higgins had done very little as far as deeds were concerned, but he had offered the ultimate sacrifice of his own life, and Parker had to give what comfort he could to the family.

Your son was one of the most popular men in the squadron. He was well liked by all of his fellow pilots. He was courageous in that way one rarely sees. He gave his life defending his country.

Parker stared down at the words, which had become almost meaningless. He forced himself to finish the letter, then signed it and stuffed it into an envelope. He posted it at once. He had made a habit of this on the occasions when men had been lost from his squadron. The longer he put it off, the more he brooded over it, and now he knew that in a few days he would be unable to even recall clearly what the young man's face looked like. Men were here one day and the next day were gone—obliterated. He hated the unfairness of it and tried to put it aside as he changed out of his flight suit into his dress uniform and left the station.

★ ★ ★

Lord Gregory Braden had always preferred the smaller of the two dining rooms at Benleigh. Now as he sat down at the table across from his daughter-in-law, who flanked the twins, he felt, once again, the comfort of the room. Glancing around, he took in the fine old walnut paneling that had taken on a royal patina after so many years. At the far end of the room, two large windows reached from the floor almost to the ceiling, admitting abundant light that illuminated the blue-and-gold carpet. A magnificent buffet made of rosewood held stacks of gleaming white china and crystal goblets that sparkled like diamonds.

"Would you care for some more of the beef, Lord Braden?"

Looking up, Braden saw that Mrs. Sophie Henderson, the housekeeper, was standing over him. She was a handsome woman in her midforties and had become a fixture at Benleigh.

"I don't believe I would, Sophie."

"You're not eating well enough. You need to force yourself."

"Well, just a bit more, then." Gregory was used to being bullied by the housekeeper, but then everyone was. He waited until she had put a slab of beef on his plate and then listened to the conversation of his wife and daughter-in-law as he cut it. But his attention was on the twins, who were perched in high chairs between the two women. He positively doted on his son's adopted children, whom he had come to regard as fondly as if they were his own grandchildren. He had always wanted a large family with a house full of children, but when their second child had died at birth, his wife was unable to have any more. They were left with their only son, Parker. Now Parker's children filled that void for Gregory, and he threw his affections toward the twins with all possible enthusiasm.

"I hear it's going to be one of the best musicals ever produced." Parker's wife, Veronica, was doing most of the speaking. She was a small, well-shaped woman of thirty with dark hair and dark brown eyes. She was rather sharp-featured but attractive enough in spite of this. Her voice was somewhat shrill, but although it ground on Gregory, he never mentioned how much he disliked it. "I've got to hurry," she added, checking the grandfather clock in the corner.

"Are you going alone?" Lady Grace Braden, at the age of fifty, was fourteen years younger than her husband. Grace's blond hair was still rich and full, and her blue eyes were clear. She had never been a real beauty, but there was a winsomeness about her that made her attractive.

"No," Veronica said. "Charles is going to pick me up. Such a bore. I offered to bring our car, but he wants me to try out that new one of his."

"What's he doing now?" Gregory asked. "Still producing musicals for the stage?"

"Yes. His new production is going to be great. I expect it to win every prize in sight."

Gregory despised Charles Gooding, considering him an effeminate parasite. Veronica kept company with a group of actors, writers, and artists, and Gregory had little patience with them. He himself had been given to a life of hard work building up the family business of aircraft manufacture. To him, writing a play did not constitute work. Making a fitting for an airplane—now, *that* was work.

Paul suddenly reached out toward his mother, but unfortunately the back of his hand struck his glass of milk. It fell right in his mother's lap, and she cried, "Look what you've done!" Her face was red, and she reached out and shook the toddler, who began to cry loudly.

"It was an accident," Gregory's sister Edith said at once. She got up and put herself between Veronica and the child. "He didn't mean to do it."

"I'll have to go change now," Veronica whined. She whirled and left the room angrily.

"It's all right, Paul," Edith soothed. "You didn't mean to do it."

"Here. Let me clean up this mess," Mrs. Henderson offered. She busied herself bringing towels to mop up the milk, and while she was engaged in this task, they heard the front door open.

Millie, the eighteen-year-old maid, went to the foyer, and Gregory and Grace looked up eagerly when they heard the maid greet their son. Almost immediately, Parker appeared at the dining room door and headed straight for the twins, who were calling loudly for their daddy.

"Having a little supper, are we?" Parker managed to get Paul out of his high chair, then with the boy in one arm did the same with Heather.

"Yeth!" Paul cried out. "An' I spill milk all over Mum."

As he held them both, all the darkness of the war faded. "I've got to hear what you two have been doing."

"How long can you stay, Parker?" Grace asked.

"Only overnight, I'm afraid, Mother. I'll have to be back tomorrow afternoon."

"I don't see why you can't take longer leaves," his father said.

"Well, it wouldn't be fair for me to do it when the rest of the men can't. Let's sit in the parlor and you two can tell me what you've been doing."

For the next ten minutes the twins swarmed over Parker, filling him in with stories about what they'd been up to and demanding that he perform all sorts of favors for them, including a trip to the zoo.

Veronica entered the parlor, having changed clothes completely. "Hello, Parker," she said coolly. "How long is your leave?"

He got to his feet and came to her. She offered her cheek, and he kissed it dutifully. "Just until tomorrow afternoon."

"Well, that's not much, but tonight you belong to me. I want you to come to the new musical. Charles is coming by to pick me up in just a few minutes. We can get another ticket."

A shadow crossed Parker's face. "I'm beastly tired, dear. It's been a hard day."

Veronica shook her head impatiently. "It will be good for you. Come, now. Don't argue."

But he stood his ground. "I'd really rather stay home and be with you and the children. We get so little time together."

Veronica's face assumed a martyr's expression. "All right, then," she sighed. "I'll just have to miss it."

Across the room Gregory was watching this scene closely, anger smoldering on his face, for he had witnessed it often.

Parker shrugged and said, "I wouldn't want you to miss your outing. You go ahead. I'll stay here with the children."

"Well, if you insist," Veronica said quickly, with obvious relief. "After all, we have tomorrow."

"Yes. We have tomorrow."

Gregory was furious. His eyes met those of his wife, and he was thinking, *What kind of a woman is she? Her husband risks his life every day, and she'd rather go to a stupid musical than be with him.*

Charles Gooding came by ten minutes later and invited Parker to join them, but Parker was adamant. "Maybe next time I'll be able to take in a play, but not tonight."

"Well, if you insist. Are you ready, Veronica?"

"Yes. We'll be back late." She kissed each of the twins but merely spoke to her husband. "I'll see you when I get in, Parker."

As soon as the two had left, Parker turned to find his parents watching him. His mother was rather good at covering her feelings, but he could see the disapproval in his father's eyes. Yet there was nothing much his parents could say, really. He had married Veronica largely at their insistence, as well as the encouragement of his aunt Edith. The whole family was involved, knowing they had been drawn into a relationship with Veronica out of the kindness of their hearts, but learning too late that their compassion had blinded them to the full reality of the situation. Their decisions had brought their family both great joy and great anguish at the same time. Lord and Lady Braden wished things were different for their son's sake, but what was done could not be undone.

When Parker had returned home from the States in

August of 1937, he was so despondent over Katherine Winslow's refusal to marry him that he allowed himself to be drawn into a courtship with Veronica Taylor without much thought. He had known her for some time, having been acquaintances during their school days. She had always played the lead roles in the school plays, and long after they had left school, he continued to follow her acting career on the London stage. He had always admired her talent from a distance. It had not surprised him when she had married a prominent stage producer and director in a glittering December wedding in 1936, but he *was* shocked to learn of the birth of her twin children in early July 1937, only seven months after her wedding day. He had found it hard to picture Veronica willingly giving up her acting career to devote herself to being a mother of twins.

Then while Parker was traveling in the States in the summer of 1937, he had received the shocking news from his parents that Veronica's husband had been tragically killed in a car accident, leaving her alone with the newborn infants. There were rumors of his having been drunk when his car ran off the winding country road one night on his way home from London. To make matters worse, Veronica was apparently left with no financial provisions to care for herself and the babies. The highly publicized fairy-tale romance had turned into a scandalous disaster for Veronica, who saw her career and life unexpectedly plunged into ruin. Her own parents could not be of much help to her, having enormous financial difficulties of their own as her mother had to care for her invalid father. But they were people of good stock and believed their daughter's only hope was to marry into a family of wealth and stature. Parker Braden was a very likely candidate in their minds to help their daughter out of her dilemma and to give her and her children a respectable home.

No sooner had Parker returned from the States than he learned that Veronica had been visiting his family of late, expressing great interest in Parker and his whereabouts. Lord and Lady Braden and Parker's aunt Edith had taken

Veronica into their family circle, supporting her in her grief and falling in love with her darling babies. The Bradens were good people and merely concerned for this young widow in her time of great need. Unaware of Veronica's skillful manipulation of their emotions, they began to believe it was their own idea that Parker should begin courting her, in hopes that he could come to care for her and the children and help Veronica out of her desperate situation.

Parker had allowed himself to be persuaded, and before he knew it, he was deeply drawn into a whirlwind romance with the stage actress. The wedding that followed in a few months' time gave Parker a renewed sense of purpose, believing now that he was the one man who could give Veronica a new life and rescue her from her uncertain future. It concerned him a bit, however, that she talked of someday returning to the stage, for although he admired her talent, he felt the theater was an inappropriate world for a proper wife and mother to inhabit.

Just as his parents and aunt had, Parker fell in love with Veronica's two children, adopting them and caring for them as his very own. For a time he basked in the joy of being a father and family man, content with his new life. But as the conflict in Europe picked up its tempo, Parker was forced to throw himself behind the war effort, leaving his position managing his father's factory to join the RAF. As his absences became more frequent, Veronica dreamed about returning to her acting career on the London stage. Being the mother of twins was simply not enough to bring contentment to her life, and she knew she could leave the children in the care of the willing Braden family while she sought after her own ambitions.

As for Parker, his focus at home was solely on his adopted children, whom he loved desperately. They filled a deep void in him as his marriage began to fall apart. Whatever feelings Veronica and Parker might have briefly had for each other soon dissolved into nothing more than a reserved tolerance.

Such was the state of Parker's life when he greeted his

children that evening. It was far from perfect—but he did know a deep joy in coming home to the children's smiling faces after his long hours of fighting and killing in a world gone mad with hatred and warfare.

"How about a treat?" Parker said to the toddlers in either arm. "I smelled some treacle pudding when I walked in." The twins squealed in delight and bounced in Parker's arms as he carried them off toward the kitchen.

Grace meanwhile turned to her husband. "I wish Veronica hadn't gone off like that."

Gregory shook his head. "It hurt Parker. It hurts me too. I can't believe she'd do such a thing." They sat there helplessly, knowing there was nothing they could do about it.

"Let's go to the kitchen too," Grace suggested. "I could eat some treacle pudding myself."

★ ★ ★

Parker packed his kit and left the bedroom. It had been a good day. Veronica had gone with him and the children to the zoo. She had apologized, after a fashion, for leaving him the night before, but he had made little of it.

As he crossed the foyer, Aunt Edith called, "Parker, are you leaving?"

His father's spinster sister was sixty-seven now. She was a proud, strong-willed woman, successful as a historian although she had not gotten rich by it. She was a rather small woman with silver hair and came up to take Parker's kiss. "You're not going to leave now!" she exclaimed. "I've hardly seen you at all."

"You should have been with us at the zoo. You would have enjoyed the monkeys."

"I couldn't get away from my meeting." The woman was always involved in some kind of charity work.

The two stood there talking, and finally Edith said, "Oh, by the way, when I picked up my mail I got one of your letters by mistake. I think I put it right over here." She turned to the table beside the front door. "Yes. Here it is." She looked at the return address. "Who is this woman writing you from America?"

Parker hesitated for a moment. "She's the daughter of the man I bought the Black Angus cattle from." He had never told his family of his deep feelings for Katherine Winslow and his desire at one time to marry the American woman.

"But that was nearly three years ago. She's still writing? That *is* like an American, isn't it? Rather pushy."

"She only writes occasionally." He did not open the letter but leaned over and kissed his aunt again. "The next time I get any leave at all, you and I will have to spend some time together."

"You be careful, Parker."

He smiled. "I will," he said, wondering how in the world a man could be careful while flying a Spitfire against crack German fliers. He left the house and opened the envelope after he got into his car. He scanned the letter quickly and sat absolutely still for a moment. Then he started the car and drove away.

He made his way to the heart of London rather than going directly to the airfield. He parked in front of a large building with a small sign that said *International Mission*. He went inside and approached an attractive young woman sitting at a desk. "I say, I'm looking for a Miss Katherine Winslow."

"Are you, now?" The melody of Wales was in the young woman's voice. She had a wealth of auburn hair and beautifully shaped green eyes set in an oval face. "What would a flight officer be doing in this part of town? There are no German planes here."

"Just visiting."

"Ah, well, come along, then. I'll take you to Sister Winslow."

"I've always wondered why they call nurses *sister*. Do you know, by the way?"

"No, I don't. How do you happen to know Miss Winslow?"

Parker was bombarded with questions, for the young woman was not shy at all. She led him through the building, which was filled with activity. Finally she brought him into a large room with a table and a line of ragged, dirty children. Katherine was wearing a blue nurse's uniform, giving the children shots.

"You have a visitor, Sister," the young woman said.

Parker moved forward and saw the delighted recognition leap into Kat's eyes. She put the needle down and stood to greet him warmly.

"Are you surprised to see me?" he asked.

"Yes, I am."

"Aren't you going to introduce me?"

Kat turned and said, "Wing Commander, may I introduce you to Sister Meredith Bryce. Meredith, this is Wing Commander Parker Braden, an old friend of mine."

Meredith's eyes sparkled. "I'm so happy to meet you, sir."

"And I you."

Meredith winked at Kat, then said, "I'd better get back to the front desk." She turned and left, and Parker looked at the line of children. "I've come at a bad moment. You're busy now."

"Yes, I am rather."

Parker glanced at his pocket watch. "I have to be back at the station at five-thirty."

"I get off at four. That's only fifteen minutes."

"Good. I'll wait outside."

Parker left, and Meredith came scurrying back. "Who was that?"

"You heard. An old friend."

Meredith studied the face of the young nurse. "An old *married* friend. I saw the ring on his finger."

"Yes, he is."

Meredith started to say something, then shrugged. "The good ones are always married."

As she turned and left, Kat picked up the needle and said, "Come here now, darling. This will only hurt a little."

★ ★ ★

"I don't have much time. I wish I had more."

Kat was sitting across from Parker in the quaint tea shop he had taken her to. They had given their order and were waiting for their tea and raspberry tarts. "I was surprised to hear you were coming to London."

"So was I," she said. "It was all very sudden."

"How long have you been here?"

"Only a week."

"I wish you would have contacted me earlier, but then I've been rather busy. How are your parents?"

She gave him a full report about her family, and finally their order came. She stirred sugar and milk into the strong black tea and took a sip. "Tell me about the war, Parker."

He shrugged. "It's bad, Katherine, and it's going to get worse." For some reason he wanted to share some of his experiences with her, so he told her about Tommy Higgins. He found himself stiffening as he told the story, and he was aware of the sympathy in her eyes.

"Losing young men like that is the worst. It's bad enough having to shoot down the enemy, but watching our own lads die like that with their whole life before them . . . it's hard to take."

"I'm so sorry." She reached over and squeezed his hand. "I hope it will be over soon."

"It won't be. It's just starting." Parker was intensely aware of the warmth of her hand and said suddenly, "I'd like for you to meet my family."

"Oh, I'm not sure that would be—"

He headed her off before she could say no. "And, of course, Hercules. I'll bet he remembers you."

Kat's face lit up. "Oh, I'd like that! I've missed him so much." She laughed. "I've put the pictures you sent me of him on my wall back home. I took a lot of teasing for that. Most women have pictures of Robert Taylor or Clark Gable, but I've got a Black Angus bull for my hero!"

"I'll have to call you the next time I have some time off. I never know for certain when I can get leave."

"Here. Let me give you the number of the mission."

He waited until she wrote it down, and finally he looked at his watch. "May I take you home?"

"Thanks, but it's only three blocks away."

The two left the tea shop, and he turned to her. "It was good to see you, Katherine. You haven't changed a bit."

"I've . . . I've thought so often of the little time we had together."

"I've thought of it too." He hesitated, then said, "I'll call you when I have more leave." He turned and walked away, shaken at how the sight of her had awakened old memories. He tried to push his feelings away, but they came back to him strongly. When he got into the car, he slammed the door and muttered to himself, "Pull yourself together, man! You're a husband and a father. It's too late for anything like that!"

CHAPTER NINE

LUNCHEON WITH THE NOBILITY

★ ★ ★

Meredith Bryce lay propped up against the headboard, her legs stretched out, her fingers laced behind her head. She and Kat shared a one-bedroom flat in London that was close to both the mission and the hospital. They worked long hours as nurses at both places, so it really didn't matter that they didn't have much living space.

Meredith was watching Kat dress and finally remarked, "Going to luncheon with the nobility, eh? You're not doing bad for an American."

Kat had just slipped into the dress she had chosen for the occasion. Parker had called her the day before and said he would pick her up at noon. She had been nervous ever since, and now she stopped and tried to peer at herself in the small mirror fastened to the wall. She was wearing a light green wool dress and had bought a new pair of black pumps with a two-inch heel. The only other shoes she had were flat, suitable for nursing duties. She poked at her hair, which she had cut before leaving home. She wore it now in a bouffant style since it was easier to wash and care for.

"He's a good-looking chap," Meredith said. She got off

the bed and opened a dresser drawer. "Here. You can wear my jade earrings. They'll look good with that outfit."

"Thank you, Meredith. I really don't have much jewelry." Taking the earrings, she adjusted the screws and winced. "I hate earrings. They hurt my ears."

"So you're going to meet Lord Gregory Braden and his family. That's moving in pretty fast company."

"Oh, I'm really going to see Hercules."

"Hercules! Who in the world is Hercules?"

Kat gave her a quick summary of how she had raised the animal and Parker had purchased it.

Her eyelids arched. "You're going to see a cow?"

"No. A steer."

Meredith had been intensely curious about her roommate's relationship with the handsome, but married, Parker Braden. She had gotten Kat to tell her some of the story but felt there must be more. "Well, I'll be blessed, I can't believe the woman's going to see a steer while visiting nobility!"

"I've got to go."

"You'll have to tell me all about it when you come back," Meredith called.

"I will." Kat shut the door behind her and went downstairs to find Parker just arriving. "I'm sorry if I made you wait."

"No, I just got here." He looked at her outfit and smiled. "Hercules is in for a treat. He doesn't usually have such attractive visitors."

She felt her cheeks grow warm as he laughed.

"I'm anxious for you to meet my family, Katherine."

★ ★ ★

"Who is this woman?" Veronica looked across the table at her husband's aunt, who was arranging the silverware. "What's she doing here? She's an American?"

"She's the daughter of the man we bought the Black Angus cattle from," Edith explained.

"I know that, but what's she doing here?"

"Parker got to know her family while he was in America looking for livestock. They've written a few times, I understand, mostly about cattle breeding and the newest things in veterinary medicine."

Gregory was standing beside the window looking out. "She's working at a mission house in East London, Parker tells me. Ah, there they are."

"A missionary?" Veronica muttered. "That'll be dull fare."

"She writes very nice letters," Gregory said. "I've written her a few times about the cattle. She seems quite sharp."

"Well, I'll stay for luncheon, but I'm not going to be preached at."

★ ★ ★

As Parker pulled into the driveway, Kat gasped, "What a beautiful house!"

A large front porch extended across the front of the huge two-story red-brick house. Six broad pillars held up the porch roof, and on either end of the house large chimneys were putting out puffs of gray smoke. The grounds surrounding the elegant home were carefully tended.

Parker opened the car door, and when Kat stepped out, she stared at the house, obviously overcome. "It takes all we can rake together to keep it. Veronica wants to sell it and buy a townhouse for us in London and a cottage in the country for my parents and aunt."

"What a shame! Don't you just love it?"

"Well, my parents and Aunt Edith will never hear of selling it. They love this old place."

"What about you?"

"I love it too. Of course, I grew up here and it's full of memories. But sometimes I think Veronica and I and the children need a place of our own."

They climbed the steps, and the door opened before they reached it.

"Hello, Cooper," Parker greeted.

"Good day, sir."

"This is Cooper, who takes care of us all. Cooper, this is Miss Katherine Winslow from America."

"I'm very pleased to welcome you, miss. Won't you come in?"

As she stepped inside, Kat was awed by the foyer. The floor was made of a beautifully veined marble. The walls were decorated with original paintings, and there was an air of spaciousness about it that could only be purchased by high ceilings and open spaces.

"The family's waiting in the drawing room."

"Thank you, Cooper."

As they walked down the long hallway that looked like an art gallery, Kat did her best to take in all the portraits lining the walls.

"These are all of your family?"

"Yes. My jolly ancestors. Rather grim looking, wouldn't you say?"

Kat just nodded.

Parker was watching her carefully. She was obviously overwhelmed by the house and by the stern faces of the Bradens that stared down at her. Parker knew that Kat had spent her early childhood in a lovely home in New York, and had even had servants at one time, but their home in Georgia was much more modest. "I think they were really better-humored people than they appear. I believe back in those days it was considered appropriate to look very stern when sitting for a painting."

"It must be wonderful to have pictures of so many of your ancestors."

"Your family goes a long way back too. Your father told me the first Winslow went over to the New World on the *Mayflower*."

"That's true. His name was Gilbert Winslow. We don't have a portrait of him, though."

Parker stopped and motioned toward the door. "Here's the drawing room."

Kat stepped inside and saw the family that had gathered to meet her. As she was introduced to Veronica Braden, she saw something hard in the woman's eyes and didn't know what to make of her. She was impressed with Parker's parents, however. Lord Braden was much older than his wife and looked rather tired, but his wife had a warm smile and made Kat feel at home.

"And this is my aunt, Miss Edith Braden. Aunt Edith, this is Miss Katherine Winslow."

"I'm pleased to meet you," Edith said formally.

"I'm so happy to meet you too. Parker has told me so much about you."

"What in the world could he say?"

"He's told me about your books. I have always loved history, and I admire people who are able to make history come alive on the pages of a book."

Edith Braden had been prepared to dislike this young woman. She had a distaste for Americans in general, her ideas being formed by the motion pictures she saw. However, she saw that this young woman's appreciation was genuine.

"Have you read any of my books?" she inquired.

"No, ma'am, I haven't, but I would love to. I must confess I don't know much history. I'm afraid most Americans are fairly ignorant about their own history, much less that of others."

Parker covered his mouth to hide a smile. His aunt was outspoken against ignorance, especially American ignorance, and here Katherine had unwittingly spiked her guns.

"Well, I'm sure I have one or two of my books up in my room. I'd be happy to give you one."

"Oh, would you sign it for me, please?"

"Yes, of course. I've written one about chivalry in the Middle Ages you might find interesting."

"Would you like to see the grounds," Grace intervened, "or have luncheon first, Miss Winslow?"

"Whichever would be most convenient."

"Let's eat first," Parker said. "Where are the twins?"

"You don't want them at lunch," Veronica said. "They'd be too much of a distraction."

"I really would like to see them if it's not too much trouble," Kat said. "I love children."

"I'll get them, but be prepared," Parker warned her.

He left the room, and Veronica began questioning their guest. Edith eyed her narrowly, for she understood Veronica better than most. Even though Edith and the Bradens had been instrumental in getting her nephew together with Veronica, she now grieved over their role in having encouraged such a match. She was sadly aware that Veronica drank too much and that she was not a good mother. She either swamped the children with affection, usually when she had been drinking, or ignored them. Either extreme was bad.

"Here. Why don't we go into the dining room and sit down?" Gregory suggested. "I want to hear what you and your family have been doing with your livestock."

Kat took her place, but they had only started their discussion of the Black Angus breed when Parker came in, carrying his children.

"This is Paul and this is Heather. Children, this is Miss Winslow."

He lowered them to the floor, and both children clung tightly to their father's hands.

Paul said firmly, "Hello."

Kat went and kneeled in front of them.

"Hello. I'll bet you're Paul."

"And I'm Heather."

"Daddy say you come from long way away."

"Yes, that's right, Heather."

"Do you hab any wittle boys or girls?" Paul asked.

"Not yet."

"Why?" he asked.

"Don't rush her, son," Parker said. "Let's get you in your seats." He got the twins settled in their high chairs at the long dining room table, then said to Kat, "Now you can compare English cooking with American cooking."

"I've already been doing that at the mission."

They all bowed their heads, and Gregory asked a brief blessing.

"What is this?" Kat asked after she had taken her first bite of a delicious meat and potato dish.

"Shepherd's pie," Mrs. Henderson said. "It's our cook's specialty."

"I want pig in a banket," Paul said.

"Pig in a blanket! What's that? It sounds awful." Kat smiled and winked at Parker.

"It's something like an American hotdog—a sausage baked in some dough," Parker told her. "The kids love 'em."

"And they're terrible for them," Veronica said. She was observing their guest's every move. "I know you're not married, Miss Winslow. Are you engaged?"

"No, I'm not, Mrs. Braden—or do I call you Lady Braden?"

"Mrs. Braden is fine. How long do you plan to be in London?" Veronica asked sharply.

"Until the mission sends me someplace else. I have no idea when that will be."

"We'll have to show you the sights," Parker said.

"I'd love to see Buckingham Palace on the inside. Can you pull any strings to let me get a peek at the royal family?"

Lord Braden laughed. "Not too many people get to see inside the palace, but the royal family is pretty much in the public eye now. We might catch a glimpse of them out and about."

"I'd like to visit Parliament too—maybe see the new prime minister, Mr. Churchill. He sounds like a capable leader."

"He's rather wild, I'm afraid." Gregory shrugged. "Always off on all sorts of adventures."

"I think he's a good man, Father," Parker said. "He

doesn't pull any punches. All he promises us is blood, sweat, and tears."

"That's a switch from the promises politicians usually make," Edith said. "But he may be just the sort of leader we need right now. Ordinary methods won't work."

The conversation about the war continued, with everyone except Veronica and the children contributing. Parker didn't seem to care much for the subject either.

When the meal was over, Parker said, "Suppose we go take a look at your old friend Hercules." He turned to his wife. "Veronica, would you like to go with us?"

"No thank you. I've seen cows before."

The twins immediately started clamoring to go, but Parker shook his head. "No, not this time."

"Oh, please, Parker, let them go," Kat pleaded.

"You don't know what you're asking for. It's like herding a bunch of bees across the desert."

"Surely two of us can handle two small children."

"All right. You asked for it. Let's get you cleaned up a bit first, kids."

★ ★ ★

"The pasture is so lovely!" Kat exclaimed. "Everything is so green. I think the grass is even greener here than it is at home."

"It seemed that way when I was in your country. Of course in Texas the grass is usually brown. Your part of the country is much more beautiful."

Kat scanned the cattle grazing in the meadow. "There's Hercules!"

"Would you like to go greet him?"

"Yes!"

"Me too," Paul said.

"No, son, you stay here. We'll let Katherine have a private reunion with her old friend."

"I'll be right back, Paul," Kat said. She slipped through

the gate and walked rapidly toward the cattle. They were beautiful stock. She was accustomed to seeing fine Black Angus, and these made her proud of Hercules, who was the sire of most of them.

"Hercules, do you remember me?"

The massive bull lifted his head and continued chewing his cud as Kat came forward. She ran her hand along his neck, delighted at his healthy appearance. "You're still a handsome fellow." She put out her hand and the massive bull lowered his head and licked it. "You remember!" she said. She turned and called, "He remembers me, Parker! Bring the children over. Let me introduce them."

Parker took the children's hands as they came across the field. They were dwarfed by the mighty bull, but when Parker set them on the animal's back, they squealed with delight. He lifted them off and asked Kat if she wanted to see the grounds.

As they started the tour, Paul and Heather attached themselves to Kat, each insisting on holding one of her hands.

"Do you ever think of my visit?" Parker asked.

"Of course. How could I forget?"

He turned to look at her, an odd expression in his eyes. "I remember everything about it."

His statement brought a flush to Kat's face. She was thinking about the times he had held her. Since then she had gone out with several other men and had been kissed a few times, but none of the others had interested her much. Now as she stood so close, she remembered his gentleness, and she also remembered how she had responded to his kiss.

She dropped her eyes and changed the subject. "You've done a good job with the herd."

"Actually Hercules did most of it."

Kat giggled. "You are a fool."

"Everyone knows that." As they walked, he pointed out the various buildings and gave her the history of each one.

"I'm jealous," Parker told his daughter with a straight

face. "You'd rather hold hands with Miss Winslow than me?"

"You hab hard hands. Shes is soft," Heather said. She looked up at Kat and smiled. "You gonna stay long time?"

"I hope so, Heather."

"You come back and see us?"

"Yes. Bring presents!" Paul put in.

Parker laughed. "There, you see the real Braden trait. Pure selfishness and raw greed."

Kat stooped down and hugged both children. "I will come back, and I will bring you both lovely presents."

Parker looked down and saw the lissome form of the young woman. Something rose in his throat as she held the hands of the two children as they peppered her with questions. When she stood up, he said, "It looks like you've made a conquest."

"It's so easy to love children."

"Yes. Sometimes grown-ups are harder."

Kat thought this was an odd remark to make, but she made no comment. Overhead the sky was blue, and suddenly she saw a group of planes flying hard and fast. "What are those?"

"Hurricanes. Probably been scrambled to meet some of Göring's fellows coming across the Channel."

The reminder of war took some of the pleasure out of the moment, and Kat asked no more. She watched the planes as they disappeared and felt a moment's fear for the tall man who walked beside her.

★ ★ ★

"Isn't Joseph taking Miss Winslow back to her mission?" Veronica had come outside with the rest of the family. She had expected the chauffeur to be there with the big car, but instead Parker had pulled up in his little two-seater MG.

Parker got out and heard the question. "I'll have to be

back at the station by eight, so it'll be convenient for me to drop her off."

"It's been so wonderful being with you, Mrs. Braden."

"A pleasure." Veronica chopped the words off, and there was little warmth in her eyes.

"You must come back again, my dear," Grace said.

"Yes, of course," Gregory agreed. "Parker monopolized you this time. Next time I want to talk with you about a new breed I'm thinking of adding."

"I'd be happy to."

Kat said good-bye to the children, promising them the presents they demanded and then got into the car. She couldn't help noticing Veronica's sour expression as she stood holding her children's hands. Parker started down the driveway, and Kat looked back to wave at the children.

"It was such a short visit," Parker said. "I haven't shown you nearly everything."

"You have a beautiful home and a wonderful family." She held up the book Parker's aunt had given her. "I'm so proud of this book."

"It's pretty heavy stuff."

"Is she famous, Parker?"

"She is among some historians. She hasn't made a great deal of money from her work, but those who know it admire her."

They talked constantly all the way back to Kat's apartment. When Parker pulled up in front of the building, he got out and came around to open her door.

"It was wonderful. Thank you so much for having me."

"I expect you enjoyed seeing Hercules almost as much as the twins did," he said with a smile.

"You have such a wonderful family, and I love your children. They're so precious. If you ever need a sitter, give me a call."

"I may take you up on that. Well, I have to run. It was so good to see you again, Katherine."

She turned and walked into the building. She climbed the stairs to her second-story flat and found Meredith waiting. Even before Kat was fully inside the door, Meredith said, "Now, tell me all the juicy details. How the nobility lives."

"Well, Meredith, I saw the most beautiful steer in all the world!"

CHAPTER TEN

A COWBOY IN LONDON

★ ★ ★

For most of his life Parker Braden had enjoyed walking along the coast of the English Channel. As a very young boy, he had fallen under the spell of the sea, and some of his happiest memories were of sailing along the coast in the family yacht. When the war started, he had agonized over whether to join the navy or the air force. Now an officer in the RAF, he stared out over the choppy waters at Margate, Kent, and wondered if he had made the right choice.

With the smell of the sea in his nostrils, he studied the military fortifications built to withstand a possible German invasion by sea. Ever since France had collapsed and the British army had been miraculously delivered at Dunkirk, a furious activity had begun, for all of Britain was convinced that Hitler would be knocking at their door soon. Intelligence had been quick to inform their superiors in London that the Luftwaffe had moved from its home base into the Low Countries and then to France. There they were gathered, just twenty minutes' flight to Dover and an hour away from London. The German navy also was much in evidence. Barges and small craft were being rounded up, and there could be no question as to their purpose. Sooner or later Hitler would attack across the Channel, and Britain worked to prepare itself.

Churchill had known, perhaps sooner than anyone else, that Hitler would never be satisfied. He played desperately for time, organizing a home guard to patrol Britain's roads and the two thousand miles of coastline, some of them armed with only hunting weapons, others with pitchforks and golf clubs. The prime minister called a meeting of the Imperial General Staff in an underground headquarters that was simply called "The hole in the ground." It was buried beneath Whitehall, close to the houses of Parliament and government offices. As Churchill looked around at his ministers in dead silence, he took the cigar out of his mouth and said firmly, "This is the room in which I'll direct the war. And if the invasion takes place, I'll sit here in this chair until either the Germans are driven back or they carry me out dead."

Parker smiled slightly as he thought of Churchill's bulldog attitude. He had braced the people for the struggle to come, and more than any single man at this point, he held the British together.

Parker turned and walked slowly westward, heading inland now along the Thames Estuary. He glanced out at one of the most ambitious of the coastal defense installations, the Sea Forts. These towering structures were as large as the Arc de Triomphe in Paris. They resembled offshore oil rigs and were constructed on land and then floated out to sea and sunk into place. He watched for a time as men swarmed over them, for they bristled with armament— Lewis guns, Bofors, and 3.7-inch anti-aircraft cannon.

The sight depressed Parker, and he turned his back on the water and returned to his car to drive back toward London's East End, about an hour's drive away. He passed a group of civilians carrying luggage along the road, surrounded by armed British soldiers. These, he knew, were German-born citizens of England. He had heard that thousands of these men were being arrested and hustled off to makeshift camps set up on racetracks or in old factories or even in elegant country estates.

The faces of the men were grim. Some of them were obviously professional men, others workingmen clad in the rough clothing of their trade. Parker felt something stir within him, for he had known many British citizens of German derivation who were good people and loyal to Great Britain. "They're going overboard on this," he muttered. "I can only hope that the officials who have organized this will come to their senses soon."

He parked his car near the hospital where Kat worked and, as he got out, was aware of a great deal of activity. He approached a bobby who was taking down a street sign and adding it to a stack of others.

"What's going on, Officer?"

"Taking down all the street signs so those cretin Huns won't know where they are when they invade."

Parker stared at him in disbelief. "They won't likely be hunting for addresses when they come."

The man shrugged, a scowl on his face. "It's orders, you know. We've got to do everything we can to stop them."

This was only one of the measures Parker knew Britain was taking to get ready for war. All the lampposts had been ringed with white paint to make them visible for drivers and pedestrians during blackouts. Headlights had all been fitted with blackout shields that masked the light, and the windows of trains got a coat of dark blue paint to conceal the light from planes overhead.

As he reached the entrance to the hospital, he saw a crowd gathered and stopped to watch an air-raid rehearsal in progress. There were four men stretched out on the street impersonating victims, while men in white coats came to put them on stretchers and carry them off. A man in a dress suit with a derby was watching the whole thing and nodding with approval. It was all very neat, but Parker thought, *When the bombs start falling, it won't be quite this simple and organized.*

He went into the hospital and stopped to ask for help

from a horse-faced woman who sat behind a desk. "I'm looking for one of my pilots. His name is Raymond Bailey."

The woman glared at him almost suspiciously. *If a pilot in the Royal Air Force gets such a harsh glance, what would she give to a German?* he wondered. He smiled, however, as she shuffled through a list of cards.

"He's in room 206," she said. "Take the elevator."

"Thank you, ma'am."

Parker made his way across the crowded floor, which was filled with scurrying people. When he reached the elevator and punched the button, he heard his name called and turned to see Kat. She was wearing her nurse's uniform and had a smile for him. "I'm surprised to see you here, Parker."

"Why, I'm surprised to see you as well. I didn't expect to bump into you in this big place. You're still working at the mission, aren't you?"

"Oh yes, but I do a shift here four times a week as well. They're short of nurses."

"That's nice of you to give them a hand. One of my pilots is here. Maybe you could give him a little special attention."

"Of course. What's his name?"

The elevator door opened and the two got on. "Lieutenant Raymond Bailey. He was shot down last week and is in pretty bad shape."

The others on the elevator were watching the tall pilot as he spoke to the nurse, and Parker felt rather confined. He waited until the elevator stopped on the second floor and the two got off. "He's in 206."

"How badly is he hurt?"

"He was shot in both legs. The doctors are trying to save them. I'm worried about him, Katherine. He just got engaged two weeks ago, and he's worried he'll lose his legs."

The two entered a ward with eight beds lined up along one wall. One of the beds had a screen around it, and after looking around and seeing no familiar faces, Parker said, "I imagine he's behind there."

The two approached the screen, and when Parker

stepped to one side, he nodded to Katherine, and she followed him.

"Hello, Ray," Parker said.

The patient was a pale-faced man of no more than twenty. His features were drawn, and pain had etched its lines upon his face. He attempted a feeble smile and reached out his hand. When Parker took it, he whispered, "Good to see you, Wing Commander."

"How are you feeling?"

"All right."

He looked down at his legs, which were swathed with bandages from thigh to ankle. Parker saw the despair on his face and said cheerfully, "Well, now, I brought you some good company. This is Miss Katherine Winslow. She's an American, and she'll be able to help you some. Won't you, Katherine?"

"Hello, Lieutenant," Kat said. She moved forward and smiled down at him. "I'm sorry about your bad luck, but I'm sure your legs will heal thoroughly."

Bailey looked at her and barely nodded. It was obvious that he was deeply depressed, and there was no hope at all in his face.

Parker talked rapidly about the weather and his twins, trying to take the pilot's attention off of his condition, but finally he seemed to run out of topics. Kat knew little of the specifics of his case, but she knew that depression would not help him at all. She said brightly, "Parker tells me you're engaged to be married."

"I was." He looked down at his legs, and his lips drew into a tight line. "Diane won't want to marry a man without legs."

"Now, now! It won't come to that, I'm sure," Kat said quickly. "There are fine doctors in this hospital. They'll do their very best for you."

"They can't do a miracle."

"Well, of course not," she said, "but the Lord can."

"Why did God let me get hurt like this?" he asked bitterly.

Parker was at a loss, but Kat was not. "God is able to do all things, and I don't know why this happened. Things like this happen in wars all the time. You know that better than I. But I would like to pray for you, Lieutenant. I've seen God do great miracles. Would you mind?"

"I guess not," he muttered.

To Parker's surprise Kat moved forward and took the young man's hand. She held it firmly between the two of hers, and Parker saw Ray's eyes open with surprise. Kat began to pray a simple but fervent prayer.

She concluded by saying, "O God, we're not asking anything impossible. I pray that you will be with this young man and give him his legs, and I pray you will be with his fiancée and give her a loving heart. May she be a support for him. Give them a good life together and protect his life in the future when he flies again. In the name of Jesus."

Parker lifted his eyes and glanced at Kat. There was a peace on her face that he admired greatly. He shifted his gaze and saw that Raymond was staring at her. Some of the strain seemed to have left, and he managed a smile.

"Thank you, miss. I appreciate it."

"I'll be back to see you every chance I get."

"So will I," Parker said quickly. "We're a little busy right now, Ray, but the fellows will be checking on you. I know you're going to be fine."

The two said their good-byes, and when they left the ward, Kat said, "Do you have time for some tea? We could go to the cafeteria here."

"That sounds good to me."

Ten minutes later the two were sitting in the crowded cafeteria sipping their tea. Kat asked about the twins.

"I'm afraid they're expecting you to come back with presents for their birthday next Wednesday. It would be wonderful if you could come. It's a bit much for my mother, and Veronica could use some help."

"I'll try very hard to work it in. They are such lovely children."

"Hello, Parker."

Parker turned and looked up at a couple who were standing by the table. "Why, hello, Ann, Wade," he said quickly. "How have you been?"

The couple were staring at Kat suspiciously, at least so she thought. They were well dressed and obviously well-to-do. They explained that they were visiting a sick relative of Ann's.

When they left, Parker shrugged. "She's a decorator—a good friend of Veronica's."

He picked up his tea, sipped it, and did not speak for a long time.

Finally Kat said, "It's very hard on you when your men get hurt or when you lose them, isn't it?"

"Yes, of course it is. We become like brothers in the squadron. I guess I'm the father figure and these are like my sons, although we're all about the same age, really. I appreciate your prayer for Raymond. He's such a fine chap."

"I hope his fiancée is sympathetic."

"I hope so too. Raymond didn't sound too optimistic, though."

When they had finished their tea, Parker reminded her again of the birthday party. As Kat went back to her duties, she made a note to make as many trips as possible to the bedside of the wounded pilot.

★ ★ ★

Parker looked up from his desk at the RAF station, and his eyes widened with surprise. "Veronica!" Getting up, he came to meet her. "Is something wrong? Are the children sick?"

"No. They're fine." Veronica was dressed to perfection as always, and she had obviously been to a hairdresser. Parker could not conceal his surprise, for she never came to his office. "Here, sit down. Let me have someone bring us some tea."

Veronica nodded, and Parker sent his assistant to brew a

fresh pot of tea. They made small talk while they waited for the tea, and Parker wondered why Veronica had come. She did not do many things impulsively, and now as the man left, he studied her face closely. He had learned to read her very well and knew that something had upset her. "Is there anything wrong, Veronica?"

"Yes, something's wrong!" she said tersely. Her lips drew together in a tight line and for a moment she could not speak. Finally she said, "I've heard about your date with your American girlfriend."

"What in the world are you talking about?"

"Ann told me she saw you two having lunch together."

"Oh, that. I went to the hospital to see Raymond Bailey. You remember the guy who got shot in the legs? I didn't even know Katherine worked there. We ran into each other, and I asked her to go with me while I visited Ray. She seemed to care for him quite a bit, I think."

"That wasn't the way I heard it. Ann said you two seemed to be having a very good time."

"Veronica, this is ridiculous."

"Is it?"

"Of course it is. If I were going to have a date, as you put it, with a woman, I certainly wouldn't do it in the middle of a crowded hospital cafeteria."

"Where would you do it, then?"

"I wouldn't do it anywhere. That's the point."

Veronica Braden had never expected her marriage would be perfect, or even especially happy. She had not truly loved Parker when she married him, though she had made a good pretense of doing so in order to hook him. At the time she was mostly thankful to have found a means of support and a father for her children. With such a shaky basis for a marriage, their relationship had only grown terse. She knew he didn't love her anymore, but in her mind that didn't give him any right to have an affair right under her nose. She had suffered enough scandal in her life and wasn't prepared to endure any more. She glared at him, her eyes hard. "I won't put up with this sort of thing, Parker! I don't want you to see that woman again."

Parker's nerves were taut. He was upset over the losses in the squadron and was worried about the new men who were coming in with not nearly enough training. Now he said quietly, "There's nothing between me and Katherine Winslow."

"I'm going to make sure of that. Don't bring her to the house anymore."

Parker's temper was rising within him at her accusation. He knew it was unwise to argue, however, for he had learned long ago that Veronica was much better than he at domestic battles. But he couldn't help himself. The tension of his duties had drawn up his nerves to a breaking point. He put both hands on the table and glared at her. It was the expression he had when he was honing in on an enemy aircraft with his finger on the trigger. "That's ridiculous. The children have already asked her to come to their party."

"I told you I don't want her there."

"I don't care what you want, Veronica. She's coming and that's it. Don't make me say something I'll be sorry for. The discussion is closed."

Veronica's face was pale. Parker had never set himself against her like this. He had always been easygoing, eager to avoid quarrels. Now seeing the way he stared at her, she knew she could go no further. She got up and left without a word, but she was thinking, *He's lying to me. There is something between the two of them.* Even though she didn't love her husband, she had no intention of being pushed out of the way by another woman. *She may come, but I'll make it so unpleasant for her she won't ever come back.*

★   ★   ★

The scene with Veronica had not helped Parker's emotional state. He hated confrontations with her and avoided them whenever possible. He was glad when it was finally time to scramble the squadron. He took only six planes out for reconnaissance, which was uneventful. When he landed, he gave his report and then started toward his office. He pulled up short when he saw a civilian lounging in a chair beside his desk. He could not see the face at first, but something about the man seemed familiar. Not many visitors wore cowboy boots and impressive western-style hats. Recognition came when his visitor shoved the hat back and rose to his feet.

"Howdy there, Parker."

"Brodie, what in the world are you doing here?" Parker asked. "Did you come over to see Katherine?"

"Well, I plan on doin' that, but mainly I wanted to get in this here war. I come to sign up in your outfit."

Parker stared blankly at Brodie. He remembered then the man's background and said rather shortly, "The RAF is a little different from stunt flying. I know you're good at that, and I know you've had experience flying against the Germans in Spain. But the discipline is strict here. I'm not sure you'd be happy."

"Oh, I can do what I have to do," Brodie said breezily. "As a matter of fact, I already signed up and got myself assigned to your squadron."

Parker stared at Brodie with incredulity. "How in the world did you manage that?"

"Didn't seem to be too much trouble. They're takin' fliers from everywhere now. Lots of 'em from Canada. As a matter of fact, I flew over with three of those Canadians. When I told the officer who was recruitin' that I knew you and wanted to be in your squadron, he was happy to do it."

Parker looked at the American reluctantly, but then he did need fliers. And he had seen Brodie in action. "All right," he said. "We'll have to get you some uniforms, and then I'll take you through some training."

Brodie laughed. "I thought I'd done all the trainin' I need to do."

"Things are a little different here. You need to get

acquainted with our planes. You've never flown a Spit, have you?"

"Nope. But if it's got two wings and an engine in it, I reckon I can fly it."

Parker was afraid that trouble lay ahead, but everyone was desperate for experienced pilots. "All right, but I must warn you, Brodie, there are no stars here. We fight as a unit."

"Shore, that's fine with me," he said with a grin. "I just came over to help. I thought I'd try for the record."

"What record?"

"Shootin' down planes. How many have you shot down, by the way?"

"Five."

"Anybody beat that?"

"Yes. Several."

"Well, just lead me to one of them Spitfires and show me the Germans, and I'll set about breakin' the records."

Parker found the American's self-confidence refreshing. He laughed shortly and said, "All right, but you can't fly dressed like that. Let's see about getting you a flight suit and a dress uniform. But first I'll introduce you to the rest of the squadron."

"Shore. That suits me."

Most of the pilots were in the rec room, and when Parker walked in followed by Brodie Lee, he saw their eyes light up as they took him in. "This is Brodie Lee," Parker announced after everyone had quieted. "He's from America, and he'll be flying with us. Brodie, this is Bernard Cox." He indicated a small man with bright blue eyes. "Bernie wants to be a painter when the war is over."

"Paintin' houses?"

"No. Painting pictures." Bernard grinned. He was a fantastic pilot and asked innocently, "Have you ever been up in an airplane?"

"One or two."

"This is Sailor Darley." Parker waved toward a tall, strongly built man with a wrestler's shoulders and a big neck. "He was a sailor at one time, so he claims, but he can shoot straight."

"You look like a cowboy," Darley said. "Did you bring your lasso so you can rope these German planes?"

"No, but I brought armament, all right." Brodie reached inside his coat and pulled out a revolver. Everyone dodged slightly as he waved it around. "Been wantin' to try it out on one of them Germans."

"Put that thing away, Lee. It's against the law."

"Don't you fellows carry guns?"

"Not pearl-handled ones like that," Parker said.

"Pearl-handled! This here's *ivory*. Only a two-bit gambler in a New Orleans dive would carry a *pearl*-handled shootin' iron!"

"I suppose that's true enough." Parker continued around the room, introducing the rest of the squadron. When Zarek Dolenski was introduced, he declared, "You're a cowboy and that's what I will call you."

Parker grinned. "Call him anything you want, but when we're in the air, watch out for him."

"That's right. I'm here to save you fellows, so take good care of me." A laugh went around the room, and Archibald Kent-Wilkins, leader of Green Flight, shook his head. "What have we done to America that they send us a thing like this? I knew we should have won that ruddy war against the Colonists!"

★　★　★

Her day at the mission had seemed interminable, and Meredith Bryce was so exhausted she could hardly hold up her head. It had also been hot, and her uniform was crumpled and sweaty. Another half hour and she would be off duty.

Finally she finished washing the dirty cups and saucers and was reaching up to put them onto a high shelf. She was not a tall girl and was stretching as far as she could when something suddenly slapped her across the backside, and a cheerful voice said, "Hey, lemme help you with that, sweetheart."

Meredith whirled, red-faced, toward the man who had taken liberties with her. "Keep your hands to yourself!"

"Why, sorry about that. I heard you Brits liked gestures of familiarity."

She wanted to crack him across the cheek but settled for a verbal tongue-lashing. She knew he was American by the few words he had said and by his outlandish costume, including high-heeled boots and a cowboy hat.

"Hey, don't blow your top. I'm looking for Kat Winslow."

"She's not here now."

"Well, I've gotta find her. What's your name?"

"None of your business."

"I'm Brodie Lee. You work with Kat. She must have told you about me."

As a matter of fact, Kat had mentioned Brodie's name and showed her a picture. "You'll have to come back tomorrow when she's on duty."

"Wait a minute. I know who you are. Kat sent me a picture of the two of you."

Meredith could see the man wasn't going to leave without getting some information. "My name is Meredith Bryce."

"That's right. That's the name. Look, Merry—"

"My name is Meredith, not Merry."

"That's a right pretty name."

"Thank you, but you need to leave now."

Brodie protested, but finally Meredith succeeded in getting him out of the building. She was agitated over his familiarity with her and was glad when she could finally leave herself.

A light rain was falling as she left the mission. She opened her umbrella and walked the three blocks to her flat. She went inside and ran up the stairs to the second floor. "Kat, are you here?" she called.

"Yes, I am." Kat came into the living room from a door

that led to the kitchen. "Did you remember to bring the milk?"

"No, I forgot the bloomin' milk. Let me tell you—"

A staccato knock on the door broke in, and Kat started. "Who can that be?"

"I have no idea," Meredith said. She opened the door and there stood Brodie Lee.

"Hi, Merry," he said. He looked over her at Kat and said, "Hey, Kat, there you are." He brushed by Meredith, walked right up to Kat, and kissed her soundly.

She struggled to free herself. "Brodie Lee, what are you doing here?"

"I've come over to win the war for the limeys."

"Well, you haven't changed," Kat said, shaking her head but smiling at the same time. "This is my flatmate Meredith."

"Oh, sure. We met down at the mission."

"You followed me home!" Meredith exclaimed, her face pink with anger.

"Yep, I believe I did. I'm pretty hungry, Kat. Why don't you take me out to dinner?"

"I've already got dinner fixed."

"All right. Don't mind if I do," Brodie said with a grin. "I could at least help you set the table."

Kat laughed. "You're impossible. Well, I think I've got enough for the three of us."

Meredith stared at Brodie. She knew that Kat had a liking for the man, but she had seen nothing so far to admire in the crass American.

"Why don't you be a gentleman and leave."

"I'd rather be just like I am and stay, Merry."

Kat shook her head. "You can't insult him, Meredith. It's impossible. Why don't you go ahead and take your bath? I'll have supper on the table by the time you get finished."

★ ★ ★

"And so I figured I might as well come over and join up. According to what the radio said, Hitler's gonna be comin' this way. I thought I could be part of the welcoming committee."

"You can't just up and join the RAF," Meredith broke out.

"Oh, I already done that. I'm in Eagle Squadron." He winked at Kat. "Lord Parker Braden is my squadron leader for now."

"What do you mean 'for now'?"

"Oh, I figure I'll be leadin' the guys myself after I've put in a little time."

"Why, you egotist!" Meredith said loudly.

"No, I'm a democrat."

The visit proved to be a long one, with Brodie doing a great deal of the talking. He finally was ushered out by Kat, who avoided his attempts to kiss her. As she shut the door, he said, "I'll be seeing you around, sweetheart—you too, Merry."

"He is impossible!" Meredith exclaimed.

"You'd better watch out for him, Meredith. He can charm the birds out of the trees. Every girl in my hometown was crazy about him when we were kids. And since then he's acquired that romantic glow of being a pilot."

"You don't have to worry about me. I'd just like to take a pin and puncture a bit of that egotism!" She sighed and said, "Well, we are in trouble if that's the best that America can send over here to help us."

"I don't know about that. He's a good pilot." She started toward the kitchen, but a thought came to her. "But he's not much for discipline. I don't know how Parker will handle that."

★ ★ ★

Field Marshal Wilhelm Keitel, chief of the German armed forces, scanned the faces of his officers whom he had called into a special meeting. "The führer has decided that a landing in England is possible," he said tersely, "provided that air superiority can be attained. All preparations will begin immediately."

Laughter went up around the room, and one of the officers said loudly, "It will be as the British pilots say—a piece of cake."

"It will not be unless we gain air superiority," Keitel said soberly.

Colonel Multz shook his head. "The RAF will be in no position to stop us. They lost a great many planes and pilots in France. It will be a walk-over!"

The Luftwaffe was indeed the key to the invasion of Britain. The action would begin with an intensive air attack, and in Hermann Göring's view, this would be all that was needed to subdue the island nation. At this point Hitler had his eyes fixed on the Soviet Union. He would have been glad to have reached an agreement with Britain—on his own terms. He had been somewhat sobered by Admiral Erich Raeder's view that a land invasion would be very difficult, considering Great Britain had the strongest navy in the world. Nevertheless, Hitler's directive number sixteen stated, "As England is unwilling to compromise, I have therefore decided to begin to prepare for and if necessary to carry out an invasion of England. The code name will be 'Operation Sealion.'" He added further, "The air attack that must destroy England's air superiority will start on a day we'll call 'Eagle Day.'"

CHAPTER ELEVEN

THE HIGH-FLYING COWBOY

★ ★ ★

Most of the world viewed the oncoming confrontation between Britain and Germany as a David and Goliath battle. The Luftwaffe had taken on the aura of an invincible force. Every distinguished visitor to Germany was filled with stories of the invincibility of Göring's air force. These visitors returned to their homes with dire predictions.

One of them, Charles Lindbergh, toured the air stations and factories of Germany and on his return issued a gloomy prediction. He stated that he felt German air strength was greater than that of all other European countries combined. Germany had the means to destroy London, as well as Paris and Prague, if she wished to do so. England and France together did not have enough modern equipment for effective defense or counterattack.

Lindbergh's words were shored up by the ease with which the Luftwaffe wiped out the Polish air force in May. The might of such an air force no longer seemed arguable. How could Britain possibly expect to win against an enemy reputed to have forty-five hundred first-line aircraft, while the Royal Air Force had no more than twenty-nine hundred?

But though the odds were overwhelming, the struggle was not as one-sided as it seemed. Britain could compete favorably in the quality if not in the quantity of planes. Also, Britain possessed something new that would change the whole course of the war—the all-seeing eye of radar. Besides, the British would be fighting on their home ground. Any British pilot shot down that safely parachuted out could return to action, whereas the German pilots would be imprisoned until the end of the war.

Perhaps one of the factors that ultimately helped the British in this conflict was the inadvertent help they got from the mistakes made by German industry. Hitler claimed that to speed up their production of aircraft would unnecessarily alarm the German population, who had been repeatedly told they would see a string of easy successes. Hitler assigned the secret task of procuring planes and developing new models to General Ernst Udet, a hard-drinking, happy-go-lucky World War I ace. Udet was an excellent pilot, but as an administrator he was a total failure. He created a monstrous bureaucracy in which it was almost impossible to get a decision made. This slowed down the production of fighter planes and ultimately gave Britain the edge she desperately needed.

One other factor worked in the favor of the British forces. Göring and his men were the victims of tremendous overconfidence. Encouraged by past successes, the intelligence reports they received told them that the RAF would only put up a feeble air defense. Göring, always arrogant, accepted these reports at face value, which proved to be a fatal miscalculation.

Churchill placed a sixty-one-year-old Canadian-born newspaper publisher, Lord Beaverbrook, in charge of Britain's aircraft building program. Beaverbrook galvanized the production of airplanes, moving at once into a seven-day week, and announced that there would be no work stoppages. To collect the aluminum to build the planes, he sponsored a drive to persuade the women of Great Britain to donate their pots and pans, as well as anything else made of metal, to the industry. In the months that followed the evacuation at Dunkirk, British workers built more than four hundred new fighters for the RAF. These planes were produced not only in factories but in small garages and workshops. Planes were also beginning to flow in from Canada and the United States.

The Spitfire and the Hurricane were the mainstays of the RAF fighter squadrons. The Hurricane had been in service longer; almost half of England's sixty-one fighter squadrons were equipped with them, while only twenty of them had Spitfires. The Hurricane's top speed was 325 miles an hour, 30 miles per hour slower than the Messerschmitt, but it had a superior range and was more heavily armored than the Spitfire. The Spitfire owed its speed to the Rolls Royce engine, which gave it incredible horsepower and was the most maneuverable fighter plane in the air. On the other side of the Channel, Germans were flying the Me-109, a remarkable aircraft that was improved by two 20-millimeter cannons mounted on the wing's leading edges.

And so the adversaries waited, poised for the titanic struggle that was inevitable in the skies over England and the Channel.

★ ★ ★

Parker took off with Brodie Lee right behind him. After they had climbed to ten thousand feet and gone onto oxygen, Parker said, "All right, Blue Three. I want you to follow me as close as you can. Where I go, you go. You keep me covered."

"Sure. No problem, Boss."

"The answer is *No problem, Red Leader.*"

"Right. Red Leader."

Parker immediately banked and sent his Spitfire into a sharp turn. He saw that Lee had followed him easily, so he began to use more complicated maneuvers. He threw the plane into tight turns, steep climbs, every maneuver he could think of, but no matter what he did, Lee was right there beside him. "Very good, Blue Three."

"Glad you like it, Red Leader."

"Now, you try to lose me."

"Yes, sir."

Immediately Lee's plane went into a series of maneuvers. Parker was hard put to follow them, and finally he took his eye off of the Spitfire for one moment. He lost sight of the plane in a thin, wispy cloud. When he emerged into the open sky, he searched ahead of him . . . no Brodie.

"Hi there, Red Leader."

Startled, Parker looked up into his mirror and there was Brodie Lee right behind him. Brodie waved cheerfully, and Parker felt like a fool. "All right. That's enough, Blue Three. We'll head back to the base."

As soon as they landed on the airfield in the Kent countryside, Parker walked up to Brodie and said, "You're ready for combat, Brodie."

"You mean now?"

"No, not now," Parker said with a grin. "The next time we scramble. That was a good exercise up there. Remember, always protect your flight leader."

"Who's going to protect me?"

"I didn't think you needed any protecting. Not the great Brodie Lee." Parker clapped him on the shoulder.

The two men walked toward the building, where Brodie joined a card game that was in progress. Parker was stopped by Bernard Cox in the hallway. "Can he do the job, do you think?"

"He's a first-class pilot. Lots of experience."

"That's good. I'd hate to have an amateur up there with us," the Blue leader commented. "From what I can pick up, we can expect some fun pretty soon. I've heard the Germans have been bombing some ships out in the Channel."

"I expect they'll try to draw us up, but I'm not excited about protecting ships. Most of them are empty—"

A voice broke in with, "Attention, 120 Squadron. Scramble!"

"That's us. I'll find out what it is," Parker said. He was still in his flight suit, and he was intercepted by an officer who said, "They're bombing more ships in the Channel. Here's the position."

Parker grabbed the paper and ran out onto the field. He was glad to see that the entire squadron was already climbing into their planes, and he demanded, "Did you get the plane fueled, Denny?"

"Yes, sir. She's full. You think it's the real thing this time?"

"I think it may be."

"Get some of them dirty krauts for me, sir."

"Do my best."

The squadron took off and immediately arranged themselves into four groups of three each, each group in a *V* formation with the leader in front. They were identified as yellow, green, blue, and red. They flashed over the Channel, and five minutes later Parker saw planes ahead.

"Keep your eyes open, men. There they are. Take the bombers first if you can and ignore the fighters."

Parker nodded as he saw the German Stukas attacking the ships below. "This is Red Leader. We'll take those bombers over to the left waiting to go in." They had climbed high and were now overhead. "All right. Here we go. Tally ho!"

The squadron went in full force and were spotted almost at once by a 109. Ignoring them as best they could, they plowed ahead, aiming for the bombers.

They were attacked on their way in by at least twenty 109s, and a fierce dogfight began. Two of the Stukas went down in smoke, but Sailor Darley saw one of the Spits going down as well. He could not tell who it was. He glanced over his shoulder and saw that Bernie Cox was there, but he could not see Lee. "Where are you, Blue Three?"

He got no answer, then suddenly saw holes appear in his wing and threw himself over. His Spit would not maneuver—his controls had been hit. He desperately tried to shake off the new Messerschmitts and managed to avoid more direct hits, but the faster 109 was zeroing in on him.

Suddenly, as he went into a turn, he saw a Spitfire coming from out of nowhere. The plane got so close to the German flying straight at him, guns blazing, that Sailor shouted, "Watch it, Cowboy."

But Brodie plunged straight ahead. Sailor saw the tracers enter into the nose of the 109s and dance along the fuselage before the canopy was smashed. He knew the pilot was killed instantly.

"You got him!" Sailor cried. He watched as Cowboy pulled up close, waved at him, and then plunged back into the melee.

"He may be a show-off, but he's a killer," Sailor muttered to himself.

When the squadron landed, several of the planes were damaged but none critically. Jimmy Fitzwilliam, the smallest and youngest pilot in the squadron, had been shot down, but he had been fished out of the Channel and was safe. As the pilots gathered in the report room, they were excited.

"Cowboy, I was glad to see you out there," Sailor said. "Congratulations on your first kill. Not many pilots get a kill on their first mission."

Brodie shrugged his shoulders. "Should have gotten another one, but they're slippery devils, aren't they?"

Parker spoke to the pilots after they had given their reports. "I'm very pleased with your work. We've got a fine squadron here. Everyone looked out for his wingman, and we shot down four of their bombers and two of their fighters with the loss of only one plane."

He went on praising them, and after the meeting broke up, he pulled Brodie aside. "Congratulations. Sailor tells me you saved his life."

"Don't know about that. I should have gotten more than just one, though."

"I'm very happy you got the one."

"Well, I aim to be a hero, and it's a pretty slow start. But you just watch my smoke. When do you reckon we'll scramble again?"

Parker could not help but laugh. "At least give us time to

get our planes patched up and refueled. But you did fine. I'm very happy with your work."

★ ★ ★

Kat and Meredith both had Monday off, since they had worked on Sunday. They were spending the day catching up on some reading. Kat scrambled for the phone when it rang Monday afternoon.

After a brief greeting, Grace Braden said, "The twins will be turning three on Wednesday, and I was hoping you could come to their party. Paul and Heather keep asking about you. You made quite an impression on them."

"Why, yes, Lady Braden, I'd love to come." She didn't mention that Parker had already invited her.

"It'll be a very small gathering. Parker says he doesn't think he can get the time off. My husband has been down with the flu or some such thing, so I don't know if he'll be up to joining us either."

"I'm so sorry to hear that. Is there anything I can do to help with the party preparations?"

"Oh, that would be lovely! I'll send the car for you—say, one o'clock on Wednesday?"

"Yes, that would be fine. I'll be in front of the mission."

Kat hung up the phone and turned to face Meredith. "Well, I'm going to a birthday party for Parker's twins. I've got to go get them something. What do you get for a three-year-old?"

"I have no idea. But something indestructible, I would think."

"I'd better go shopping right now. I won't have time tomorrow."

Kat left, and thirty minutes later Meredith got up from her chair to answer the door. When Meredith saw Brodie Lee, she said, "Kat's not here."

"Do you mind if I wait for her?"

"She may be gone quite a while. It's probably not a good idea."

Brodie frowned for a moment, then said, "Well then, maybe you could show me the sights."

"I'm not about to go out with you!"

"You're not? I can't think why."

"You are totally self-centered, that's why!"

"Oh, come on. Be a good sport."

"You're Kat's boyfriend, not mine."

"I wish you'd tell her that! Anyway, I'm not gonna ask you to marry me or anythin'. Just keep me company."

Suddenly Meredith, who had disliked Brodie from the very start, found herself smiling. "You're such a scoundrel."

"Who, me? I'll be on my best behavior."

★ ★ ★

" . . . and so that's what it was like over in Spain."

"It sounds terrible."

"It wasn't much fun," Brodie said with a shrug. The two of them were sitting in a little eatery near Meredith's flat enjoying their dessert of gooseberry cobbler with vanilla custard. She had been quiet at first, and he had begun to tell her of some of his experiences. She had become interested, and finally he grinned and said, "That's enough about me. What about you?"

"What about me?"

"How come you're not married?"

"I was married."

Brodie had been lifting his cup of tea, but he stopped abruptly. "You're married?"

"I said I *was* married."

"You're divorced, then?"

"No. My husband was killed in action in northern Africa."

Brodie set the cup down and laced his fingers together and stared at them. When he looked up there was a different expression in his eyes. "I'm sorry about that."

"Not your fault."

"Has it been pretty hard?"

"Yes."

Brodie felt a wall of resistance from the young woman, but despite her rather brusque manner, he admired her. She had a wealth of beautiful auburn hair and large green eyes. He knew she was Welsh, and as he studied her, he tried to think of some way to express his feelings. "I'm right sorry about your husband."

"Well, I've learned not to take any more chances."

"What kind of chances?"

"I'm not going to get tied up with anyone ever again."

He turned his head to one side and studied her. "You gonna live in a cave, go to a deserted island?"

Meredith lifted her head, her eyes sharp and alert. "I'm just not going to allow myself to get too close to anyone. It doesn't pay. Especially not during a war."

Brodie continued to sip his tea, but he was aware of her charms. She was not tall but was shapely in a way that would appeal to any man. She even looked good in the simple cotton dress she wore. "Let's you and me go see a movie or something tonight."

"I'm sorry. I have a previous engagement."

"Well, maybe I'll go along with you."

A small dimple appeared at the corner of Meredith's mouth, and a glimmer of light danced in her eyes. She lifted one shoulder and a hint of a smile touched her lips. "All right," she said. "I'll see how dependable you Americans are. You can come with me if you promise to stay with me. You won't run out on me?"

"Scout's honor. Come on, lady, lead on."

★ ★ ★

"This is a pretty rough part of town," Brodie noted as they passed a number of tough-looking men loitering about who gave them rather calculating looks. "You wouldn't come down here by yourself, would you?"

"Yes, I have," Meredith said casually.

Brodie was curious. "Where are you taking me?"

"Right over there."

She pointed toward four men and two women standing on a street corner with musical instruments. "I don't see anything but that Salvation Army bunch."

"That's it."

He missed a step. "What do you mean, 'That's it'?" he demanded.

"I sometimes come down and help the Salvation Army with their work."

Brodie Lee suddenly felt uncomfortable, but he had promised Meredith he would stay with her. When they were a few yards from the band, she looked at him oddly.

"Aren't you going to run away?"

"Merry, I've never run away from anything in my life!"

A light of approval swept across her face and she continued toward the band, where she greeted a tall, gangling man wearing a threadbare black uniform.

"Good evening, Miss Meredith. It's good to see you. Who's this with you?"

"This is a new addition to our band. May I introduce Brodie Lee. Brodie, this is Harry Jenkins."

"I'm pleased to meet you. What instrument do you play?"

"I'm sorry," Brodie said quickly. "I can't play a thing."

"Yes you can. You can play the bass drum." Meredith's eyes were sparkling as she turned to a small man with a bass drum strapped to his chest. "Charlie, let Brodie have your drum. That'll free you up to play the trombone."

"Right you are, miss."

"But I can't play a drum," Brodie protested.

"All you have to do is pound out a rhythm with a big mallet," Meredith said. "Here, let me help you put the drum on."

Brodie wanted to run, but Meredith had already taken

the instrument from Charlie and was standing in front of Brodie with it. He suddenly laughed. "All right." He slipped his arms into the straps and tried to get comfortable with the big drum sticking out in front of him. Meredith handed him the mallet and he tapped at the drum tentatively.

She took her flute case out of the canvas bag she had been carrying. After taking a moment to tune up, she said, "We're ready, Harry."

★ ★ ★

Meredith turned to Brodie outside her apartment building. She was still amused at his enthusiastic banging of the drum. He actually had a good sense of rhythm, and after a time, the leader had asked him not to hit it so loudly. Brodie had even stayed for the street-side sermon, where they had received the typical reaction from the passersby—some positive and some negative.

"Well, I must admit," she said, "I didn't think you'd go through with it."

"It was fun. We'll do it again sometime." Before she could stop him, Lee reached for her shoulders and kissed her right on the lips. She pushed him away gently. "That's enough of that, Brodie. I told you I have no interest in getting involved with anyone."

"I thought you mighta changed your mind by now." He laughed and then shook his head. "I gotta go. Thanks for showin' me around."

"Thank you for coming, Brodie. I'll tell Kat what a good drummer you are." She went inside and climbed the steps to the second floor. As she thought about Brodie, she found herself wondering what it would be like to date again, but she shook her thoughts off and unlocked the door.

CHAPTER TWELVE

THE FACE OF DEATH

★ ★ ★

"One wouldn't think that a couple of three-year-olds could bring such devastation!"

Lady Grace Braden was smiling as she looked about the drawing room, which was in considerable disarray. The twins had torn into their gifts like hurricanes, including the picture books and stuffed animals Kat had brought, scattering paper and string all over the floor. The table that had held the cake and ice cream was also cluttered.

Veronica Braden was trying to stop an argument between the birthday celebrants. "Turn loose of that, Paul. It belongs to Heather."

"No, mine!"

Veronica slapped Paul's hand. "Let go of it, I say!"

Paul drew his hand back quickly and looked up reproachfully at his mother. "You're mean! Don't be mean, Mums!"

Veronica shook her head impatiently and straightened up. "I'll have the servants clean up this mess," she said crossly.

"Oh, I'll help. I don't mind," Kat said quickly.

"They're paid to do such things—but as you please." She stared at Kat for a moment, an unreadable expression in her eyes. "Thank you for coming," she snapped before turning and abruptly leaving the room.

"She always gets flustered at things like this," Grace told Kat. "She's much better with adults, I think." She smiled then and added, "But you seem to have no problem handling three-year-olds."

"I practically raised triplets. My father married late in life, and he and my stepmother had triplets. I've had a lot of experience changing diapers, mixing formula, and separating the boys between battles."

She stooped down next to Paul, who was sitting on the floor looking hurt. "Look, Paul," she said. "I'll tell you what. You let Heather have this stuffed toy and I'll read you a story when it's naptime."

"I wike stories," he said.

"I want story too," Heather piped up.

"Then if you're both good children, I will not only read a story, I'll make up one just for you."

This fascinated the twins, and they at once announced that they were ready to take their nap.

"Well! *That's* never happened before," Grace said, an astonished smile on her face.

"You look rather tired, Lady Braden. Why don't you go lie down for a while. Three-year-olds can put you in bed."

"Indeed they can, Katherine. But I think I'd rather stay up. It makes me sleep better at night. I'll run along and see that the twins are properly dressed for their nap."

Kat almost smiled. She had never heard of dressing properly for a nap. When she used to put her little half brothers to bed, she'd simply tossed them in and warn them to go to sleep or she'd strangle them. "I'll just clean up some of this mess, and then I'll come and tell them some stories."

Grace left the room, and Katherine began cleaning up. It had been a strange birthday party. There had been no guests except for herself. Grace and Veronica and she had been the entire group. Grace had told her that her husband wasn't feeling well enough to attend. Veronica had mentioned that they hadn't invited any other children because it was hard enough to keep two children from tearing the house apart.

Kat worked quickly and efficiently, picking up the papers and ribbons from the floor and stuffing them into a sack. When she had finished, she started for the kitchen to get a damp cloth to wipe the table. She stopped, however, when she heard voices in the kitchen. The young maid, Millie, was saying, "Well, I think it's awful that Mr. Parker couldn't come for his own children's party."

"He can't come and go as he pleases," the housekeeper, Mrs. Henderson, said. "None of the pilots can."

"You can say what you like, but I think it's disgraceful the way Mrs. Braden treats the children."

"Millie, I've told you a hundred times not to speak poorly of our employers."

"Well, I'm not the only one. Cook and I were talking about how the mister and the missus don't get along. Why, they fight all the time."

"Millie, stop that!"

"But they do! At least she does. Poor Mr. Parker doesn't say a word. It would serve her right if he went and got himself a girlfriend."

"They have their troubles, but that's ridiculous. Now, I don't want to hear any more about this. If the master and the missus are having troubles, so are lots of other people."

Kat hesitated, then went back into the drawing room. She was disturbed by what she had overheard and felt guilty for having eavesdropped. But when servants talked openly about marital problems between their employers, things were serious indeed.

Finally Millie came in and smiled brightly. "Oh, you've cleaned up all the paper. You didn't have to do that, miss."

"I don't mind. But now I promised the children I would read them a story." She picked up one of the books and said, "Where's their room?"

"Right down the hall there. Second door on the left.

Don't worry. You'll hear them screeching," she said with a smile.

Kat walked down the hall, impressed, as she always was, by the richness and opulence of the furnishings. Everything was tastefully done, and she knew it was the work of many years. She did indeed hear Paul's voice demanding something when she reached the door. Opening it, she went inside and found the two children jumping up and down on the bed with their grandmother begging them to stop.

"Here, you two, I thought you wanted to hear a story."

"Yes, a story!" Heather cried.

"Well, lie down and you shall have one."

"I'll leave you with them, but we'll have a cup of tea before you leave, my dear."

"That would be wonderful."

Kat settled the children down on the large bed, noting that they were dressed in pajamas. She drew up a chair and said, "Now, if you're very quiet, I will read you a story."

"We will be," Paul insisted.

"Very well. Here we go." She began reading the story and was interrupted several times by both Paul and Heather. They were very bright and attractive children. Paul was going to be tall and looked quite similar to his adoptive father with his light brown hair and blue eyes. Heather, although she had the same coloring and the same facial characteristics, was small-boned and almost fragile.

Finally, when Kat had finished the story, she saw that both of them were still wide awake. "All right," she said. "You've been very good. Now I'll tell you a story that's not in any book."

"Not in a book?" Heather asked, her eyes large and inquisitive.

"No. It's one I made up myself. You close your eyes, and I'll tell it to you."

It took three made-up stories to get the children to sleep. Kat pulled a light blanket over the children and then tiptoed out of the room. *Why, they love attention! You'd think they didn't get any, but that can't be so. It seems all the adults in this home dote on them.*

She quietly closed the door and went back to the drawing room, where she found Lady Grace reading a book.

"Did you finally get them to sleep?"

"Oh yes. They were very good."

"Sit down. I'll have Millie bring us some tea."

Ten minutes later the two women were sipping their tea and Grace was saying, "You're perfectly marvelous with children, Miss Winslow."

"Oh, please, just call me Kat. That's what everyone at home calls me."

"Yes, Parker told me—but he says he prefers Katherine."

"Well, it does sound a bit more dignified. My family has called me Kat since I was a little girl."

Kat enjoyed their conversation immensely. Grace was very curious about her American visitor, and Kat found herself telling about her background at great length. Finally she laughed and said, "Heavens, I've become an egotist and a bore."

"Not at all, my dear. It's so refreshing to have you here. Parker told us a great deal about you, in letters, of course, when he visited your home."

Kat finished her tea and told her hostess that she had to leave. The two women arose, and Grace walked her visitor to the door. She had said very little about Parker and Veronica, which seemed strange to Kat, but it reinforced what she had overheard the maid saying about the couple.

Grace opened the door and called out, "Joseph, I need you to take Miss Winslow home."

"Yes, ma'am."

"I'm so grateful to you for coming, and I know Parker will be also," Grace said.

"It was such fun."

"You must come back soon. The children love it so much."

"I would like that very much."

Grace looked troubled for a moment and shook her head,

grief coming to her eyes. "Parker's all we have now."

"Shall we have a prayer for him before I leave?"

Grace Braden was surprised at the suggestion, but she agreed. "Yes, if you please."

The two women bowed their heads, and when Kat had finished her brief prayer, Grace reached out and gave her a hug. "Thank you so much," she whispered.

As Kat walked to the car, she thought, *It's probably very unusual for this aristocratic woman to hug strangers, especially an American*. The whole family seemed strange, and all the way back to town she wondered what really went on behind the doors of Benleigh Estate.

Looking up once, she saw planes overhead going south. She could not tell what kind they were, but she wondered briefly if Parker might be in one of them. *Their lives are so fragile*, she thought. *But then again, I guess life is fragile for all of us.*

★ ★ ★

The pilots of Parker's squadron were a mixed bag indeed. David Deere, tough and husky with black eyes and black hair, was the leader of Yellow Flight. He had found their new recruit rather odd, and Deere was outspoken with his opinions.

"Do all Americans dress like you?"

"Only the wealthy ones can afford that." Brodie was, of course, wearing his flying suit now, as they were expecting a scramble. But his high-heeled boots and Stetson had aroused Deere's interest.

Deere stared at Brodie curiously. "You think your country will come in and help us with this fight that's coming?"

"Well, I'm here, ain't I?" Brodie grinned rashly.

"Yes, but you're only one."

"There's only one war!" Brodie shrugged. He was lounging in a chair, looking absolutely relaxed, with his feet propped up and leafing through a magazine.

Deere was about to say something else when Bernie Cox, leader of Blue Flight said, "You can't carry that ruddy pistol. It's not regulation." Cox had learned to respect Brodie Lee's flying ability and trusted him now to guard his flank, but like the other pilots, he was somewhat put off by Brodie's eccentric mannerisms and dress.

Brodie did not look up from the magazine but murmured, "Regulations say to carry a sidearm. That's what I'm doing."

"But it's not a regulation sidearm."

"Shoots straight, though."

Cox threw up his hands, and even as he did, the call came over the loudspeaker: "One-twenty Squadron, scramble!"

Every pilot in the squadron came out of his chair, some of them pulling on their flight gear as they did.

"All right," Parker announced as he came into the room, "this is a big one. Reports say that over a hundred Jerries are headed our way."

"Is that all?" Brodie said. He had tossed the magazine down and was stretching lazily. "We'll have to teach those morons a lesson."

"When we go after them," Cox said abruptly, "you stay in formation."

"Yes," Parker agreed. "That goes for all of you."

As they went out to their planes, Brodie nudged Sailor Darley. "When we go after a bunch that big," he said under his breath, "formations go out the window."

"Better do what the skipper says, Brodie," Sailor warned.

"Why? You don't."

"But I've got seniority. You have to play by the rules until you've been in service for a year. Then you can throw them out the window."

Parker stopped Brodie before he climbed into his plane. "I meant what I said, Brodie. You stay in formation."

"Right, Skipper," Brodie said breezily. "Anything else?"

"Watch yourself."

"You too. Say, after we shoot down these planes, what

d'ya say we go out to a pub and throw some darts? That's what you Brits do, ain't it?"

"If we shoot down a hundred of them, I'll pay for the beer."

"You're on."

Brodie climbed into his plane humming "Oh! Susanna" and checked his instruments. He knew some of the pilots were tense when going on a mission, but he had apparently been born without nerves. He could not understand other men's fears, for when it came to flying, he had never had any, but he was not brash enough to say this publicly.

★　★　★

Parker led the squadron and at once set out to gain height. The highest planes always had the advantage, so there was a constant struggle between the German and British fighters. Before long all twelve planes in the squadron had the height that Parker sought.

His radio crackled: "Fifty plus bombers, one hundred plus fighters coming in over Portsmouth at fifteen thousand feet headed northeast. Your vector nine zero degrees."

Parker acknowledged and then surveyed his squadron. They were flying in four *V* formations of three. Red Flight, Parker's own, was in the lead position. He noted with satisfaction that the wingtips of the different flights were almost touching. The roar of the twelve Merlin engines drowned out all other sound as they skimmed over the Kent countryside.

Once he caught a reflected glimpse of himself in his windscreen and thought, *You're looking pretty grim, old boy*.

The green fields and the roads now were far beneath as Parker scanned the sky ahead for the first sight of the enemy. He got a new vector on the radiotelephone and then swung the group around to get the sun behind him. Suddenly he heard Brodie's voice saying, "Hey, Skipper, there they are."

"Report properly, Blue Three."

"Oh . . . Blue Three reports enemy ahead, Red Leader."

Instantly Parker found the dots coming across the Channel. Brodie had better eyes than any other man in the squadron.

The sun caught the Germans as they came in, and finally he could see the bright yellow noses of the Messerschmitt fighters sandwiching the bombers. The sky seemed full of them, packed in layers thousands of feet deep.

Leaning over, Parker switched on the reflector gun sight, flicked the catch on the gun button from Safety to Fire, and then lowered his seat until the circle and dot on the reflector light shone dark red.

"Here we go. Pick your targets." He swung the squadron around in a great circle to attack into the thick of the German planes. He put his thumb on the gun button, and the engine screamed as he went down in a steeply banked dive onto the tail of a forward line of Heinkels. It all happened very quickly then—in a matter of seconds. He touched the button, and the Spit shook as he fired three short bursts. He missed the Heinkel with the first two, but the third struck one of the engines, which immediately burst into black smoke.

Not good enough! He leveled his plane and fired another burst at the Heinkel. He thought he had hit right into the pilot's face, but he had no chance to analyze it. The air was suddenly filled with swarming fighters, and he was relieved to see that two squadrons of Hurricanes had joined the fray. He was much happier to have thirty-six planes on his side than the twelve they had started with.

He lost all awareness of time as he focused his energies on chasing the bombers. He had one in his sight, and when he pressed the firing button, a short burst followed and then nothing.

He pounded his fist on the dashboard in frustration and shouted, "This is Red Leader. Out of ammo!"

"Blue Three," Brodie reported. "Me too, Boss."

"Let's go get some ammo." Parker turned and was on his

way out of the melee when he suddenly felt the Spit shudder and saw bullets riddle his engine canopy.

Got my engine!

But the engine was not completely gone. He fought to keep the plane aloft. Spitfires were a precious commodity, and Parker grimly decided not to bail out. "Come on, we can make it," he told himself.

The Spit shuddered violently, and Parker desperately hung on to the stick. His airspeed dropped under one-fifty, but if he could maintain that speed, he could land in one piece.

But suddenly he glanced up in his mirror and saw a Messerschmitt coming up fast. Parker tried to evade it, but the Spit would not answer to the controls. All he could do was wallow all over the sky.

Parker knew what was coming. He reached up and started to slide his canopy back. Before he could bail out, however, he looked over to his right and was shocked to see the German plane keeping pace with him. The pilot had his goggles up on his forehead so that Parker could see his face.

Parker knew there was no hope. He could not imagine why the pilot hadn't shot him out of the sky. Even as he watched, the German's white teeth flashed against his tanned face. The man laughed as he drew his gloved forefinger across his throat.

Parker knew his life was over. All the German had to do was pull away and then come back and riddle him. Fear seized him, but that emotion was quickly replaced with grief. He thought of what he would be losing. He thought mostly of his children. Other things that he would never see again flashed before him, but then, even as he watched the German, an amazing thing happened.

A dark object had come between Parker's Spit and the Me-109. Parker could not believe that a Spitfire had sandwiched itself between the two. The third plane was slightly lower than Parker's, so Parker still had a good view of the German pilot's face. He saw shock sweep across the man's face, and then Parker saw the canopy of the other Spitfire open.

The next sight was one he would never forget, even if he lived to be a very old man. Brodie Lee raised himself up until his upper body was free of the canopy. He was holding his ivory-handled pistol and taking dead aim. Parker could not hear the shots with his canopy closed, but he saw Brodie's hand kick up with the recoil—and he saw the shots hit the canopy of the 109. They all appeared to hit their mark, and he watched the German's face dissolve into a bloody mass before he slumped face over the stick. The 109 nosed over and headed straight for the earth.

Brodie followed the fighter plane down until it crashed, setting off a red blossom as it exploded. He pulled the nose up and found Parker again, settling in just off his wing. Brodie laughed and blew imaginary smoke away from the pistol's muzzle. "Let's go home, Boss, and get some more bullets," he said into his radio.

Parker still could not believe what he had seen. He was overjoyed that he was not going to die, at least at this moment.

The Spitfire was shaking badly, but he was able to get it back to the airfield. "Come down, Blue Three."

The two Spits landed, and three mechanics ran over to greet the pilots. Parker gave instructions concerning his plane and then came over to meet Brodie.

"Can we get back in time, Skipper?"

"No. It'll be over. Those 109s only carry enough fuel for a four-hour flight." He put out his hand and gripped Brodie's warmly. "You were a welcome sight up there, Brodie."

"Glad to be there."

"It's your third kill." He suddenly laughed. "I'm going to have a hard time getting headquarters to believe that you shot down an Me-109 with a pearl-handled pistol."

"It ain't pearl-handled. It's ivory."

"All right. Ivory, then. I was a dead man until you showed up."

"I hope the rest of the boys are all right." He looked up

at the sky and was quiet for a moment. "I think I saw Neville Sutton go down. I hope he made it."

"Me too. He's a married man."

Parker had not seen a parachute and neither had Brodie. Parker was dreading the letter he would have to write. "The worst is coming, Brodie. A lot of us won't be here when this is over." He shook his head. "Just be glad you're not married."

★ ★ ★

Parker found Raymond Bailey in much better condition than he had been after being shot down back in June. As he entered the man's hospital room, he saw Diane Weber, the pilot's fiancée, sitting with him.

"It's so nice of you to come, sir," she greeted.

"I've got to keep up with my best flier."

"How was it today, Skipper?"

"I've had better days." He laughed suddenly and said, "I saw something I never thought I'd see."

"What was that?" Raymond asked.

Parker told him how Brodie had squeezed his plane between Parker's and the German's and shot the pilot with his ivory-handled pistol. Raymond, of course, found the whole thing hard to believe.

"Fortunately there was a witness. Archie Kent-Wilkins was on his way to help, and he saw the whole thing. I was afraid we'd both be thrown out of the air force with a story like that."

The three made small talk for a while, and it appeared that Raymond was making good progress. Much to everyone's relief, the doctors had been able to save his legs, and he was well on his way to recovery.

"Kat Winslow has been by several times," Diane mentioned. "It made me jealous, it did."

Parker knew what visits from a friendly face meant at times like this. He was glad that Katherine had stopped in to see Raymond. Parker visited for a few more moments and then went off in search of Kat. When he found her, she was filling in her replacement, Meredith, for the next shift.

The two greeted him warmly, and he told them about Brodie's feat. "I'm putting him up for a decoration. He's probably the only man to shoot down an enemy plane with a pistol since the Great War!"

"He'll be impossible now," Meredith said. "No, he was already impossible. His head will be as big as that plane he flies."

"I'm proud of him," Kat said with a warm smile.

"So am I," Parker said. "If he hadn't showed up, I wouldn't be here."

Kat felt a sudden chill of fear and said quickly, "Would you like to walk me home?"

"Be glad to."

The two left the hospital and as they walked, Parker said, "I haven't had a chance to thank you for what you did for the children. From what my mother tells me, they had the best birthday party imaginable. They loved the stories you told them. They insist you just made them up."

"I did make up some of them. Your children are delightful, and it's fun to see their eyes light up when you do something so simple for them."

"Well, it was wonderful of you to do that."

They had almost reached the door of the apartment building when Kat said, "I got a letter from my folks with a few snapshots. Would you like to see them?"

"I'd love to."

The two went up to the apartment and sat together on the couch. Relaxing and looking at the pictures was a welcome relief after the pressure of the day. He could still not believe how close to death he had come.

He turned his attention to the photographs. "The triplets have grown so much. Look how big they are."

"They're going to be big like their mother, I think."

As they looked at the rest of the photographs, Kat gave him some details about what everyone was up to at home, but his mind was elsewhere. Finally he thanked her rather absently and then got up. He said good night and started to open the door.

"What's wrong, Parker?"

"It's . . ." He could not finish, and to Kat's surprise she saw tears gather in his eyes. "What is it?" she whispered.

"We lost a good man on the scramble today. Neville Sutton." The grief that he usually managed to conceal was suddenly impossible to hide. "He's been married only a few weeks, and now he's gone."

She put her arms around him and whispered, "I'm so sorry, Parker. So very sorry!" She saw that grief had reached down into the very depths of this tall man. She also knew instinctively that he would never have revealed himself to anyone else.

There was a strength in Parker Braden she had rarely, if ever, seen in a man. But now that strength seemed to be gone. The grief over the young man he had obviously loved had robbed him of it. She was looking up at him, her lips broad and maternal, her warm eyes full of compassion, and she whispered again, "I'm so very sorry."

He leaned forward and, without meaning to, kissed her on the lips. He had not intended to do any such thing, and his sense of loss was suddenly joined by memories of long ago when he had held her and kissed her. He was also faintly aware that she was responding to his kiss.

Suddenly Kat put her hands on his chest and stepped back. She knew she had stepped over a forbidden line. "Good night, Parker."

"I'm . . . I'm sorry, Katherine. I didn't mean—"

"It's all right. We're all vulnerable at times, and you had a shock today. We'll talk later. Good night."

He turned and left without another word. Kat stood motionless, shaken by what had happened. She realized she still had strong feelings for this man. This only made her miserable, for she knew they could never pursue a relationship.

"It will never happen again," she whispered fiercely.

"Not ever!" Blindly she turned, knowing there would be little sleep for her this night. She thought she had buried the memories of her time with Parker three years earlier. But now they came back strong and vigorous. She knew there would be no hiding from them, but she also knew she had to build a barrier against her feelings for this man she had found again—and now must lose a second time.

PART THREE

July–September 1940

★ ★ ★

CHAPTER THIRTEEN

COWBOY BREAKS THE RULES

★ ★ ★

Steel cots had been placed around the walls of the ready room, and most of the pilots spent considerable time in them. Their sleeping quarters were farther away from the field, which meant either walking or catching a ride on a truck, and too often they no sooner were in their own bed than the radio began squawking for a scramble. The remaining furniture of the ready room consisted of an odd assortment of chairs ranging from overstuffed leather easy chairs to cheaply made straight-back kitchen chairs, all the worse for wear.

The walls were lined with pictures that matched the tastes of the pilots. Many of them were pinups of scantily dressed women peering coyly over their shoulders, but some airmen with classic tastes had also put up prints of *The Blue Boy* by Gainsborough and Whistler's painting of his mother. These seemed rather incongruous, and the ears of both the boy dressed in blue and the gray-haired mother must have burned at the sizzling language that went on in the ready room.

The longer walls of the rectangular room contained three

windows each, which admitted the mid-July sunlight. The light was filtered by smoke from cigars, cigarettes, and pipes, and there was a distinct odor of raw alcohol in the air as well. Drinking was not expressly forbidden as long as the pilots could control their appetites. Each flight leader was supposed to monitor the habits of the two other pilots of his flight. A radio propped on a shelf was blaring forth the voice of Ray Noble woefully crooning "A Nightingale Sang in Berkeley Square."

Trevor Park was engaged in a loud argument with his flight leader, Archibald Kent-Wilkins. Park was a handsome man with blond hair and bright blue eyes who had been a budding actor before he had given it up to join the air force. He had never been a big star, but he had been in one movie in which he kissed Marlene Dietrich, which gave him some stature. Jimmy Fitzwilliam, number two man in Green Flight along with Kent-Wilkins and Park, had found a movie poster of Park kissing Dietrich and had put it up on the wall. Park had taken a great deal of ragging over it, but actually he enjoyed this. The three now were arguing about the relative merits of the Hurricane and the Spitfire.

"Look, Trevor," Jimmy insisted, "I know the Spit can turn quicker and has a bit more speed, but the Hurricane has a steady gun platform. Why, every time I fire my guns in the Spit, I jockey all over the sky. The plane is almost impossible to keep steady."

Trevor disagreed vehemently, raising his voice over the hubbub of voices. "You're batty, Jimmy. The Spit can outfly the Hurricane any day of the week."

"That's right," Archie Kent-Wilkins agreed. The three were lined up watching a Ping-Pong game between Bernie Cox and Brodie Lee. "If you want, I can get you transferred to a Hurricane squadron." Kent-Wilkins was an aristocrat. He disliked Americans simply because they were Americans. Now as Brodie missed the ball after Bernie Cox drove it so fast it was a mere blur, Kent-Wilkins said, "I say, Lee. Why don't you give up? Ping-Pong is just not your game."

Brodie grinned. "I know it's not my game. My game is shootin' down Germans."

The remark brought color to Kent-Wilkins face. He himself had shot down only one enemy plane, while Brodie had shot down six, a record in the squadron, except for Parker Braden's eight.

David Deere of Yellow Flight ambled over to watch the game. "You don't have steady enough nerves, Kent-Wilkins. That's your problem."

Brodie disliked David Deere—a tough, husky fellow with black hair and blacker eyes—almost as much as he disliked Kent-Wilkins. "I bet you don't know who has the steadiest nerves in this whole squadron," Brodie said.

Kent-Wilkins looked down his nose. "Who?" he said icily.

"You wouldn't care to make a little bet, would you, Archie?"

"There's no way to prove such a thing."

"Sure there is. I've got two quid that says I can prove who has the steadiest nerves in the whole squadron."

Zarek Dolenski, who flew wing for Parker Braden, said, "Impossible! Nobody could prove such a thing unless you went head-on into a flight of Me-109s."

"No. There's another way. What do you say, Archie? Two quid?"

"Take him up, Archie," David Deere said, his black eyes gleaming. "Teach the Yank a lesson."

"All right." He fished into his pocket and came up with the bills. "Put up or shut up."

"That's an old Yankee sayin'," Brodie said. He fumbled through his pockets and came up with two bills. "Here, Jimmy. You hold the stakes."

Jimmy Fitzwilliam, the smallest and youngest member of 120 Squadron, grinned. He had rosy cheeks, cornflower blue eyes, and was the shyest man around women that any of the men had ever seen. "All right, but I don't think you can do it, Brodie."

"You wait right here."

"Where's he going?" Trevor asked. He ran his hand over his smooth blond hair and grinned at Kent-Wilkins. "I think you're going to be sorry. That fellow has got more self-confidence than anybody I've ever seen."

"Nonsense. There's no way to prove such a thing," Archie grunted.

Brodie came hurrying back, holding something up in his hands. "Here it is. I saved it from my Fourth of July celebration." They all remembered the day two weeks ago because Brodie had bought all the fireworks he could afford, and the squadron had shot them off with great glee. "I saved a firecracker for a special occasion. I guess this is special enough, don't you think?"

"How is that supposed to prove something about a man's nerve?"

Brodie nodded over toward the end of the ready room. "There he is, fellows. The man with the strongest nerves in the squadron."

"Al?" Bernie Cox said. "His nerves are no steadier than mine."

"You're wrong, and I'll prove it. I'm gonna light this firecracker and put it right under his bunk. He won't even turn over."

"That's impossible!" Kent-Wilkins said.

"It'll cost me if he comes off that bed as most men would. Watch this now." The other men watched as Brodie pulled a match out of his pocket. He lit the two-inch fuse and then hurried down toward the bunk where Albert Tobin lay asleep. Tobin had been a dustman collecting trash before he had signed up for the armed services. There his skills had been discovered. He had knocked the top off every test that a pilot needed. He was a crack flier with three kills, and he had a wife named Polly and three children whom he adored.

He was a sound sleeper and now lay with his mouth open, snoring softly, oblivious to the noise of the ready room.

Brodie put the firecracker under Tobin's bunk and then

stepped back and grinned. "Watch this."

All the men watched the fuse as it burned down, holding their breath as it disappeared. The firecracker exploded with a resounding boom, and they all kept their eyes fixed on Tobin.

The smallish man closed his mouth, and his shoulders shook one time, but then immediately his mouth opened again and the snoring recommenced.

"That's impossible!" Bernie Cox cried out. "I can't believe it!"

"Fork over the cash. I win. Ain't that right, Archie?"

Kent-Wilkins's face was flushed. He hated to lose at anything, and he had lost consistently to Brodie Lee—at poker, at Ping-Pong, and at every other contest.

Jimmy gave Brodie the money he'd been holding just as Parker came in, his eyes snapping. "What's going on here? I heard a gunshot."

"No, Skipper, it was just a firecracker," Jimmy said. He idolized Parker Braden, but he was also very fond of Brodie, and he smelled trouble in the air.

"Firecracker! You think this is some kind of a boys' school? Who set that thing off?"

"I did," Brodie said, grinning broadly, "but it was all part of a scientific investigation."

"What are you talking about?" Parker asked, his eyes fixed on Brodie. He had felt for some time that the American was a bad influence on the discipline of the squadron and had determined to pull him up short the next time he stepped out of line.

"We were tryin' to discover who had the steadiest nerves in the squadron, and I proved it was Al."

"And how did you do that?" Parker listened as Brodie, his eyes sparkling with fun, repeated the details of the incident. When he had finished, Parker said, "If you've got so much time to horseplay, we'll do some formation flying."

A groan went up from the squadron.

"It was just a bit of fun, Skipper."

"You're not here to have fun, Lee!" Parker bit the words

off. "And furthermore, your formation flying is rotten." Everyone knew that Brodie's experience in acrobatic flying and fighting in Spain had given him mastery over aircraft such as few men in the entire RAF possessed. He could do anything with a Spitfire that could be done, but he was notoriously bad at formation flying.

Brodie stood straight as Parker continued to reprimand him. It was not the first time he had been singled out, and anger began to build up in him. He knew, of course, that he was guilty. He had made the argument many times that flying tight formations while on a mission was ridiculous, but he said it again anyway.

"Look, sir, when a man's trying to keep his wingtip jammed up into the armpit of another plane, what's he going to be looking at? Why, he's going to be watching that plane—and he shouldn't be. He should be looking out over his head and behind him trying to spot the enemy coming in."

"We've argued about this before, Lee, and I'm not going to have it. You're going to fly formations properly or you'll sit out the flights in the future."

Sailor Darley laughed aloud. "That'll fix you, Yank. You won't get a chance to risk your life if you're not good."

"You keep quiet, Sailor," Parker snapped. "You're almost as bad as he is. As a matter of fact, I'm thinking about disciplining both of you, and I will if you don't keep tighter formations."

The room had gone quiet. None of the pilots had ever seen Parker Braden so tense and angry. When he'd left the room, Trevor Park shook his head. "Something's biting on the skipper. That's not like him."

"I think he's exactly right," Kent-Wilkins said. "Your formation flying is terrible, Lee."

Brodie stared at the aristocratic flier and for one moment the room was absolutely silent. Then Brodie turned and walked off toward Al Tobin's cot. The conversation gradually picked up again, the men speaking amongst themselves about Parker's lecture and the Ping-Pong game picking up again.

Ignoring the talk behind him, Brodie reached over and slapped Al Tobin on the shoulder. The man's eyes opened immediately and he winked and whispered, "How'd I do, Brodie?"

"Great. Here's your cut."

"I nearly jumped off the cot when that crazy thing went off."

"You did just fine." Brodie had set up the whole thing with Al, knowing he would get a rise out of Kent-Wilkins.

He started for the door, but Bernie Cox, Brodie's flight leader, came over to him. "Where are you going?"

"London."

"You can't—we haven't stood down yet. We may be scrambled."

"Let Braden get somebody who can fly formations better than I can. Don't worry about me, Bernie."

Cox tried to reason with Brodie, but it was impossible. He watched as the American left, then murmured to Sailor Darley, the third member of their flight. "I'm afraid Brodie's headed for trouble, Sailor."

"You want me to go keep an eye on him?"

"No. That'd be two of you drunk. Just hope he gets back in plenty of time for the next scramble."

★ ★ ★

The tongue-lashing he had received from Parker Braden had bitten more deeply into Brodie Lee than the members of his flight could have guessed. Brodie took pride in his ability and skills and record as a member of his squadron. He led the squadron in kills and by consensus was the best pilot in the squadron. Now to be pulled up and picked to pieces because of what Brodie considered an unimportant and even dangerous maneuver had disturbed his easygoing ways.

By the time he had made his way into town from the airfield, the first flashes of anger had settled into a dull resentment. He had no intention of missing a scramble, for he had great loyalty to Blue Flight and did not want to get Bernie Cox into trouble. He had become great friends with Cox and with Sailor Darley as they had repeatedly faced death together and defeated it.

He went into a pub, intending to have just a few beers. But he was joined by a pretty girl with snapping eyes and hair that appeared to be genuinely blond. He offered to buy her a drink and from there, everything went downhill. The girl moved closer to him, and he found that everyone wanted to buy the RAF fighter pilot a drink. They also wanted to hear about the air war, and Brodie, who usually didn't discuss the war with civilians, drank so much that his tongue was loosened.

Time slipped by, the drinks mounted up, the blond girl was attentive, and before long Brodie found himself dazed.

He never knew later exactly how the fight had started. He had a vague memory of someone saying his companion was his girlfriend, but after that it was all a blur. The only thing he knew for sure was that his adversary had struck him a powerful blow that had turned the lights out. He had awakened in a jail cell occupied by six other drunks, all of them in poor shape.

Trying to focus his eyes, he looked at his watch and saw with horror that he had been away from the station for eight hours. He ran to the barred door and cried, "Let me out! I need to get back to my squadron!"

The jailer, a sad-eyed man in a blue uniform, answered in a mournful voice, "You might as well calm down. You'll have to wait until morning to go before the judge."

"But they need me."

"Then you picked a poor way to get ready for it. Just calm down and try to sober up. You're goin' before Judge Nelson. If he has a mind to do it, he'll put you in jail instead of just levelin' a fine. So make yourself look presentable and be humble."

★   ★   ★

"What's wrong, Kat?"

She put the phone back on the receiver. "It's Brodie. He's in jail."

"What's he done?" Meredith asked her flatmate.

"He got drunk and wound up in a fight." Kat shook her head with distaste. "They allowed him one call. He wants me to come down and bail him out."

"I wouldn't do it if I were you."

"I'll have to, Meredith. He begged so pitifully, and they do need him back at the squadron."

"I didn't know he was a drunk," Meredith said, disappointment tingeing her voice.

"He doesn't drink that often. Brodie had plenty of faults growing up, but he didn't used to be a drinker. Something must have set him off. I'll have to go. Will you cover for me at the mission in case I'm late?"

"Yes, sure. Come back and let me know how it comes out."

"I'll do that."

★   ★   ★

Kat made her way straight to the jail, where she found the sergeant in charge and made her plea. The burly man with a bulldog face had heard excuses of every kind. He turned his faded eyes on her and listened as she explained the need for getting her friend out. Finally he sighed, "I don't reckon it'd do any good to keep him locked up."

"I'll be glad to pay his fine."

"All right. That'll be five pounds, miss."

Kat paid the fine and waited for the sergeant to release

Brodie. The collar of his shirt was ripped half off, and his eyes were underscored by deep circles.

"Thanks for comin', Kat."

"That's all right, Brodie. You need to get back to the base, I take it?"

"Yes. I wish I had a place to get cleaned up first."

"Maybe we can sneak you back in."

"No chance of that. I've been gone too long. I'll have to face up to Parker."

"Well, come along. I'll go with you."

"You don't have to do that, Kat. But I did lose all my money somewhere. Just give me cab fare."

"No. I'll go with you."

Actually Brodie was glad for her company. He sat in the cab feeling hung over and ashamed. "I hate drunks, and the drunk I hate the most is me."

"Then why did you do it?"

"Well, it was like this. Parker peeled my potato in front of the whole squadron. It was all about flying in close formation, which I've told him before I think is stupid. I just got sore and walked out."

"You shouldn't have done that."

"Don't preach at me, Kat." He shook his head wearily. "I know I was wrong, and I feel terrible."

She did not argue, and they sat quietly until they arrived at the airfield. "You go get cleaned up. I'll find Parker and try to explain."

"Would you, Kat? That'll help a bit, maybe. Skipper thinks the world of you."

The two divided then, Brodie sneaking as much as he could to his quarters to change his uniform while Kat went directly to the operations room. When she entered she asked for Parker, and the lieutenant nodded toward a door. "He's right back there, miss."

"Do I need to be announced?"

"No. Just knock on the door."

Kat knocked and opened the door when Parker called for her to come in.

She saw surprise flare in Parker's eyes. He was sitting behind his desk, and he got up at once. "Kat!" he said, and he smiled as he came around to greet her. "I wasn't expecting you."

"No. I expect not. I have a favor to ask."

"A favor? Well, you certainly have one coming. You've been so good to the children."

"It's about Brodie."

"Brodie? What about him?" Parker frowned and shook his head. "He's been off the station without permission."

"I know. He got into trouble, Parker. He was arrested."

"What for?"

"He got drunk and got into a fight."

"I can't believe he'd do a stupid thing like that! He knows he wasn't supposed to leave the station."

Kat almost said something about the argument over formation flying but did not feel she was qualified. "He feels awful about this, Parker. You know how it is when you pilots go into pubs. Everybody wants to buy you a drink."

"Most of us manage to say no before we get blind drunk."

"I know, but apparently Brodie's got a problem with this."

Parker was angry over the man's misbehavior, but he saw the concern in her face. "You're very fond of him, aren't you?"

"We've known each other so long, and he's been a good friend to me. I know he's very sorry for what he did. He'll be coming to tell you so as soon as he gets cleaned up." She stepped closer. "Please, Parker. I can't interfere with your policies as his superior officer, but Brodie's not the kind of man that responds very well to harshness."

"I can't gloss over this, Katherine. It would set a bad precedent."

"I know that, but I just wanted to put in a good word for him."

"Well, I'll make the punishment as light as I can."

"Thank you, Parker."

At that moment Parker Braden found Katherine Winslow most appealing. There was a freshness about her that never seemed to change, and now he stood for a moment wondering if he dared ask her to have tea.

Seeing that he wasn't ready for her to leave, Kat agreed to his unspoken offer. "Yes, thank you—I could use a little refreshment."

"Fine. I'll have tea sent in, and we can have some of the cake my mother sent over."

Ten minutes later the two were seated in his office drinking tea and nibbling at the cake. They said no more about Brodie, but Kat was sure Parker would show clemency.

"I'll be going to see Paul and Heather later this week."

"Really?" Parker brightened at once. "How did that come about?"

"Your mother called me and invited me out for dinner this Wednesday."

"I wish I could be there, but I'll be tied to the station." He suddenly got up and said, "I got the children some stuffed toys. Maybe you could take them to them."

He pulled a sack from behind his desk and showed her the stuffed animals. One was of a fuzzy bear with bright button eyes, and the other was an elephant with a trunk that curled up. "They'll probably fight over who gets which one," he said. "You'll have to sort it out."

"But, Parker, you ought to give these to them yourself."

"I know. I wish I could be there."

Kat stayed for ten more minutes before leaving. As Parker watched her go, he saw Brodie coming across the field. Just the sight of the man irritated him, but he shook his head. "I'll have to make it easy on him. Kat's right. He's not the kind of chap who responds to a whipping."

★   ★   ★

"Oh, that was a marvelous production, Charlie!"

Charles Gooding was sitting across from Veronica at the

best steak house in London. She had agreed to attend the production and then later they had gone out to eat. "It was rather good, wasn't it? But the leading lady left a little bit to be desired."

"Oh, I don't know. I thought she did rather well."

"You could do better."

Veronica looked up suddenly. "What do you mean, Charlie?"

"I mean it's a shame that you are wasting your talent." He gave her a warm smile and shook his head. "You had a great future before you. I've always been grieved that you weren't able to continue. Isn't it time you made a comeback?"

At one point it had appeared that Veronica was headed for a top career on the stage when her work had been interrupted first by marriage and pregnancy, then the tragic death of her first husband and second marriage to Parker Braden in close succession. She had known Charlie Gooding for some time, having met when they had both had small parts in the same production. He had been married at the time, but he had befriended her and encouraged her acting ambitions. Now Gooding was divorced and had become a successful producer.

"Why, that's out of the question, Charlie."

"You ought to think about it."

Veronica looked down for a moment, and when she looked up there was almost desperation in her eyes. "I would love to, but how can I? Parker would divorce me."

"But other married women go on with their stage work."

"I have two children."

"You know as well as I do that some married women with children do very well on the stage."

The conversation went on for some time. Veronica had been surprised when Charlie had brought the matter up, but she herself had thought of it many times—especially as her marriage to Parker became increasingly frustrating. She missed the stage desperately, and now that Charlie had mentioned it, her old desires came rushing back.

All the way home Charlie Gooding kept speaking of how easy it would be for her to return. "I'll be going into production with a new play soon, and we're looking right now for people. You'd be perfect for one of the roles. Not the lead but the second. But it would be a good career move for you, and you and I could work together."

"I'd love to, Charlie. There's nothing I would like better. But I don't see how I could do it. You don't know what I would have to face at home."

"It might be hard," he agreed with a shrug, "but wouldn't it be worth it? And if you were successful, they'd be proud of you."

"Not Parker. He wants me to stay home all the time—be a nice homey woman. I'll never be the kind of woman he wants."

When Charlie pulled up in front of her house, he said, "Don't go. Let's talk about this a bit more."

"It's getting late, Charlie."

But he was persuasive. They talked for twenty minutes, and she realized that his interest in her was more than just professional. She saw it in his eyes, and when he pulled her into his arms, she did not protest, returning his kiss with the same passion he gave to her.

Finally she whispered, "I've got to go in, Charlie."

"Think about doing the play. I believe it would be right—for both of us."

He got out and walked around the car to open her door. Veronica stepped out, and he took her in his arms again. It was late and there was little chance that anyone would see, so she allowed it and kissed him fervently. Then she stepped back and said, "Good night, Charlie."

"We'll talk about this again."

He got into his car then and drove off as Veronica entered the house. Neither of them had seen the man who had witnessed everything. The chauffeur, Joseph, had been coming in late from a date and had been on his way to his quarters when the car had pulled up. Moving into the shadows, he had watched the two as they talked and finally watched as they kissed. Then when they had embraced again just before the man left, Joseph noted the license number.

He had never liked Veronica, but he was intensely loyal to the family—especially to Parker. He muttered a curse under his breath. "You ain't a proper wife, you ain't, and I'm gonna do somethin' about it!"

At once he turned and went to his room. He pulled out a sheet of paper and a pen and wrote a note, being careful to write in plain block letters. He added the license plate of the car and then folded the sheet and put it in an envelope. He determined to get the note to Parker the following day.

"That oughta fix her," he muttered, a grim smile shaping his lips. He undressed and went to bed, and the last thing he thought of was how happy he would be if the sorry woman got her comeuppance.

CHAPTER FOURTEEN

"I Shouldn't Have Come Here"

★ ★ ★

Kat stood holding the receiver of the telephone to her ear, pressing against it so hard that it hurt. The caller was Lord Braden, and she had been caught off-guard to hear his voice on the other end of the line. Even though she had spent some time with him and found him to be very easy to be around, the mere idea of speaking with a baron on the phone made her nervous.

"As my wife mentioned the other day, Parker won't be able to come," he was saying, "but Paul and Heather have been asking for you to come back. Demanding, I should say."

Relief washed through Kat. As secretly attracted as she was to Parker, she was determined not to spend any time alone with him. "Well, I'm looking forward to seeing the twins."

"Good. I'll send Joseph to pick you up at the mission tomorrow. Shall we say five o'clock?"

"That will be fine."

"Splendid! The children will be so excited. We'll look forward to seeing you then."

"Yes. It will be nice. Good-bye, Lord Braden."

Replacing the phone, Kat turned slowly and saw that Meredith had paused from the task of filing her nails to watch her. She had told Meredith at a weak moment that she did not feel quite safe around Parker, and then, of course, the whole story had come out about his proposal in America three years earlier. She had also promised Meredith she would take all precautions to keep out of situations that would throw her alone together with Parker.

"That was Lord Braden confirming our dinner plans for tomorrow. He and his wife and the twins will be there, but not Parker."

Meredith studied her carefully, a smile suddenly coming to her lips. "You're playing it safe, aren't you?"

"I don't know what that means."

"Oh, I think it's a good idea. You really shouldn't be around Parker. I've seen the way he looks at you."

"There's nothing to that," Kat said stiffly. She started across the room, but Meredith asked, "What about Brodie?"

Kat turned. "What do you mean 'What about Brodie?'"

"I think he's been in love with you for a long time from what you tell me."

"No. We're just friends."

"Really? I think you might be wrong. He keeps coming around."

"We're from the same part of Georgia. We've been friends for a long time."

"He's a very attractive man."

"He has enough bad habits for a squadron, Meredith. He's not even a Christian, and he would give a wife nothing but trouble."

"That wouldn't stop some women, a good-looking chap like that."

"You have such a romantic streak. You're always seeing romances that simply don't exist. I've got to go get ready for work."

★ ★ ★

The next day, Parker stood at the window staring at the note that was before him. *Watch out for your wife*, it said. *She's seeing other men. One of them drives a car with the license number ANV483.*

As Parker read the note, his hands were not steady. There was no way of tracing it, and he was not sure that he wanted to. Who would send a note like this? He had no idea, and he wanted desperately not to believe it. Still he stared at the license number and wondered if he should have it traced. He had no idea how such things could be done, but he had a friend at Scotland Yard who would be glad to find out for him.

He looked out the window and watched as a flight of bombers took off from the field. They were headed for Germany to destroy Hitler's munitions factories. Part of him demanded action, and he had the impulse to trace the number. But another part of him resisted. What if he learned the man's name? What if he knew him? What would he do then? He remembered a young man, Gerald Barnett, who had been a member of his squadron. Before the man was shot down over France in the early part of the war, he had said once to Parker, "I don't want to know bad things. There's enough bad things that happen to us without going and digging up more."

As he stared out the window, Parker tried to remember Barnett's face but found that his memory was fuzzy. It was that way with other men he had flown with. While they were alive their faces were sharp and clear, but after they died, the memory seemed to fade so that he could not hold on to them.

"Maybe Barnett was right," Parker murmured. Turning

back to the desk, he sat down and tried to study the records of the replacements who would be coming in to his squadron. He had not lost a man in over a month, but the way the Jerries were stepping up their attacks, he knew he would before long. Finding it impossible to concentrate, he put the papers back into the folder. He did not move for a long time and just sat, elbows on the desk, leaning forward against the palms of his hands, hands over his eyes. He tried to blot out the note and the license number, but he knew that the number had inscribed itself on his memory and that he would probably remember it forty years from now, if he lived that long.

He was aware of muffled voices outside his office, and from time to time a flight of planes took off or landed. Automatically he identified them as Hurricanes, Spitfires, or Wellingtons, but this was all second nature. His mind would not leave what the note had implied. He had been unhappy in his marriage for some time and was well aware that Veronica was equally unhappy. He had fancied himself in love with her when they had married, and he had thought they were happy at first, enjoying the physical side of their relationship for a few months, but that had quickly faded with the stress of everyday life during wartime. Less and less often did he seek Veronica's arms at night, and he became aware that this was actually a relief to her. They performed as a happy couple publicly, and Veronica, being an accomplished actress, pulled it off better than he himself did. Parker was painfully aware that his parents were disappointed in Veronica, although they never said so.

Wearily Parker dropped his hands and sat up straight in the chair. He opened the drawer, found a schedule, and studied it for a moment. *I'll go home tonight and have it out with Veronica,* he decided.

The decision brought no peace of mind. On the contrary, he dreaded it much more than risking his life in an airplane. But perhaps the note was all a lie. He could not imagine who would invent such a fabrication. He tore the note into shreds and dropped the pieces into the wastebasket. Then putting on his hat, he left his office, his jaw set.

"I'll be back in the morning, Lieutenant."

"Yes, sir. Going home, are you, sir?"

"Yes. Just for the night. If anything comes up, call me there."

"Yes, sir. Looks like the Jerries have quieted down a little."

"Let's hope it stays that way."

Parker left the station and drove slowly toward home, oddly aware of the greenness of the grass and the brilliance of the flowers. Everywhere were riotous bursts of reds, blues, and yellows so bright they almost hurt his eyes. Every house he passed seemed to have a small flower garden, some only three or four feet square. Somehow people had an instinct to bring a little beauty into life amidst all the horrors of war that lurked just over the Channel and sometimes flew overhead to drop its deadly load upon the peaceful land beneath.

When he pulled up in front of Benleigh, a heaviness rested on him. *I wish I hadn't come.* The thought came unexpectedly but very strongly—so strongly that he almost turned and drove back to the station. But it was too late, for the door had opened, and his mother was waving to him and calling his name. Sighing, he got out of the car and went up the steps. "Hello, Mother."

"Parker, I'm so glad to see you. Can you stay the night?"

"Yes. I'll have to get back fairly early in the morning, though."

His mother held on to his arm as if she were afraid he would run off and leave her. Parker had noticed the tendency of both his parents to touch him more often than they used to, as if finding out if he were real solid flesh and not some phantom.

"Where's Veronica?" he asked as soon as they were inside the house.

"Oh, she's gone into London."

Parker waited for his mother to explain why Veronica was gone, but he saw that she was nervous and fidgeting.

She probably doesn't know. "Well, where are the children?"

"They're playing out at the pond with your father. He bought them a little boat. They've gone crazy over it. I expect they're in mud up to their eyes by now."

"I think I'll put on some comfortable clothes. Maybe I can splash around a bit myself."

Lady Grace put her hand up and touched Parker's cheek. "That would be good," she said. "I'll come out and watch you. Oh, you did know that we're having Katherine Winslow to supper tonight?"

"She did mention something, but I'd forgotten the day."

"Joseph is picking her up at five."

"Let me see what I can change into." Parker went to his room, where he changed into old clothes and then left the house. When he got to the pond, he called out, "What's going on here?" Immediately Paul and Heather ran to him, their legs muddy to the knees. The mud was even in their hair, but despite that, he caught them up into his arms, mud and all, and spun them around. "You two are filthy."

Heather was squealing with delight. "Daddy, come see the boat!"

"Yeth, ith *my* boat!" Paul shouted.

Parker carried the children over, and their argument continued as he set them down. "Hello, Father."

"Son, it's good to see you. We weren't expecting you." Gregory had a considerable amount of mud on himself. He looked down at his white shirt and shrugged. "Well, it's washable, I suppose. I'll tell you what. They've about worn me out, son. Why don't you take over?"

"Yes. Why don't you go on inside?"

"I believe I will."

"Now, who's the captain of this boat?" Parker asked the twins.

"I am!" both Paul and Heather shouted at the same time. They both waded into the water up to their shins to show him how they propelled the boat around the pond.

Parker laughed. "Now I think it's my turn to be the captain." He took off his shoes and socks and waded in with them. "And if you argue with me, I'll stuff mud up your nose."

Heather squealed with delight. "Yes, mud in the nose!" She reached down and got a handful of mud and handed it up toward Parker.

Laughing, he said, "No. No mud in the nose. Let's see about this boat now. . . ."

★ ★ ★

When Kat arrived she got out of the car and thanked Joseph for picking her up.

"You're welcome, miss. Whenever you're ready I'll take you back to your flat."

"That will be fine. I expect I'll stay at least until the twins are in bed."

"No problem at all, miss."

Kat walked up the steps, but before she could ring the bell, Millie, the young maid, opened the door. She was smiling brightly and said, "Hello, Miss Winslow. We've been expecting you."

"Where is the family, Millie?"

"Mr. Braden is in the library reading to the—"

"Mr. Braden—as in Mr. Parker Braden?"

"Yes, miss."

"I didn't expect him to be here tonight."

"Neither did we, miss. And Lord and Lady Braden are getting ready for dinner. It'll be served very soon."

"Thank you, Millie." Kat walked down the wide hallway and followed the high-pitched voices to the library. Parker was on his hands and knees with both Paul and Heather on his back. Heather was in front and was leaning forward, holding two handfuls of Parker's hair. Paul was busy slapping his father, yelling, "Gittyup!" at the top of his lungs.

"Have I interrupted a rodeo?" she asked loudly so they could hear her over the noise.

The twins at once scrambled off Parker's back and came over to greet her.

"Did you bring us presents?" Paul asked brightly.

"Yes, I did," she said, holding out the bag. "But they're not from me."

"Who they from?" Heather asked as she snatched the package.

"From your father."

Parker got to his feet, making a face as he did. "I'm too old to be doing a thing like this."

He doesn't look like an old man, Kat thought. Fatigue did show on his features, but his skin was smooth, and his eyes, though somewhat troubled, were bright.

"I'm glad you could come," he said.

"I didn't expect you to be here."

"I decided to take a little holiday. Here, stop pulling at that elephant! You'll tear his ruddy trunk off, Paul!"

As Parker had assumed, the two were arguing over the two stuffed toys. But Parker settled it at once by playing a game with them, giving the winner first choice.

Finally Mrs. Henderson, the housekeeper, came and hauled the children off to wash up for dinner.

Kat watched them go and then shook her head. "I wish I had their energy."

"So do I. They never run down."

"How have you been, Parker?"

"Very well, considering."

"I worry about you."

Parker turned and asked quietly, "Do you really?"

"Of course I do!"

"That's good to know. I've had to give up worrying about myself. There's no point in it."

The two stood there talking quietly, and finally she said, "Tell me the truth, Parker. How do you keep from being ter-rified every time you go up?"

"Oh, I suppose you get used to anything. I've had men in the front-line trenches say that the first few times a bullet came anywhere close to them they tried to dig a hole. But after a month under fire, they walked around with bullets whipping everywhere. It's a psychological necessity, I suppose. You can't go around stiff with fear all the time. Couldn't fly an airplane that way." He cocked his head to one side and said, "You know there's a poem I had to memorize when I was a schoolboy. I think Byron wrote it. For some reason I say it to myself."

"What is it?"

"I don't know the name of it, but it's fairly short:

"So we'll go no more a-roving
So late into the night,
Though the heart be still as loving,
And the moon be still as bright.

"For the sword outwears its sheath,
And the soul wears out the breast,
And the heart must pause to breathe,
And love itself have rest.

"Though the night was made for loving,
And the day returns too soon,
Yet we'll go no more a-roving
By the light of the moon.

"I don't know why I like that, but I do."

"It's a sad poem."

"It's a poem about loss. We lose pretty much everything, don't we? There's always the last trip to the country. The last kiss. The last meal. And death, of course, is inevitable."

Kat studied him carefully. "You're tired," she said. "I can see it in your eyes."

"We're all tired. It's an occupational hazard for all military men."

A tiny warning sounded in Kat. She had vowed to keep herself separate from this man, but she couldn't help the way she felt about him. "God will keep you safe."

"That's the only hope I have, or any of us, for that matter," Parker said simply. "I don't know why one man dies and another lives. God is sovereign, and I'm rather glad it's in His hands. It makes me feel good to know that. He may choose to take me tomorrow, or He may choose to let me live to be an old man. But whichever, it's God's will. That's what I'm embracing."

"That's wonderful, Parker. Do many of your men feel like that?"

"Not too many. Most of them are rather wild young fellows. They never seem to give a thought for tomorrow and certainly not for eternity. I think they've blocked it out of their minds."

At that moment Edith Braden came in. "Parker, it's good to see you!"

"Aunt Edith, it's good to see you too," he said as he kissed her on the cheek.

"It's nice to see you again too, Katherine. Come. Dinner's on the table. Let's all make utter gluttons of ourselves."

The three went into the dining room, and Kat immediately noticed that Parker's wife was not there. Lady Grace made a quick statement that Veronica had an engagement in London, and Kat noticed that Parker looked uncomfortable as his mother said this.

The meal was excellent, and Parker's aunt was at the top of her form. She had a quick wit and a way of drawing others into her stories. Before long Edith had them all laughing at tales of her struggles with publishers. After they had dessert they moved to the drawing room, where the twins greedily clamored for attention. Finally Kat looked at her watch and exclaimed, "Goodness, I must go!"

"No!" Paul cried out. "Stories."

"Yes! Stories!" Heather added.

"If you wouldn't mind," Grace said. "They're fascinated with your stories. Just a few minutes?"

Kat was really in no hurry to get back to London. She was merely being polite. "Of course," she said with a smile.

Fifteen minutes later the twins were in their pajamas and Kat was sitting at the side of their bed. She was aware of Parker standing with his back against the wall. She told ridiculous, implausible stories, and the children loved them.

Finally she saw that they were getting sleepy, and she kissed them both and stroked their hair. "Go to sleep now."

"More stories," Heather whispered.

"Not now. Some other time."

She stepped back, and Parker came and said his good-nights. She saw the affection in his face as he touched them, and a quick fear came as she thought, *What would happen if he were killed? They would be without this man who loves them so dearly.*

Kat left the room and Parker accompanied her to the front door. "Joseph will be pulling the car around in just a moment."

It was a beautiful evening, so they waited in front of the house. "I just wanted to tell you how much I appreciate your taking time with the children."

"It's such a pleasure to be with them. They're lovely children."

"I don't want to take advantage of your kindness, but any time you could come back and be with them, I would consider it a favor."

"Why, of course. I'll come as often as I can."

Impulsively Parker took her hands in his own and kissed them. "Bless you, Katherine."

A car pulled into the driveway, and Kat pulled her hands away as she saw Veronica Braden staring at her out of the window. She instantly felt guilty. "I shouldn't have come here, Parker. It's not right—I mean, I shouldn't be spending any time alone with you."

"You've done nothing wrong," he said.

The chauffeur pulled his car up behind Veronica's and got out to open the door for Kat.

"Here you go, Miss Winslow."

"Hello, Mrs. Braden," Kat said as Veronica got out of her car, but Veronica only glared at her. Kat got into the car, and Joseph shut the door.

She watched as Veronica walked up to Parker but could not hear what she said as the car pulled off.

★ ★ ★

"You're going to have to stop seeing that Winslow woman," Veronica said adamantly as she got ready for bed.

"What about the man you're seeing?"

"What are you talking about?" she cried.

"It's getting bad when I have to get notes telling me you're seeing other men."

"That's a lie! Whoever said that is a liar!"

"I even have the license number of his car, Veronica— ANV483. All I have to do is get Jack over at Scotland Yard to run a check, and I'll know who it is."

Her face went pale, but she stood up straight. "Well, what about your precious Miss Winslow?"

"She's just a friend. She's been very kind to the children."

"Kind to the children, I'll bet! You were in love with her three years ago, weren't you?"

Her words had touched on the truth that lay deep within him. He tried to cover, but she had seen him falter, and the argument grew more and more bitter. Finally Veronica said, "Get out of this bedroom! Find yourself another place to sleep!"

At that instant Parker knew that something had irrevocably changed between him and his wife. It was as definite as the sound of a door closing.

"That won't be hard to do, Veronica."

As he left the room, she called out, "I don't want to hear any more of your accusations!"

Parker closed the door and knew he could not spend the night in the house. He left a note for his parents and drove back to the station. He felt something like seasickness, except it was spiritual rather than physical. He had seen other marriages break up, even between men and women who had once truly loved each other, and now he knew that he and his wife were heading in the same direction.

CHAPTER FIFTEEN

EAGLE DAY

★ ★ ★

The month of July had worn the Royal Air Force thin. The Germans had thrown wave after wave of planes against them, and only by intense effort and sacrifice had the RAF been able to stem the tide.

But Hitler was not satisfied. On July 30 he told Hermann Göring to have his forces in readiness to launch a more powerful attack: "The great battle of the Luftwaffe against England."

The following day during a conference at Hitler's mountain retreat, the Berghof, Admiral Erich Raeder made it plain that the earliest possible date for launching an invasion of England would be September 15. On the first day of August, Hitler issued directive number seventeen. "In order to establish the necessary condition for the final conquest of England, the Luftwaffe will overpower the English air force with all the forces at its command in the shortest possible time." The order commanded attacks against flying units and ground installations, as well as against the aircraft industry. This was given the code name of *Adlerangriff* and was intended to crush all RAF opposition and clear the way

for Sealion, the invasion of Britain. The first day of the operation was dubbed Eagle Day, and Göring issued his directive to all units of air fleets two, three, and five: "Within a
short period you will wipe the British air force from the sky.
Heil Hitler!"

The fliers of Parker's squadron felt the brunt of Eagle
Day. They scrambled four times, coming back in between
each flight for fresh ammunition and petrol. The one advantage they had was that the German fighter planes had small
fuel tanks. After flying to England and returning to their
bases, they had only ten minutes of actual fighting time.

The action was furious, and Parker lost his first pilot in a
month on Eagle Day. Dick Summerton was not the best pilot
in the world, but he had always been eager and willing. He
had gone up against no fewer than five 109s alone, and they
had simply blasted him out of the sky.

The sight of the young man going down had sickened
Parker, and it did not encourage him to know that he himself had downed two Germans. Both his and Brodie's score
of kills stood at ten now, but all of this was meaningless to
Parker. His only thoughts were of the letter he would have
to write to young Summerton's parents.

★ ★ ★

Every radio in England probably was tuned in to get the
results of the battle. Meredith Bryce had listened all the previous day, and the next morning she came to her superior at
the mission, Reverend Amos Chatworth, and told him about
the idea she had been working out most of the night.

"The poor pilots are exhausted," she told him. "Why
don't we take meals and drinks out to the station? Good hot
meals, Reverend."

"I can't spare the manpower, or the womanpower either.
We've got our hands full taking care of all that's going on at
the mission on a day-to-day basis."

"If you'll give me the authority, Kat and I will work extra

shifts to see that our responsibilities at the mission are met while we minister to the pilots as well." She had already told Kat about her plan, and she had been excited about the possibilities.

Chatworth agreed, and by eleven o'clock that morning, Meredith and Kat were on their way to the airfield. Meredith had managed to commandeer a truck, and the two women had worked hard to cook hot meals and even had portable heating units on the truck in case there were no facilities there.

When they got to the field, they found that 120 Squadron was gone on a mission, but that did not deter Meredith. She went up to two mechanics who had their heads buried in an airplane.

"Excuse me," she said. "My name is Meredith, and my friend here is Kat."

"Denny Featherstone, ma'am. This here's Keith."

"We brought some hot food out for you and the other men."

"You mean for the pilots, mum?"

"When they come in yes, but for the mechanics too. I know you men are working day and night to keep the planes serviced."

She had heard that ground crews worked almost around the clock, some of them not even taking the time to go back to their bunk but rather simply finding a quiet spot to lie on the ground and go to sleep. These men got very little credit or glory except from the pilots themselves. Those who flew the planes knew just how worthy these men were who worked until they dropped.

"Well, glory be!" Denny said. "Did you hear that, Keith?"

"I sure did!" Keith said, straightening up and wiping his hands on an oily rag. "Anything we can do to help, mum?"

"Where can we set up some tables?" Meredith asked.

"Right this way," Denny said. "Me and Keith will help you ladies."

The mechanics gathered around and gratefully ate the hot soup and sandwiches served with coffee and tea. The women had also brought plenty of sweets.

As they were finishing the meal, Featherstone yelled, "Here they come!"

Kat watched the skies, and soon little black dots appeared. She saw the squadron come in and asked nervously, "Are they all there, Denny?"

Denny was counting the planes anxiously, "Yes, mum, they're all there. They're all safe!"

Some of the planes were riddled with bullet holes, and one had the tail fin practically shot away.

But all of the men were all right.

As the pilots approached the gathering, Denny said, "Right this way. These ladies from the East End Mission have brought some hot food."

Meredith saw the fatigue on their faces pulling them down, their faces gray with strain. But she kept a smile on her face as she stepped forward and said, "Right this way. I have plenty of hot food for all the heroes. Any among you not heroes?"

Brodie laughed. "No, we're all heroes here!"

"Good." Meredith and Kat greeted each man as he received his food, and gave them each a tract as well. Some of the men flirted with the two young women, and they all gulped the food down.

Parker looked terribly weary as he finished his meal. He managed a smile and said, "This is awfully nice of you two ladies."

"It's little enough," Meredith said. "Here, have another piece of cake."

Brodie seemed to have no strain at all in contrast with the others. While Parker was talking with Kat, Brodie took it upon himself to refill coffee cups, and Meredith made sure everybody had all the cake they wanted. "I have to treat these lads like children," Brodie said with a grin. "I'm the closest thing to a father they've got."

A rouse of insults went up at this, and Meredith enjoyed the camaraderie that bound these men together.

After they had all had their fill of cake, most of the pilots went off to get some sleep before the next scramble, but Brodie stayed behind. While Kat started cleaning up, Brodie said, "Come on, Meredith. I wanna show you my plane."

"I'd like to see it. Do you mind, Kat?"

"Not a bit. You go ahead."

Meredith walked around the plane as Brodie pointed out its features.

"Why don't you get inside? You can see what it feels like."

"In this skirt?"

"Nobody to see but me, and you know how modest I am."

"I know all about that."

"Take your shoes off. Those high heels might punch a hole in the wings."

After removing her shoes, Meredith took his hand, stepped up on the wing, and then managed to slip into the seat. "It's so small!"

"Not very big." Brodie had crawled up and was leaning over her. "Some of the big fellows have a hard time closing the canopy."

Meredith was fascinated. Brodie showed her all of the instruments and explained the function of each one. Finally she climbed out of the plane and put on her shoes.

"I'll show you the rest of the operation," he said, taking her by the hand.

He took her on a tour, and Meredith could not understand how he could be so lighthearted. "Aren't you afraid, Brodie?"

"Scared pink."

"No, really. Aren't you afraid of death?"

"About as much as everybody else. Now Parker, *he's* the one that's got a big load. He has to keep up with all of us and make split-second decisions. All I have to decide to do is to get in a Spit and shoot at Germans."

Meredith couldn't understand how he could live under such strain and remain so calm. He leaned back against a fence. "You look pretty today."

She smiled. "I believe you'd flirt with a woman even if you had one foot in the grave."

"I hope so."

"Brodie, answer me something honestly. Aren't you afraid of death?"

He did not answer for a time. He took out a package of gum and offered her a piece. She refused it. He peeled one of the sticks and began to chew it. "Actually, Meredith, I'm more afraid right now than I am when I'm going into action."

"I don't understand that. You're in no danger here."

"I know it, but that's the way it is. When I'm in action I can't think of anything but what's right in front of me. No time to worry. Some of the fellas don't feel like that, but I do."

"But you're in danger of dying every day. Don't you ever think of God or eternity?"

Again there was a long silence. When Brodie lifted his eyes, he was entirely serious. "Yes, I do." Then his eyes crinkled. "But sometimes I beat the drum for the Salvation Army."

"You are crazy," she laughed. She put her hand out and touched his chest, and he captured it.

"That's enough talk about me. It's boring. Tell me about you."

"Nothing to tell about me."

"Yes there is. Tell me what you plan to do after the war."

"I suppose I'll put any decisions off until the war is over."

"You still got yourself shut up, not letting any men inside that little box you made for yourself?"

Meredith bit her lower lip. "I can't think about that."

"You're still grieving for that husband you lost."

"Yes, of course I am."

Brodie dropped her hand. "I guess we're both loners, then. You don't want a man, and no woman would put up with me."

"You could change, Brodie."

"I'm not sure that I could. Come on. Let's go back and get some more coffee."

★ ★ ★

Parker could hear the pilots outside laughing. It had been awfully nice of Kat and Meredith to feed his men. He knew they appreciated it. He picked up the phone and called home. His mother answered, and he asked about the children.

"Actually, they aren't feeling well. I think they're coming down with something. I hope it's not the mumps or measles. I'll have them see the doctor tomorrow."

"Yes. Please do that, and let me know what you find out." After a brief discussion of their symptoms, Parker asked to speak with his wife.

"Why, Parker, she's not here."

"Is she in London again?"

"I . . . I think so."

There was a silence then, a clear sign to Parker that his mother knew more than she was saying. He had checked the license number written on the note through his friend at the Yard and knew that the car belonged to Charles Gooding. "I'll try to get home as soon as I can," he said, "but it's busy here."

He hung up the phone and then sat at his desk, a sense of depression and futility grasping him. He thought about going to find Veronica and having it out with her and making her go home, but he knew that would never do. He finally got up, put on a face that was suitable for company, and left his office.

CHAPTER SIXTEEN

Missing in Action

★ ★ ★

Lady Braden stared blankly at her daughter-in-law, too stunned to speak. The two were standing in the foyer, where Grace had caught Veronica just as she was preparing to leave. She had merely wanted to find out how long she would be gone, but Veronica had spoken bluntly, shocking Grace to the core.

"Going back on the stage?" Grace finally managed to say. "Why, that's . . ." She was so stunned, she couldn't even form a sentence.

"I don't know why you should be so shocked, Grace. Surely you realized I would someday return to my career."

"But things are different now, Veronica. You're a mother. . . . What will you do about the children?"

A defensive light leaped to Veronica's eyes. "They're not babies anymore, and the money I make will be more than enough to hire a nanny for them."

"But a nanny isn't the same thing as a mother."

Veronica smiled bitterly. "According to what Parker says about my care of them, a nanny would be even better."

"He doesn't mean that. He's just on edge these days."

"He means it, all right," Veronica said grimly.

Grace tried desperately to think of something that would change Veronica's mind, but she had little hope of success. "You know Parker will be totally against it."

"I know. He believes a woman's place is in the home having babies and taking care of them." Bitterness touched the edge of her lips, and she gave Grace a direct stare. "You might as well know it, Grace. Parker and I are going different ways."

Grace had seen it coming, of course, but spoken aloud, it had an ominous sound. "Please think it over before you make any major decisions."

"I have thought it over." Veronica opened the door. "I'm late for my meeting." She shut the door firmly behind her.

Grace walked rapidly to the library, where she found her husband reading a book at his desk. "Gregory," she said unsteadily, "Veronica's told me something I think you need to hear. . . ."

★ ★ ★

As the Germans stepped up their attacks on Britain, both Kat and Meredith felt more and more certain that they should continue taking hot meals to the fliers and mechanics. They could not maintain a regular schedule, and it had taken a great deal of persuasion to convince Reverend Chatworth, their director, of the importance of what they were doing. He had finally given in to their persuasion, and both women arranged their work so they could go out as often as possible.

They arrived at the airfield one day to find the maintenance men totally exhausted, trying to grab some sleep on the grass by the runway. Denny Featherstone and Keith Poe, Parker's two lead mechanics, roused themselves when the women arrived, very glad to see them. Featherstone, burly and as muscular as a wrestler, filled them in on what had been happening as he munched on a fish sandwich, while the much smaller Poe filled up on cakes and cookies.

"Well, it's like this, you see," Denny said. "The Germans have been sendin' bombers over at low levels to knock out our radar towers."

"That's very bad, isn't it, Denny?" Kat asked.

"You've got that right. A lot of the women who work in the stations got killed. Men too, of course." He took a huge swallow of his coffee and then bit an enormous plug out of his sandwich. The hand he held it in was full of grease stains, but that didn't seem to matter. "We've been awful busy around here. The planes come in all shot up, and we have to get 'em ready to fly again."

"That must be very hard," she said. "What do you do if they can't be fixed?"

"We rob 'em for their parts. One of the things we had to do was put armor plating behind all the pilots and under the seat. That took a bit of doin' to get 'em all ready."

Denny seemed to be enjoying explaining his job to a civilian, and he pointed to the other crew members in the area as he explained their various jobs. Some of them were lying flat on their backs on the grass sound asleep, while others were helping themselves to the food Kat and Meredith had laid out. There were the armorers, who were responsible for the ammunition and flares. The fitters were in charge of the engines and related controls, and the riggers were responsible for the overall structure of the plane. Denny told her that many of them had never been outside of their base, and many more went for days without even seeing their bunks or the inside of their mess hall.

"Does it bother you that you don't get any credit for what you do?" Meredith asked. "I mean, the pilots get all the headlines. People never see the work you do."

"Nah, that don't bother us much," Poe said. "The fliers, *they* know what we're doin'. They're quick to tell us how much we mean to them."

"Our boys are doing real good," Denny said. "Brodie's got fourteen kills now. That's four more than Wing Commander Braden."

Kat just nodded. The business of killing the enemy seemed a necessary evil in the present conflict, but it was not something she felt she could rejoice over.

Poe grabbed a sugar cookie and washed down a big bite with a cup of scalding coffee. He appeared to have asbestos lining in his mouth, for no coffee was ever hot enough to suit him. He smacked his lips, but there was a worried look around his eyes when he said, "Been a little friction between the wing commander and Brodie Lee."

"That's enough of that," Denny said roughly. "We don't tell tales out of school. They'll be all right. Natural enough there'd be a little fuss now and then as tough a job as they've got."

Both Kat and Meredith were intensely curious to hear more, but Featherstone had shut the conversation down, so they didn't ask any more questions.

Ten minutes later Featherstone cocked his head. "They're comin' in. Hey, you lazy blokes, get up!" He went around prodding the remaining sleeping men with his toe while Kat and Meredith moved to the edge of the field. Both of them watched the dots that were appearing to the south, and long before they could identify anyone, Featherstone growled, "Only eleven. One of them's missing."

"Can you tell who's missing?" Kat asked as the planes got closer.

"Number two. It's Blue Three."

"Who's that?" Kat asked.

"Brodie Lee."

Both women stared at the burly crewman, but neither said anything. They watched as the planes came in and rolled into place, the pilots crawling wearily out.

"They'll have to go give their reports first, miss," Keith Poe said. "Then they'd probably appreciate a hot meal."

One of the pilots, however, did come over as the others filed toward the building where they would be debriefed. "Hello, Miss Winslow, and you too, Miss Bryce," Bernie greeted. "I see you've brought some goodies for us again."

"Hello, Bernie," Meredith said. She smiled nervously

and poured a cup of coffee for the pilot. "What happened to Brodie?"

Bernie Cox was the smallest man in the squadron. He looked more like a jockey than a pilot. He sipped his coffee and shook his head, a worried look in his eyes. "We met a flight of Stukas and pretty well whipped up on 'em, but you know we only have fifteen seconds of firing time with our guns, and all of us were pretty much out of ammo, and nearly out of fuel too. We had to do a long chase." He sipped his coffee again and seemed reluctant to continue.

"What happened, Bernie?"

"Well, we saw a flight of German bombers, Heinkels, and Brodie took off after them. I called him back and so did the wing commander, but he didn't answer." He cast his troubled eyes up to the sky. "He should have been back by now. I'm worried about him." He finished his coffee and set the cup on the table. "I'll have to go in and give my report."

As Cox left, Kat said, "We'd better go make more coffee." She started toward the truck but soon realized Meredith hadn't followed her. She turned and saw that Meredith was staring at the ground. Kat went back to stand in front of her, noticing the strain on her face. "What's wrong, Meredith?"

She shook her head and looked down at her trembling hands that were clasped together.

"Are you worried about Brodie?" Kat asked, putting her arm around the shorter woman.

When Meredith looked up, Kat was surprised to see her eyes were moist and her lips were trembling. "I can't go through it again. I just can't!"

Kat knew that Meredith was thinking about the loss of her husband. She knew little of the circumstances, but she knew that the death of Donald Bryce had been terrible for Meredith. They had not been married for long, and although Meredith rarely spoke of him, her voice was often unsteady when she did. Quickly Kat made up her mind. "Look, I can handle this alone. I want you to take a cab and go home and get some rest. Sleep if you can."

Meredith did not argue. She said not a word as Kat took

her to the edge of the field and called a cab for her. When she put Meredith inside, she said, "Try not to worry. I'll call you if we hear anything."

Meredith still did not answer, and as the cab drove off, Kat saw that her friend was slumped in the back seat. Kat went back to the truck and began to make more coffee. Fifteen minutes later the pilots all emerged from the building and headed straight for the truck. David Deere, leader of Yellow Flight, was in the lead, along with the two men who flew with him, Al Tobin and Orin Morris. Morris was a rather timid man, but David Deere made up for that with an oversupply of confidence.

"Hello, Miss Winslow. What have you got for us today?" David asked.

"Fried fish sandwiches with hush puppies and apple pie."

"Hush puppies? What's a hush puppy?"

"Here." Kat picked up one of the round balls and handed it to him. "See how you like it."

David popped it into his mouth, and his eyes opened with surprise. "This is *good*! What's it made of?"

"It's just corn bread fried in fat with some green onions added."

"Why do you call them hush puppies?"

"The story I've heard is that back in the old days on the farm when the dogs would crowd around the table to try to get something the people were eating, someone would toss some of these little corn bread balls to them and say, 'Hush, puppy.' They've been called that for a long time where I come from."

The pilots gathered around, and Kat was kept busy dealing out the sandwiches and hush puppies. The men ate like starved wolves, and all of them complimented Kat mightily.

"I'll tell you what, Miss Winslow," David Deere said. "I think I'll marry you so I can get hush puppies all the time."

"Don't listen to him, miss," Trevor Park said, his eyes gleaming. "He's already married."

"Sure, I am, but the Bible says two wives are better than one."

Kat laughed outright. There was a cheerfulness about David that was welcome in the sometimes tense environment. "Where does it say that? I don't remember reading that."

He shrugged his burly shoulders. "It actually says *two* are better than one. Somebody forgot to put the word *wives* in there."

"You can't even take care of one wife, much less two," Parker said. He had joined the group and was enjoying listening to the banter. When he'd had his fill, along with the rest of the pilots, he told the men to try to get some sleep. He had a feeling they wouldn't be able to sleep long.

The men all thanked Kat again, and when they were gone, Parker said, "Let me help you clean up."

"Oh, you don't have to do that."

"I don't mind." As they began to clean up, he asked, "What happened to Meredith?"

"She was upset. I sent her home."

"You mean over Brodie?"

"Yes."

"I didn't know she was that close to him."

"I'm not sure she is. She's still mourning the loss of her husband. I think she suffers when anything like that happens again."

Even as she spoke, the noise of a plane coming in caught Parker's attention. He shaded his eyes with his hand but then shook his head. "I thought it might be Brodie, but it's not."

"You're worried about him too, aren't you?"

"Yes, I am. He shouldn't have gone after those Heinkels by himself. He couldn't have had much ammo left." He saw that she was watching him with a nervous expression, and he tried to be more positive. "He might be all right, Katherine. Maybe he had to bail out. We'll probably hear that someone's picked him up."

Kat continued gathering the dirty utensils, but she could

not forget Brodie. Finally she said quietly, "He's not a Christian, Parker. It would be . . . terrible if he were dead."

Parker turned to face her at once. "You care for him, Katherine?"

"No, not like you mean. But I do care for him in another way. We got very close after you left Georgia, Parker. He would stop in and cheer me up, and he was always upbeat and happy. Or seemed to be. I can't even fathom the thought that he might be . . ." She could not bring herself to speak the word. "Well, we'd better get this mess cleaned up."

But Parker took her by the arm and turned her around, his face set with a peculiar expression. "Have you ever had second thoughts, Katherine, about refusing to marry me three years ago?"

She could not answer, for in all truth she had wondered if she'd made the right decision. She could not admit this to Parker, however. "I try to put things like that behind me."

"You were looking for a high calling then from God. Have you found it?"

"I . . . I'm not sure. I thought God wanted me to work with the mission here. It's good work I'm doing, and I'm glad to do it. But I've always thought I would be doing something more than serving fish sandwiches and hush puppies."

Parker did not speak for a moment, and finally he said, "I don't want what I'm going to say now to be a burden to you, Katherine—but I've never gotten over what I felt for you."

"You shouldn't say that, Parker. You have a wife and a family. God's given you a great gift. Your children are wonderful."

"Yes, they are, and I love them with all my heart. But I think you know that my marriage is a travesty, and I know you feel as I do that marriage is forever." He started to say something else but then caught himself. He shook his head as if he were angry, then pulled himself together. "I should never have mentioned this. Please forget it."

He turned and walked away, and Kat watched him go.

She knew that what he had asked would be impossible, that she would not be able to forget what he had just said. Not for weeks or months or maybe forever.

★ ★ ★

Meredith had been tossing and turning for two hours. She did not want to have to take a sleeping pill, and more than once had almost decided to get up and read a book or pace the floor. She had come home from work the day before at Kat's insistence but had been unable to sleep no matter how hard she tried. Kat would not hear of letting her go to work today, so she had stayed home again. While Kat worked the night shift at the hospital, Meredith had endured the loneliness of the evening and had finally gone to bed when it was almost midnight.

There had been no letup from the grief she had felt at the airfield. She had willed the phone to ring, for somebody to call to say that Brodie was safe, but it had remained silent.

Just as she was about to get up, a rap sounded on the door. She leaped out of bed, grabbing her robe. As she hurried to the door, she thought, *What if someone has come to tell me he's dead?* She stood there for a moment in the darkness unable to move. "I can't face it again," she whispered. The knock was repeated, and she turned on the living room light. She slipped the latch and for one moment wished she did not have to open it, but she knew she had to hear the news, whatever it was.

She opened the door—and caught her breath, for there stood Brodie Lee, grinning at her.

"Sorry to come so late, but—" He broke off suddenly and the smile left his face when he noticed how pale she was and that her lips were twitching. "What's wrong, Merry? Are you sick?"

She did not answer. She couldn't! She wheeled and walked over to the window, leaving Brodie standing there. He put his hat on a chair and followed her. "What's wrong?"

"Go away."

But he was entirely serious now. "Have you had bad news?"

"*You're* bad news! Now please go away!"

He did not know how to take what was happening. "I went to the mission and you weren't there. Then I went to the hospital, and Kat told me you weren't feeling well. She wouldn't say what was wrong. I came by to see how you were." Brodie stood waiting for her to answer, but she did not move. He could hear a muffled sobbing and finally he reached out and turned her around. Her face was pale and tears were running down her cheeks.

"Here. Sit down before you faint or somethin'." He pulled her to the couch, keeping his arm around her. "Can't you tell me what's wrong, Merry? Can I help?"

"I thought . . . I thought you were dead," she said in a muffled voice.

Brodie had grown tremendously fond of Meredith Bryce, and with his arm around her, he could feel the tenseness of her body and the tremors that were going through it. "I'm sorry to worry you." She did not answer, and he began to explain. "I chased some Germans out over the Channel, and my engine conked out. I bailed out, and I got picked up almost right away by a British destroyer that was headed for Scotland. They couldn't stop to let me off, and they couldn't break their radio silence. Some kind of a secret mission. Anyway, there was no way I could call in. They let me off in Scotland. I had to catch a train back. I'm all right. Nothing to cry about."

But Meredith had not moved. She was obviously still struggling, and the tears were now running freely down her cheeks. Brodie felt entirely helpless. "Do you want to talk about it?"

She whispered, "I never cried once when Donald was killed."

Parker was no psychologist, but he knew Meredith was bound up tight and headed for real trouble. "Sometimes," he said gently, "it's the best thing to cry." He pulled her into

his arms, and she fell against him, sobbing. This was no
dainty sort of crying. It shocked Brodie how she wept with
great gulping sobs and clung to him fiercely. He made comforting noises, but mainly he simply held her and stroked
her back until the sobs began to mitigate.

She finally pulled away from him and sat back, and he
reached into his pocket and gave her his handkerchief. She
took it and wiped her face with it. "I'm sorry," she said
weakly.

"It's all right," he said with relief. "I don't think anyone
ever cried for me like that before."

"It wasn't just you, Brodie. I was worried, of course, but
it's all mixed up. I was thinking about Donald and about the
other men who don't come back, and it all caught up with
me."

Brodie took the handkerchief from her and wiped away
more tears that she had missed. "I don't like to see you cry."

The room was quiet, and for a moment the two stared at
each other. Something passed between them, and then suddenly color started to rise on Meredith's cheeks. "You'd better go, Brodie. No man likes to be around a weepy woman."

But he shook his head. "No, not unless you'll go with
me. Let's go get something to eat."

"It's too late, but I'll fix you something."

"All right, but I can't help. I can't even boil water without burning it."

"It won't be much," Meredith said as she got up. "How
does a ham and cheese omelet sound?"

"Sure, and anything else you find. Throw it in there."

Relieved to have something to do, Meredith moved
around the kitchen putting the simple meal together. True
enough, she had not wept over Donald when he died, but
now she realized she should have. She marveled at the
strength she had, even though she still felt a bit weak.

As she fixed the omelet, Brodie began telling her stories
of his youth in Georgia. Before long he even had her laughing. She put the omelet on a plate before him, and he ate
heartily while she drank some of the tea she had made.

Afterward they sat talking quietly, and the mood turned serious again. "I'm glad you're all right," she told him.

"So am I." He looked at her intently. "Are you okay now?"

"Yes."

"Well, I'd better go. We'll have the neighbors gossipin' 'bout us—and I got my reputation to think of, you know." He got to his feet, and she followed him to the door. He put his hat on and opened the door.

"You've been a comfort to me, Brodie." She looked at her feet for a moment. "And you didn't try to take advantage of me—as most men would."

"I must be close to achieving sainthood." He hesitated, then nodded. "Thanks for caring about me."

She did not answer, and her eyes looked enormous by the dim light.

"I never told you how beautiful you are, did I?"

Meredith suddenly smiled. "In this ratty old robe, no makeup, and spilling tears like a waterfall?"

But he did not smile. He reached out and touched her cheek. "Yes, you are." He turned and left without another word.

Meredith closed the door and went to the window. After a moment he appeared in front of the apartment building and got into a military truck. As she watched him drive away, she realized that she felt more for this man than she should.

CHAPTER SEVENTEEN

BERNIE

★ ★ ★

The noise in the ready room was dominated, as usual, by a raucously blaring radio. A Ping-Pong tournament had attracted several of the fliers. A few were reading, and Brodie and his flight leader, Bernie Cox, were engaged in a fast-moving chess game. Although Brodie could beat Bernie at anything involving strength or dexterity, he had never beaten him at a game of chess. Chess was Bernie Cox's delight, and next to his art, he loved it better than any other activity on the face of the planet.

Bernie leaned forward, his hand poised over the board delicately—almost like a surgeon preparing to open a patient's body. He picked up a chess piece and moved it. Then he leaned back and locked his fingers behind his head. "Checkmate. I win again."

"I'll never play another game with you, Bernie!" Brodie said, frustration written on his face. "I don't see how you do it. I can never beat you."

"It's all in the mind, old boy."

"I don't think you're that much smarter than me."

"Perhaps not in everything, but I happen to be a genius at chess."

Bernie puffed out his chest proudly and tipped back in his chair, but he went too far. He started flailing wildly, but it was too late to stop the chair from crashing backward. Brodie laughed uproariously as his flight leader got to his feet. "You might be great at chess, but you're sure as shootin' the clumsiest guy I've ever seen!"

Bernie looked embarrassed but quickly righted his chair. "Let's play again," he challenged, sitting down again and setting up the board. "If I can beat you once more, I think it'll be an even hundred that I've taken from you."

Brodie rolled his eyes and helped set up the board again, thinking about how close he'd gotten to the two men in his flight—Bernie Cox and Sailor Darley. They had grown to know each other so well that they hardly needed the radio when they were flying. They had practiced their maneuvers more than most of the flights, but it was almost eerie the way the three could move into action, each always knowing what his two wing mates were doing.

Brodie felt particularly close to Bernie because Bernie had taken him to his home to introduce him to his parents. It had been an enjoyable day for Brodie, and he liked the parents a great deal. Bernie was their only son, and he knew, despite the smiles, they were deeply concerned for his safety.

Brodie had also been impressed with Bernie's talent for painting. He was not the best pilot in the squadron, but he painted amazingly well. One of his paintings had been of a Spitfire attacking a lone Me-109 high in the clouds. The painting caught the spirit of battle, with beauty and violence married together high above the earth. He had admired it so much that Bernie had given him the painting, refusing any money for it. He had also painted a picture of Brodie leaning against the wing of his plane with his flight suit on and his helmet in his hand.

As they set up the board and began to play again, their individual styles of play reflected their personalities. Brodie moved quickly and impulsively, as if he could not wait to get the piece from one square to another. He sometimes made amazing moves, and that won him games against lesser players than Bernie. Bernie, on the other hand, was meditative and thoughtful. He loved the order and the precision that Brodie lacked.

★ ★ ★

Parker was speaking with his group captain, Howard Monroe, over the noise of the radio and the Ping-Pong tournament. Monroe had come to make an inspection, and now the two men stood in one corner of the room discussing the fliers.

Monroe took his eyes off the pilots to face Parker. His brow furrowed and he shook his head. "You look terrible, Braden. Why don't you take some time off?"

"I'm no worse off than anyone else, Captain."

"It looks to me like you are. The responsibility for the squadron rests with you. You need to try to spare yourself a bit."

Parker had heard this before. "I'll try to do that, sir."

"See that you do. Tell me about the men. What's their condition? Are they holding up well?"

"Yes, sir. Very well indeed."

"There's been a lot of talk about the one called Cowboy."

"That's him over there playing chess. The taller one. He's the best pilot in the squadron. He's shot down fourteen planes. Well, at least he's credited with that many. I'm sure he actually has more that weren't identified."

"A good pilot, eh?"

"The finest."

"How does he fit in? I mean, being an American and all."

"Very well. But I might say he's not much on discipline."

"I suppose that comes from being an American."

"It might be. What I would like to see—"

The loudspeaker interrupted Parker's words. "Scramble, 120 Squadron, scramble!"

"I'll have to go, sir."

"Yes. I'll wait around until you get back from this mission. We need to talk some more."

★ ★ ★

As Brodie looked ahead, he saw a tight formation of enemy bombers guarded by what seemed to be a great many 109s. His radio crackled, and he heard Parker's voice say, "All right, lads, there they are. Let's go get them."

Even as Parker spoke, Brodie saw a flight of RAF Hurricanes attack the German formations, their guns ablaze. Soon several of the German bombers and fighters were headed for the ground in flames.

"Bandits at twelve o'clock!" Bernie's voice came sharply. "Close up!"

They closed the distance that lay between planes. "Number five, attack!" Parker commanded.

The squadron altered shape, altered course, and then changed again. Suddenly the German bombers also changed course, banking steeply to their right.

"They're breaking up," Parker said. "Go at them and watch out for one another, chaps."

A calmness came upon Brodie as it usually did for a few seconds before making contact. His whole mind was fixed on the bombers, and as he made one pass along with his wing mates, Bernie and Sailor, he saw his tracers mark the path between his plane and one of the bombers. He knew he had hit the pilot when he saw the bomber veer and start flying erratically.

From that point on the squadron fought with everything it had. Finally the battle became merely a blur.

"Get into formation!" Cox barked. "We've got a signal there's a group of Jerries just over there. I think I can see them."

Brodie pulled in tight next to Bernie. He noticed that some of the other Spitfires were also working to get into formation again.

As they approached the new crew of bombers, Bernie said, "Watch out for fighters. I don't see any, but they're probably here. Watch my back as we go in."

The three planes wheeled almost as one, with Bernie Cox in the middle and Sailor on the other side. Brodie followed Bernie's movements exactly, although everything in him yearned to simply go in after his prey.

"All right, chaps. Here we go. Let's hope you're better at shooting than you are at chess, Blue Three."

"I'll beat you next time. See if I don't," Brodie called back.

The flight went in, made one pass, and shot down one of the bombers. "There's no fighter cover," Brodie said. "Let's just go get 'em."

"No. Stay in formation. We've got to cover for each other."

Brodie had a great affection for Bernie Cox, but what he saw ahead was entirely too tempting. He was supposed to cover Bernie's rear to be sure nothing came up from behind, but when he saw one of the enemy bombers veer off and streak away toward the Channel, he said, "I can get him. You guys wait for me."

Wheeling his Spitfire around, Brodie caught up with the bomber, which could not match his speed. He had him in his sights, and he had sent two short bursts when he suddenly heard Sailor yell, "Look out, Bernie! Bandits behind you!"

Brodie wheeled the Spitfire around. It was his job to watch his flight leader's rear, and he had wandered away. By the time he got back to his position, he saw Bernie's Spitfire heading down in flames, and a cold hand seemed to constrict around his heart. "Bernie," he yelled, "bail out!"

But Bernie Cox could not bail out. He had been taken from behind by a 109, and the first burst had killed him instantly. He had collapsed on the stick and went down like a lead ball.

"Watch yourself, Brodie," Sailor shouted. "They got Bernie. There's too many of 'em for us."

But Brodie did not answer. He was following the fall of Bernie's Spitfire, willing it to straighten up, repeatedly calling out, "Bernie, pull out!"

But he did not pull out. His Spitfire hit the earth with such force that the wings flew off and the rest of the frame shattered.

Numbly Brodie turned his Spitfire back. The dogfight was still going on, and a red rage enveloped him. He threw himself back into the battle, totally disregarding his own safety. The world was filled with the clatter of machine guns and the scream of planes, and death reigned in the sky over the battered body of Bernard Cox.

★ ★ ★

Parker stood staring at Brodie, and the silence in his office seemed thick. Bernie Cox's death had brought grief to the whole squadron, for he was one of the more popular pilots. Parker had heard the story from Sailor Darley and others who had seen the plane get hit.

Brodie's face was pale, and there was no laughter in him now. "There were no fighters at all when I pulled away, Parker." His voice seemed harsh, and his eyes contained an anger that went beyond normal. "I'll get them for it. You see if I don't."

"You're not going to help Bernie by getting yourself killed."

"It was my fault! Why don't you throw me out of this outfit? It's what I deserve."

Actually, that was exactly what Parker had intended. He felt sick over the death of another good pilot and had looked forward to giving Brodie Lee the roughest speech he had ever given any pilot. But now as he stood there, he saw that it would be useless. Bernie was gone. They needed another flight leader, but he well knew it would not be Brodie. He contemplated grounding him for a while, which was seeming more and more like a reasonable action. "Maybe you'd better take a few days off."

"I don't need time off. Just get me back in action, Parker."

He shook his head. "You can't go at them mindlessly. You've got to think."

Brodie did not answer, and for some time Parker tried to reason with him, once more emphasizing the benefits of flying in formation, explaining that mere madness would just bring disaster.

"I'll make them pay for it." Brodie's face was grim, and his usual happy-go-lucky attitude had changed.

Parker nodded wearily. "All right. That's all."

Brodie turned and walked out of the office stiffly, and Parker wondered if he had done the right thing in keeping the American on. He had based his decision on the need for experienced fighter pilots. Brodie was by far the best in the whole wing—perhaps even in the RAF—and he could not afford to lose him.

"I'll just have to watch him more closely," he muttered grimly, "before he kills somebody else—probably himself."

Parker was exhausted, but he took the time to compose a letter to Bernie's parents before heading for a bunk for a few minutes of much-needed rest. He knew a piece of paper was useless to a couple who had lost the joy of their lives, but it was all he could offer the family at the moment.

He fell asleep instantly and knew nothing until a soft voice said, "Wing Commander, wake up."

He came slowly out of the sleep, feeling groggy. He sat up on the cot, rubbing his eyes.

"What is it, Lieutenant?"

"Your wife, sir. She's waiting to see you."

"Where is she?"

"I had her wait in your office."

"Thank you."

Getting to his feet, Parker tried to shake off his grogginess. He had flown numerous missions with little downtime in between. It was not the flying itself nor the danger that had worn him down but the burden of command and the loss of life. He had taken the death of Cox harder than he had ever taken a loss before.

When he stepped into the office, Veronica was standing waiting for him. "I have to talk to you, Parker. It won't take long." Her voice was tight, and she sounded determined. She had made up her mind about something, but he could not imagine what.

"Have a seat, Veronica."

"I know you're not going to like this, but it's something I feel I need to do." She glanced at him nervously but saw nothing in his face to reveal his feelings. "I'm going to pick up my career again. I've not been happy since I left the stage. I should never have given that up."

"You know I don't want my wife having a career like that, Veronica. If we didn't have children, perhaps it would be different."

"Parker, why don't you admit it? Things will never be different between us. Our marriage was a mistake. We each need to get on with our own lives." She looked at her hands on her lap. "I'm not sure we ever really loved each other."

He felt fatigue drag him down. He was too exhausted to try to decipher her comment. Was she telling him she was going to leave him? "We can stay together for the children" was the best he could do at the moment.

"We'll try it for a while if you like. I don't think it will work. I'm not even sure it's worth the effort." She shrugged, and he saw regret in her face. "The children need us, so we'll try to do the best we can, but I need to go back to work. I hope you won't hate me because of it."

He could not think of an answer, and finally Veronica, without another word, turned and left the office. Parker locked his fingers together and pressed them as if he could squeeze the present out in some simple way. The breakup of the marriage, he recognized, had been coming for a long time. He leaned forward and put his forehead on his hands, sitting absolutely still.

★ ★ ★

"Darley, you'll take Bernie's place as flight leader."

Sailor Darley nodded grimly. "If you like, sir. I'll do the best I can." He hesitated, then said, "I hate to mention this, but Brodie's gone."

"Gone? Gone where?"

"He was hit pretty hard by Bernie's death. I think he just went into town."

"Well, you'll take two of the reserves in Blue Flight until we get Brodie straightened out."

"Yes, sir."

"I'll see if I can find him. I wouldn't want him to get into trouble in town again."

★ ★ ★

Kat took the call from Parker, giving her the news that Brodie had wandered off the post. "If he comes to see you, try to talk some sense into him."

"What's wrong with him? What happened?"

"His flight leader was killed. The two were very close. Sometimes it hits men like this. Call me if he shows up."

"All right, Parker."

Kat put the phone down and looked over at Meredith, who was sitting beside the window reading a book. "That was Parker, Meredith. There's a problem with Brodie."

"What kind of a problem?"

"He left the base after losing a good friend—Bernie Cox."

"Oh, that nice man!" Meredith exclaimed. She put the book down and stood up. "How terrible!"

"I have a feeling that Brodie's in trouble. Parker says we're to call him if we see him."

"What will they do to him?"

"I don't know. I think Parker wants to avoid any direct action. I have a feeling that if we just find him and get him back, Parker will take care of it."

"But we wouldn't know where to look for him."

"No, but I think one of us ought to stay here. I've got to go on duty at the hospital."

"You go ahead. I'll stay here in case he calls."

Kat left the flat a few minutes later, and Meredith could no longer concentrate on her book. She set up the ironing board and began ironing. The radio was on with Frank Sinatra singing "I'll Never Smile Again." It was a plaintive melody, and she hummed along with it.

There was a rap at the door, and she put the iron down. "Brodie!" she exclaimed as she opened the door. "Come on in."

"I don't know why I came here," he muttered as he shuffled in.

"Come in the kitchen and sit down. I'll fix you something to eat."

"Not hungry."

Meredith got him to sit down while she brewed some tea and kept up a steady stream of idle talk. She put his tea in front of him and noticed that his hands were unsteady. "Is something wrong, Brodie?"

"Yes, there's something wrong. There's something wrong with me!" He put his palms on the table. "I killed the best guy in the whole RAF."

"What are you talking about?"

"I killed Bernie, my flight leader." He clasped his hands together and said bitterly, "I wish it had been me that was killed instead of him. It was my fault."

"Why don't you tell me about it?" she said gently. She prodded him on and asked questions until finally the whole story spilled out.

"But you mustn't blame yourself. You told me before what chaos it is up there when planes are going everywhere."

"I shouldn't have left his back unguarded. It was my job to cover him, and I didn't do it."

Meredith felt a surge of compassion for this man who had always been so sure of himself. All confidence was gone now, and his face showed only bitterness. She let him talk for a long time, and when he seemed to have finished, she said, "You know, Brodie, you're carrying a burden of guilt, and it will destroy you."

"I *am* guilty. I oughta bear the burden." He suddenly jumped to his feet. "I gotta get out of here."

"No, sit down. Let's talk some more."

"There's nothin' more to talk about, Meredith." With his fists clenched, he stared at the wall, fixedly avoiding her gaze. "I'll get 'em for killin' Bernie!" He started for the door again. Meredith got up quickly and tried to stop him, but he shook his head and left, slamming the door behind him.

As he ran down the stairs, his only thought was that he wanted to kill as many Germans as possible. "They killed Bernie, the best guy that ever lived," he snarled under his breath, "but I'll pay 'em back!"

CHAPTER EIGHTEEN

DEATH FROM THE SKIES

★ ★ ★

August 1940 brought heavy raids from German bombers to RAF airfields, as well as radar stations, ports, and aircraft factories. Most of the leadership in Britain regarded this as a prelude to an invasion. Never had the Luftwaffe made such a determined effort to wipe out RAF airfields, and never had the defense shown more courage and determination. Not only were pilots dying, but now civilians were being killed as well.

America's interest in the war was intensifying, and one headline in an American newspaper said, "If Great Britain loses the present battle, she will in effect have lost the war, at least as far as the mother country is concerned."

One American behaved in a particularly shameful manner. The American ambassador in London, Joseph Kennedy, ensured that a continuous stream of pessimistic news reached the United States. "England," he said, "will go down fighting. Unfortunately I am one who does not believe that it is going to do the slightest bit of good." To President Roosevelt's disgust, Kennedy ordered the embassy and all its staff to flee London, and of course, Kennedy fled with them.

Britain's defensive capabilities during the months of July and August had been severely tested, but so had those of the Luftwaffe. The loss of planes, both bombers and fighters, had been enormous. The Luftwaffe lost more than 450 dive bombers and fighters during this period, a little over a sixth of its original operational strength. It was at this point that Hitler changed his mind about the bombing of London itself. His refusal to bomb England's greatest city had puzzled the German officers, particularly Göring, but now Hitler called his marshals in and gave them a specific order: "Destroy London."

No one understood Hitler's reason for refusing to bomb London in the early days of the battle. Some had thought he might want to make a triumphal ride past an undamaged Buckingham Palace, while others suggested he feared the outburst that the destruction of London's ancient monuments would bring, but the die was cast, and engines of Luftwaffe bombers and fighter planes were warming up, preparing to strike London and create as much damage as possible.

★   ★   ★

Veronica studied her face in the mirror and then applied a darker shade of lipstick. Straightening up, she walked quickly to the large bedroom that had been made into a playroom for the twins. Her father-in-law was trying to break up an argument over possession of a stuffed toy. Coming between the children, she said, "Now, stop that fighting!" She stooped over and kissed each one of them on the cheek. "Mum has to go into town for rehearsal."

Once she had made the decision to get back into acting, she had wasted no time and had immediately auditioned for and won a part in Charles's latest production. It felt so good to be back on the stage, surrounded by other creative, energetic people.

"I wanna go," Paul demanded.

"No, you can't go this time. But tomorrow you both have to go to the doctor for a checkup, and after that, I'll take you someplace you'll like."

"Where?" Heather demanded.

"How about to the zoo?"

"Yeah, the zoo!" Both twins were ecstatic. Their parents had taken them to the zoo once, and they constantly begged to return.

"All right. Now, you be good today for your grandparents." Veronica tousled Paul's hair and patted Heather on the back.

"When you coming back, Mum?" Paul demanded.

"It'll be a little late, so I'll see you both in the morning. Don't forget. If you're good, we'll go to the zoo tomorrow. If not, only the doctor's."

"I'm good," Heather promised.

"Me too," Paul said. "I'm very good."

Veronica looked at them with fondness for a moment and then turned to leave, making a mental note to spend more time with them in the future. She went to the door and found the chauffeur waiting for her.

"Should I drive you in, Mrs. Braden?"

"No. I'm taking my own car, Joseph."

"Yes, ma'am. Be careful if you come back after dark. They've put up some barricades where they're replacing the bridge."

"Yes. I know. Thank you, Joseph."

Veronica got into the car and started the engine. Gregory brought the children out to the step, each of them holding one of his hands. She waved at them and they waved back as she drove out of the driveway and started for the theater.

★　★　★

Parker looked up at a knock at the door and said, "Come in." He stood up when he saw who it was. "Well, hello, Katherine. I wasn't expecting you."

"No, but I wanted to talk to you about Brodie. I'm worried about him."

"Here. Come sit down. Can I send for something? Tea, perhaps, or coffee?"

"Nothing." Kat was wearing her nurse's uniform, and her face was somewhat flushed, for the first week of September had been unusually hot. "I haven't seen Brodie for a while. He usually stops by the hospital or the mission every now and then."

"Well, I wish I had better news for you, but he's not doing well at all."

"What's he doing? Is he drinking?"

"No, I don't think so. But ever since Bernie Cox was killed, he's blamed himself. He's focused on one thing and that's killing Germans, and I'm afraid he's going to lose his focus and get himself killed."

"Oh, Parker, that's terrible!"

"He lost something when Bernie went down. Of course, these things happen, but most men are able to shake it off. I was surprised when Brodie wasn't able to."

"He's always been a very single-minded person. If he's got revenge on his mind, it's going to be hard for him to think about anything else."

The two spent several minutes trying to think of ways to help him, and finally Kat said, "You look so tired, Parker."

"Well, I am a bit weary. The Jerries are really stepping up their attacks."

"Is there never going to be any end to this?"

Parker's answer was cut off when his phone rang. "Excuse me." Picking up the receiver, he said, "Braden here." He listened for a moment and then said, "Thank you. I'll be right there." He replaced the phone, shock written on his face. "There's been a bombing in London."

"In London? But they haven't been bombing the city."

"Well, they have this time, and the bombs fell right in the area where Veronica was going for rehearsal today." He seemed stunned, then shook his head. "I've got to go."

Seeing the strain on Parker's face, Kat said, "Let me go with you."

He appeared not to have heard her, but he did not protest. She followed him out to the car, and he did not say a word as they got in. They were well on their way when they looked up and saw a group of planes flying high overhead.

"Those are Germans," he said. "I believe Hitler has changed his strategy. He's never bombed London before."

Almost at once they began hearing bombs detonating and the sky filling with aircraft fire. Parker glanced out his window and said, "Those are our boys going to stop them."

He spoke no more, but as they approached the section of town where the theater was located, they were stopped by a police officer. Parker stuck his head out the window. "I've got to get through, Officer. My wife's in there."

"You can't take your car in, sir. I'm sorry. We have to keep the way clear for ambulances and fire trucks. You'll have to park it and walk."

Parker did not argue. He found a place to park, and when he got out of the car, his face was pale. He looked ahead at the smoke that was boiling up and muttered, "Katherine, they've hit it hard."

"I pray she's all right," Kat murmured.

Parker began running toward the area. It was all Kat could do to keep up with him. As they got closer, they couldn't deny that the damage was extensive. "I'm afraid it's bad," Parker said over the wailing fire engines. "Look, there's where she was going."

The building he pointed to was almost completely destroyed. Fire blazed out of the windows, and a steady stream of wounded and dead were being carried out by firefighters and ambulance workers who had already arrived.

Parker ran toward the building and was grabbed at once by a burly firefighter. "Sir, you can't go in there. It's too dangerous."

"My wife's in there."

"She was in this building?"

"I think so," he said.

"Go over there, sir. She might have already been brought out."

Parker and Kat went to find the officer in charge. Stretchers lined the street, some with blankets covering the faces of the victims. Parker quickly moved down the line, looking at each face. He turned back and said, "She's not here, thank God."

"Let's wait over here," Kat said. "We can watch for Veronica as they bring out the injured."

Parker and Kat stood and watched as workers went through the rubble. It was not going to be a quick job, and for the next two hours they watched as body after body was brought out. Parker said almost nothing, and Kat could not think of a remark that would give a great deal of comfort.

Two men were coming out carrying a stretcher with a blanket over the victim. Parker moved forward and said, "Hold it a minute." Kat watched him pull the corner of the blanket back. When his face froze, Kat stepped over beside him. Veronica Braden lay on the stretcher. There was one smear of dirt on her right cheek. Otherwise, she seemed to be simply sleeping.

Parker stared down on the face of his dead wife. He finally lowered the blanket and said to the stretcher bearer, "This is my wife."

"Yes, sir. Will you come with us, then?"

Parker seemed incapable of making a decision, so it was Kat who spoke. "Yes. We'll go with you." The two men immediately started off, and Kat said, "Come, Parker. We'll have to go see that she's taken care of."

Parker nodded, but his feet seemed bonded to the cement. Kat took his arm and urged him on. He began to move, and the two followed the emergency workers and the stretcher containing the body of Veronica Braden.

PART FOUR

September–October 1940

★ ★ ★

CHAPTER NINETEEN

"No Time-Outs in a War"

★ ★ ★

Kat did not know most of the hymns that the congregation sang at Veronica Braden's funeral. At funerals back home in Georgia, it seemed to Kat that most of the hymns were chosen to make the family and other mourners feel even sadder than they already did. The success of a Georgia funeral was judged by how many tears were shed and how many women collapsed beside the coffin. Kat was very glad that the Braden funeral was a more dignified affair.

As she looked around the chapel, she saw that most of the squadron had managed to get to the funeral. She studied their faces and especially Brodie's. *I wonder what he thinks of all this? Probably doesn't like it any better than I do.*

Although she was seated halfway back in the chapel, she had a clear view of Parker's profile. His face was set, as it had been since the death of his wife. A slanting beam of light from one of the high windows seemed to throw a spotlight on him, and he was so very still that there was something almost frightening about it. Kat had dutifully visited at Benleigh, but she was doubtful about whether her presence had meant anything. The family had been grateful and thanked her for coming, but afterward, she'd had the odd feeling that something was very wrong.

Kat noticed the musty odor in the ancient stone church in the little village near Benleigh, where the funeral was being held. As were so many churches in England, this one was centuries old. The hand-hewn wooden beams that crisscrossed overhead were dark with age, and the marble aisles were worn by the feet of countless worshipers. The stained-glass windows were beautiful, expertly crafted, but somehow Kat felt uncomfortable with them. She studied the one that portrayed the baptism of Jesus. John the Baptist was bringing Jesus out of the water. The faces of both figures were looking straight ahead with wide-open eyes. The two figures were so stiff and artificial that Kat wondered what it must have been like to be there when Jesus was baptized and the Spirit of God came down like a dove. Her vivid imagination picked up the details, and she was only called back to reality when the minister's voice broke through to her.

The sermon was brief and not particularly comforting to Kat. The elderly minister had a voice that was as dry and brittle as his body appeared to be. He read several lengthy Scripture passages, but there was no excitement or life in his voice. It was as unemotional as if he were reading names out of a telephone book. His delivery was at the opposite end of the spectrum from some of the preachers at the country churches she had attended who ranted and raved and wept. *I don't know which is worse,* Kat thought, *too much emotionalism or not enough.*

Finally it was over. She decided it would not be a good time to express her sympathy to Parker. He was standing frozen in place, his face wooden, no light in his eyes. He was a man carrying out a duty, and when people came by and whispered some meaningless words of comfort, he gave a signal of assent that was equally meaningless. What could be said at such a time, and how would one be able to respond?

Kat joined the crowd that was heading out the door and caught up with Brodie. Touching his arm, she whispered,

"Parker looks terrible, doesn't he, Brodie?"

"Sure does, but I reckon it's always that way."

She shook her head. "Wouldn't it be wonderful if funerals could be more of a triumph than a defeat?"

"I don't know how that could be."

"Well, for Christians, dying isn't the end. It's really just the beginning."

"I guess so. I never thought of it like that."

"I want my funeral to be something like when celebrities leave to go on a long voyage. You know, a big crowd shows up at the dock to see them off. There's shouting and singing, and after the celebrity gets on board, he laughs and waves to the crowd. Then pretty soon the ship leaves the dock and sails away out of sight. I'd like my funeral to be something like that."

Brodie was strangely moved by her words. He turned to study her face, and although she had a curtain of reserve, there was a spirit in her eyes he had always admired. She had the soft depth of a woman, but at the same time, she had a strength that went beyond that of most women.

"I suppose that's foolish, but then I guess I'm just a foolish woman."

"Not so foolish," he said. "That's a better taking-off than most of us have." He dropped his eyes. "Not everybody has faith in God like you do."

"I wish you did, Brodie. I don't mean to preach to you, but I think about you so much, and I pray for you too."

He smiled at her. "I guess your prayers have kept me going, Kat. I've always known that you were praying for me. You made it pretty plain."

The two watched as people got into cars and left. "Not like the funerals back home," Brodie remarked. "Remember? After the service we'd all go out to the cemetery, and there'd be a little tent up over the grave, and the preacher would preach some more."

"It's different here." She noticed that his face was drawn, and she thought, *He's wearing himself out, but so are all of the pilots.* "Come along," she said brightly. "I'll let you buy me some lunch."

"That sounds like a winner to me."

★　★　★

As the raids on London grew more intense, more homes were destroyed, which meant people had no place to live. Some of them had relatives who could take them in temporarily, but the mission was making an all-out effort to help those who had nowhere else to go. Kat and Meredith worked long hours at the mission every day for the two weeks following Veronica Braden's funeral.

On a blustery Wednesday afternoon, Kat stopped at an abandoned factory building to see if any of the families staying there needed any help. She had been talking with Edna Smith, who had a month-old baby, as well as five other children from age two to ten. Her husband was in the navy somewhere in the North Atlantic, and she had not heard from him for weeks. Her face showed the strain that came from caring for six children on her own.

Suddenly the alarm blasted out an urgent warning.

"Come on," Kat said. "We need to get to the Underground."

"Yes, come on, Mum," the oldest boy said, a ten-year-old with bright blue eyes and a shock of yellow hair. "It's fun down there."

Two girls came running over from a corner where they had been playing with dolls, fear in their eyes. "Mark, you take your sisters' hands," Edna directed.

"Here, let me carry Helen, Mrs. Smith," Kat said.

"Okay. If you want to take her, I'll carry Mark and the bag."

Edna picked up a huge canvas bag that she had at the ready for these situations and pulled two-year-old Mark onto her hip.

Kat led the party, helping to herd the children as they

made their way to the Underground, where they joined a host of other families that were already settling in. Many of the weary citizens were stretched out on blankets, even though it was not time for bed. Most of them had learned quickly to take food, blanket rolls, and books to make it through the night. Two women were passing out sandwiches and hot tea, and a priest wearing an air-raid helmet was helping everyone find a space.

"Let's sit down over here, children, and I'll tell you a story," Kat said.

"Can't we have something to eat, Miss Katherine?"

"It's rather crowded right now. Let's wait until things quiet down a bit."

"Tell the story about the porcupine," Evelyn piped up. She was an adorable child with the same blond hair and blue eyes as the rest of the children. Her cheeks were rosy, and since she was only five, she did not grasp the seriousness of the situation.

"No, I'll tell you a brand-new one," Kat said quickly. She had already forgotten the story about the porcupine she had made up, but her fertile imagination began to work, and soon all the children were gathered around her listening to the stories of a raccoon named Henry.

She was well into her story when they heard the muffled booms of bombs going off. The children were beginning to look frightened, so Kat picked up the tempo of the story. "Henry knew that he had to get the giant to leave his castle so he could get in and take the treasure back home. . . ." She spoke quickly, gesturing with her hands, and was reassured to see the children's eyes were on her again.

The bombing seemed to go on for a long time but finally it mitigated, and Kat wrapped up her story. "Now let's go get a sandwich and some tea."

Eating occupied the children for a time, and as Kat nibbled on a sandwich, she tried to comfort the weary mother.

"I just don't know what we're going to do, Kat."

"God will be with you. He's always with us."

Edna shook her head. "I can't believe our home is all gone. Everything! When Jack comes back there won't be any of the pictures or the furniture that he loved."

"But you'll be here and so will the children." Kat leaned over and put her arm around the woman. "God spared your lives and his. This won't last forever. One day you and Jack will have a new place and the children will be with you, and it'll be wonderful."

Edna laughed and shook her head. "Now you're telling me fairy tales that you're making up just like you do for the children."

"I'm not doing any such thing!" Kat protested. "I really believe that we're going to survive this. You and the children and Jack."

Edna's eyes glistened in tears. She said in a tight voice, "You're a blessing to me and my children, Kat."

The two women sat there until the all-clear sounded, and then Kat accompanied them back to the abandoned factory. Kat gave Edna and the children each a hug and then left. Her mind was reeling with the problems this family faced, and there were hundreds more just like it. Kat had learned to admire the courage of the Londoners who were enduring the worst that Adolf Hitler and his henchmen could send at them. "They'll get through somehow, God. Please be with them and help Jack to come home safely."

★　★　★

Parker spotted the 109s far over to his left. There were eight of them, four pairs, in a long saw-toothed line. At once he passed the information to the squadron—half a squadron, actually. Only the red and blue flights were taking this patrol. "Bandits! Do you see them?"

"I see them, Red Leader." Sailor Darley's voice came through loud and clear.

The Spitfires banked and then angled down, and the formation of 109s turned and headed toward them. The action came quickly then, with everyone firing at the same time. Bullets flew between the two formations and then the planes broke up into individual dogfights.

Parker made a hard turning climb, and a yellow-nosed 109 showed its belly to him. He went after it, but he was too slow. The 109 rolled and dipped and then slipped away.

Parker had no time to think. He heaved his Spit on its side in an effort to drag it around, and for a moment the strain dimmed his vision so that he could not see. All around him were dogfights, and he looked desperately to find the other two members of his flight. He saw Zarek Dolenski engaged in a furious battle on the tail of a 109. He couldn't see Alan Miller, the man who had replaced Dick Summerton. Miller didn't have as much combat experience as some of the other men did, and Parker worried about him.

For a few seconds the action went on furiously, but such things could not last long. A Spitfire had ammunition enough to fire for only fifteen seconds. Most of those were in short bursts. Fifteen seconds was not much time, and the Messerschmitts carried about the same amount of firepower.

"All right. Let's go home," Parker said, and the two flights fell into formation. He saw that Miller had survived and heaved a sigh of relief. But he knew he would not have missed that 109 if it had been two weeks ago. The strain of Veronica's death had slowed him more than he could have imagined, and his timing was lousy. He had thought once of grounding himself, but they were short of manpower, and now as he led the squadron home he felt weary and drained.

The twins were just beginning to understand that their mother was gone forever. At first they'd had the idea that she had only gone on a short trip, but now the reality was beginning to sink in, which made a double burden for Parker's parents, who had taken over their care completely. He could not help with this burden, which made him feel miserable. As the Spitfire streaked toward home, he had nothing to look forward to but a brief rest and then another encounter in the sky.

★ ★ ★

Brodie climbed out of his plane, and Keith Poe was there at once. "Did you take any bullets, sir?"

"Not a one, and she's running like a watch. Good job, Keith."

"She's a fine craft, sir. You just be careful."

Brodie slapped the diminutive mechanic on the shoulder and then joined the others who were going into the debriefing room. When they were dismissed, the pilots made their way to the truck and the table that Meredith had set up. She was smiling at them, warmth and welcome in her eyes.

Brodie took the doughnut and the cup of tea she offered. "Where's Kat?"

"She went inside."

"To see Parker?"

"Yes."

"He's having a hard time."

"Death is never easy. Especially when it's your spouse." She handed a doughnut to another pilot. "Was it bad up there today?"

"Oh, just the usual stuff." He took a bite out of his doughnut. "I wonder what they do with the holes."

"The holes of the doughnut?"

"Yes. I mean, do they mash all the holes together to make one giant doughnut?"

She grinned. "I have no idea."

She served the other men until everyone had their fill, and then she began to clean up. Brodie watched and sipped his tea, and finally she came and sat down beside him.

"I'm worried about Parker," Brodie said. "He hasn't been the same since his wife died."

It was the opening that Meredith had been waiting for.

"No, he hasn't. And you haven't been the same since Bernard Cox died."

"I don't know what you're talkin' about."

"You're living for revenge, and that's not a good idea."

He shook his head. "Nothin's really changed."

"That's not what the other pilots say. They say you're taking enormous chances up there, Brodie."

He knew he had been throwing himself into battle in a reckless fashion. He was always careful to guard Sailor's back, for he was determined not to lose another friend, but whenever he had the chance, he would take on the enemy with the wildest abandon.

"One of the guys told me that you attacked eight German planes all by yourself."

"Who said that?"

"It doesn't matter. You shouldn't do that."

"I know it sounds bad, but I had the height on them. I came down and made one pass, and they had no chance at all. I got one of 'em too."

Meredith did not understand much about aerial warfare, but she knew about people. And now she studied this tall American, thinking how fragile his life was, as were the lives of all of them. She felt a sudden start of fear at the idea that he might have been shot down on the sortie this very day. She had been meaning to speak to him more directly about becoming a Christian, and now she said quietly, "I know you feel bad about Bernard Cox. Nobody can help that. But you can't let your sorrow dominate you. You can't change the past, Brodie, but you can do something about the present."

He well understood what he was doing and knew that it was wrong, but like a drunk who couldn't refuse one more drink, he could not seem to get rid of the hatred that burned in him when he saw a German plane. He felt that each German he attacked might have been the one who killed Bernie.

"I would so love to see you come to the Lord Jesus," Meredith said.

The simplicity of her words and the clearness of her eyes and everything about this woman seemed to fit into a pattern that Brodie found admirable. He chewed his lower lip for a moment and then shrugged his shoulders. "Kat's been preaching to me about Jesus for years."

"You should have listened to her."

"Maybe I will."

"I don't . . . I don't want anything to happen to you."

He was surprised at the unsteadiness of her voice. "Nothin's gonna happen to me, but it's good to know you care."

Meredith was a very straightforward person—too straightforward for some people's taste. She looked at him and said bluntly, "I think I might be falling in love with you."

Brodie was completely taken aback. He gave her an astonished look and said, "Well, that's comin' right out with it!"

She laughed. "There, now you can start running away. Kat tells me you do that when women fall in love with you."

He grinned. "Well, you don't want for grit, I'll say that for ya."

And then Meredith grew serious. "But I can't let myself fall in love with you, Brodie. I couldn't spend my life with a man who doesn't love God."

This might have offended him at another time, but he knew he was talking with a woman who had a great capacity for love. She was also full of fire and had a temper that could swing from laughter to anger. He knew she was proud too. It couldn't have been easy for her to admit her affection for him. "You're some woman, Meredith."

"I know you don't need any husband-hungry women chasing after you."

"Wait a minute," he said, growing serious once again. "Tell me more about how you came to know God."

Her eyes opened wide with surprise. "You really want to hear about it?"

"Yes, I do."

"Well, I was thirteen years old and had no more idea about God than a rabbit. . . ."

★ ★ ★

"You didn't come, so I brought you some doughnuts and tea. No extra charge for the personal service."

Parker had been staring out the window when Kat came in after a quick rap on the door. He took the doughnut wrapped in a napkin and put the tea on his desk. "Thanks, Katherine." He bit into the doughnut. "That's good."

"Well, I didn't make them. I don't know how to make doughnuts." She sat in the chair across from his desk as he settled into his own. "You look so tired," she commented.

"We're all tired, Katherine."

"How are things at home?"

He shook his head and stared at the doughnut. When he lifted his eyes, she saw the misery in them. "Paul and Heather are just beginning to understand that their mother's not coming back. At first they didn't. It was like she was gone on a vacation, but it's beginning to sink in now."

"The poor babies!"

"And Father is down with a cold or something, so the burden's all been on Mother."

"I wish I could do something."

"Well, there might be something you could do. The kids would love to see you. They miss your stories."

"I'll try to get out to see them, Parker. How is the squadron doing?"

"Everyone is doing fine—except me."

"Why, that can't be true!"

"It is, though. I made a bad mistake this afternoon. I could have brought great harm on myself or one of my men. I don't have that fine edge anymore."

Kat knew this must have been hard for Parker to admit. "Can't you take a little time off?"

"There are no time-outs in a war, I'm afraid."

Kat watched while Parker finished his doughnut, although it didn't look as though he was even tasting it. "I know that you must grieve over Veronica."

He lifted his head and something flickered in his eyes. She could not tell what it was. He shrugged his shoulders wearily and said, "We were going through a bad time. I feel awful that I didn't do something that could have helped her."

He gazed into his tea as if there might be some comfort there. "I didn't really have the love for her that a man should have for his wife. I should have been much kinder."

Kat wanted to put her arms around him but knew this was not the time. "We always say that after we lose someone." She sought for more words and finally said, "I know it sounds foolish to tell someone to be careful in a time of war, but please do try to take care of yourself." She stood up. "I'll make some time to go see Paul and Heather."

★ ★ ★

As Parker brought the Spitfire in for a landing, he felt groggy. They had scrambled four times in the past twelve hours. They had been engaged in combat on only one of the sorties, but the fatigue was always there even if there were no enemy fighters to contend with. As he came in for a landing, he was thinking about Paul and Heather, wondering how he could spend more time with them. Suddenly a voice crackled in his ear, "Red Leader! Red Leader!"

It was Brodie Lee, but there was no time to respond. Suddenly, instead of wheels hitting the ground, there was a crash of metal. Instantly Parker knew he had committed the stupidest error a pilot can. He had forgotten to put down his landing gear!

He hauled back on the stick to try to gain air space, but the propeller smashed against the ground and skewed the plane around. Desperately Parker held on, but he had no control now. The plane was only obeying the laws of physics as it skidded along the runway, and Parker could do nothing.

As the Spit shot along the field, the tip of one wing dipped, and it spun the plane around in the opposite direction, throwing Parker to one side.

He never saw the pole that he hit, but he heard the crash of metal, and then he was flung forward and a terrible pain struck him right in the forehead. He knew nothing more.

★ ★ ★

He came out of the darkness shivering and with a feeling he was falling. He started to twist, and his head seemed to be splitting open.

"Take it easy."

He opened his eyes and could see a blurry face.

"Lie back, Wing Commander."

Parker obeyed, closing his eyes again, and his memory came swimming back. "I piled it up, didn't I?" he gasped. He tried to reach up and touch his head, but a hand seized him. "Leave your head alone. You're all right, but you had a bad bump."

Parker obeyed. He opened his eyes again, and this time he recognized the flight surgeon, a tall man named Peterson.

"Something's wrong with my eyes, Doctor."

"What do you mean?"

"I can see two of you."

"You've got double vision and a bad concussion. Close your eyes, Parker." Peterson's voice was soothing. "You're going to be all right. I'm going to give you something to make you sleep."

"But I can't see."

"That'll take care of itself in time, but in the meantime you're not flying."

"But I've got to."

"No. Darley will take your place."

Parker could not think clearly. The double vision frightened him. He had always had excellent eyesight and now that was gone. "What if my vision doesn't get any better, Doctor?"

"It will. I promise you. You're going to take at least a week off, so make up your mind to that. You need it."

CHAPTER TWENTY

A CALL FOR HELP

★ ★ ★

The phone rang abruptly, breaking the silence. Kat sat straight up in bed and looked at the clock. Eight forty-five. She had worked until midnight last night and had been sleeping soundly. She picked up the phone as her head started to clear. "Yes? Who is it?"

"Katherine? This is Parker."

At once Kat grew alert and lost all grogginess. "What is it? Is something wrong?"

"Yes. Really there is."

"Tell me!"

"Well, it's several things all come together. You heard about my crash yesterday?"

"Oh yes. I'm so glad you were all right."

"Stupid thing to do. I can't believe I forgot to put my landing gear down. The greenest pilot in the squadron can laugh at me now."

"How do you feel?"

"Not too bad. But I'm having trouble with my vision and I feel pretty tired. The flight doctor grounded me for a week, so I'm recuperating at home. I'm wondering—" He broke off and then continued in a voice tight with strain. "The twins are sick, Katherine. I don't think it's serious, but you know how kids are when they're sick. They require a lot of care, and of all things, my father is down too with bronchitis, and the housekeeper had to go off and help her daughter, who's having a baby. Sounds like a bad movie, doesn't it?"

"Oh, I'm so sorry, Parker. Your poor mother. Would you like me to come over and help?"

"Could you?" he asked with relief. "Even for a day or two until we can find somebody."

"Don't worry about that. I think I can get off from the mission, and I'm not due to work any shifts the rest of this week at the hospital. Has a doctor seen the twins?"

"Yes, and he says it's the mumps. Not serious, but they're very fussy."

"I'll come at once."

"Did you have the mumps when you were a child? We wouldn't want to expose you to something you haven't had."

"Yes, I think I had them when I was seven or eight."

"That's great. Then I'll send Joseph into town to pick you up. Say, in about an hour?"

"All right, Parker. I'll be ready."

"Katherine. . . ?"

"Yes, what is it?"

"I hate to ask you to help like this, but I can't think of anybody else."

"Don't worry about that. I'll pack a bag so that I can stay long enough to see the twins get their bearings."

"Thank you, Katherine. I'll be here waiting when you come."

★ ★ ★

"Let me hold this umbrella over you, Miss Katherine. You'll get soaked."

"Thank you." Kat got out of the car, and Joseph held the

umbrella over her as they made their way to the front door. "Now you're getting soaked, Joseph."

"No matter, miss. I'm just glad you could come. Mr. Parker has been worried half to death, and Lord Braden and his wife too."

The two of them reached the shelter of the porch, and the door opened at once.

"Terrible weather," Parker said. "You must be soaked."

"No, Joseph took very good care of me." She turned and said, "Thank you very much, Joseph."

"You're welcome, miss."

"Joseph, you can take Katherine's bag up to the guest bedroom," Parker instructed.

"Yes, sir."

"The only good thing about this rain is that there won't be any raids by the Jerries," Parker said. "Come in and let me take your coat."

"How are you feeling, Parker?" Kat asked as she slipped out of her coat.

"Well, my eyes still trouble me at times, but not nearly so much. Come into the drawing room. We've got a fire going in there. It's terrible to get you out on a day like this."

"No. It's no trouble."

"Of course it's trouble, but as I said, I didn't know anyone else to call."

The two went into the drawing room, where Cooper was putting a log on the fire.

He smiled at her and said, "Good morning, miss."

"Good morning, Cooper. My, that fire looks good."

"It feels good on a day like this."

"Could you bring us some tea, Cooper?" Parker asked.

"Certainly, sir."

As the butler left the room, Parker said, "Stand by the fire and get some of the cold out of you."

"You say your father's sick?" Kat said as she backed up to the fire and felt the heat soaking in.

"Yes. Bronchitis." He shook his head, and his brow furrowed. "He's had it before, and it always worries us. It could go into pneumonia so easily. It's all Mother can do to take care of him."

"Perhaps we should get him to the hospital."

"He hates hospitals." He shoved his hands deep into his pockets. "The doctor is doing his best to keep him comfortable. He says just don't let him go outside or tire himself. He's hard to keep down, though."

"That was a pretty bad bump you took."

"It split my forehead open. I had to have twelve stitches." Parker reached up and touched the bandage on his forehead. "Good thing I hit my head, where I'm toughest."

"You must feel pretty bad with a concussion like that."

He smiled slightly. "Now that you're here, I feel much better."

"Are the twins awake?"

"Oh yes. Once I told them you were coming, there was no getting them to take a nap."

The two of them went up to the twins' bedroom. "Well, here she is," Parker announced. "I hope you two will be nice."

"Mith Kat, I hurt!" Paul complained.

Kat went over at once and sat down on the side of the bed, and Paul crawled up into her lap. Of course, Heather demanded equal space. Kat adjusted them both until they were all fairly comfortable, and she could feel they had fevers. "I've come to take care of you two, so you've got to be very good."

"I'm good," Paul announced, "but I hurt."

"Well, I'll tell you what. Why don't you both lie down and I'll read to you."

This pleased the twins exceedingly. "I can handle this, Parker, if you have something to do."

"No. I don't have anything to do. The doctor said I shouldn't do anything except work on recovering. Do you mind if I stay?"

"Get in bed with us, Daddy," Heather called.

"No. I'll just come and sit on the other side." He came

over and sat down. "Let's be very quiet now so Katherine can tell a story."

Kat began making up an outlandish story and soon she was rewarded by seeing the children grow sleepy and also by Parker's smile as he listened to her impossible concoctions. When both of the children were asleep, she got up. Parker did also, and the two of them pulled the covers over the twins and moved silently out of the room.

Parker closed the door silently. "You are so good with children."

"I just like making up stories. I've never had an adult listen to one of my stories before."

"I'd like to hear how this one comes out."

"I haven't thought ahead to the ending yet. I just make it up as I go."

"Let's go down and fix a sandwich or something."

The two of them went down to the kitchen, where they found the cook making tarts. When Kat admitted she hadn't had breakfast, Parker asked, "Could you fix up a nice breakfast for our nurse, Cook?"

"That I can and for you too, sir. You sit right there. It won't take long."

When the breakfast was delivered, Kat ate heartily. She noticed that Parker was only picking at his food and made a mental note to see to it that he ate better. "If you don't clean your plate, you'll be a bad boy and Santa Claus won't come to see you."

Parker laughed but then quickly winced. "Ow, that hurt my head! You mustn't be so amusing, Katherine."

"All right. I promise to be as dull as possible."

After they ate, he showed Kat to her room. "Why don't you take some time and lie down, if you'd like? You'll probably need the rest later on."

"No, let's just go down and sit in front of the fire. I may doze off there."

The two went back to the drawing room and found Parker's mother there. She greeted Kat warmly, her relief evident. "I'm so glad you're here, my dear."

"I hope I can help."

After Grace gave Kat an update on her husband's condition, Kat encouraged her to lie down and take a nap while she had a chance.

"You know, I believe I will," Grace said.

"Is your husband awake?"

"No, he's not."

"Well, I'll check in on him later to see if he's awake or if he needs anything. You go rest."

"Thank you, dear. You're a godsend."

As Grace left the room, Parker said, "Mother's about reached the end of her rope—and so have I."

"Well, maybe you need to go rest too."

"I will after a while. Tell me what you've been doing."

The two sat down, and Kat began to speak of the activities that filled her life—helping to provide food and shelter for the homeless, taking food to the airfield for the fliers and mechanics, and nursing the sick and wounded.

The fire crackled pleasantly in the fireplace, and a large clock on the mantel made a slow, regular ticking. Outside, the rain was still coming down, making the coziness of the room all the more welcome.

"I love your home, Parker. I know it's expensive to maintain, but it's so lovely."

"It is nice, isn't it? I really don't mind spending the money."

"How's your family's aircraft business?"

"Father says there's more business than we can possibly handle. Of course, he hired a new manager when I left to join the RAF, and apparently the man is doing a fine job." He sat quietly for a time staring at the fire, and once he picked up the poker and rolled a log over, sending golden sparks flying up the chimney. He sat back down beside her on the couch that Cooper had pulled over in front of the fire.

"This is nice," she said.

"Yes, it is, isn't it? I've been thinking lately about how odd life is. You never know what's coming. One day's fine— the birds are singing and the sun is shining—and the next day the monsters come out from under the bed and out of the closet."

"No monsters today." She leaned over and squeezed his hand. "Just a nice warm room with a welcoming fire."

"And with you here to take care of us all."

The smell of burning wood was sharp in the room, and they sat there talking, both of them relaxed. "I read something the journalist Malcolm Muggeridge said once," Parker said. "I wrote it down and memorized it."

"I've heard of him. He's British, isn't he?"

Parker nodded.

"What did he say?"

" 'Every happening, great and small, is a parable whereby God speaks to us, and the art of life is to get the message.' "

She smiled at him. "Hmm. Interesting. No wonder you memorized it."

"It is good, isn't it? Sometimes it's hard to get God's messages."

"I know. He doesn't send Western Union telegrams telling us what to do. I've often wondered why He's so cryptic in His commands to us," Kat commented. "I've always thought that He likes to honor those who seek Him."

"You're probably right. I've always admired those who know the art of finding God. I've read about several of the great believers who would pray all night." He turned to her and smiled. "I tried that once."

"Did you? How was it?"

"All I discovered was that I can sleep in any position."

Kat giggled. "I had about the same experience. Every time I've ever tried to fast for a long period it doesn't work."

"You mean you can't think of anything but eating?"

"Yes. I'm not very spiritual, I'm afraid."

"Me either."

They sat silently and listened to the fire crackle. "Do you think about your home a great deal, Katherine?"

"Sometimes I do, but lately I've been so busy I haven't even had time for that." She leaned forward, staring into the fire and listening to the sibilant sound of a log releasing its moisture. "Have you heard of the new book *You Can't Go Home Again*?"

"Yes, I did hear something about it. It was written by Thomas Wolfe, wasn't it?"

"You know of him?"

"I don't know much about him, but I do remember hearing this book was published after he died."

"Yes, that's right. I haven't read it yet, but I keep thinking about that title. You can't go home again."

"What does that mean to you?" he asked.

"Why, I think it means much like the philosopher who said, 'You can't step in the same river twice.'"

"I haven't heard that one."

"Well, you see what it means. The river that flows today will be different tomorrow. The water you stepped in yesterday has now gone down to the sea."

"And you feel that way about going home? I'm surprised."

"This is the first time I've ever really been away from home, Parker." She leaned back and twisted to face him. The flickering tongues of flame from the fireplace threw a yellow corona of light over his cheek and highlighted the bandage. He looked more rested than he had when she had come in the door, and she was glad to think that, perhaps, it was due to her. "But things change so quickly."

"Yes. A fellow can bend over to tie his shoes, and when he straightens up the whole world's changed."

"Well, I never thought of it like that, but I think if you try to go back, you may rediscover an old path and wander over it. But the best you can do is say, 'Oh yes, I remember this place.' Yet it's somehow not the same."

Parker reached out and put his hand on her shoulder. She turned quickly to him, and he said, "All the words in the dictionary, and I've been trying to think of some way ever since you came this morning to say how much this means to me and to all of us."

"Why, I was glad to do it, Parker. You'd do the same for me."

He removed his hand at once, and they sat quietly for a time. "Do you like living in the country?"

"Yes, I like the country. Even when we lived in New York City, I was always trying to get my dad to take me over to Central Park so I could feel like I was out in the country. Back in Georgia I'd get up every morning and go to the window, and I'd see the sun. And I'd always say, 'You son of a gun, you did it again!'"

Parker laughed. "What a thing to say!"

"I know. I'd hate for you to see the diary I kept when I was in my teens. I went back and read it before I left for London and couldn't believe any human could be that foolish."

"And you're still searching for that high calling you talk so much about."

"I don't talk about it much anymore, Parker."

"Do you think you've found it, then? Serving in the mission and working in the hospital?"

"I . . . don't know. I'm not sure of much of anything anymore."

His face clouded. "I know that feeling," he said quietly. Suddenly he asked, "Have you seen the movie *The Wizard of Oz*?"

"Oh yes! It's a wonderful movie."

"You know what that movie means to me, the whole essence of it?"

"What?"

"That happiness is to be found in our own backyards. We don't have to go off seeking any wizard to give it to us."

"Why, of course, that's very true. Most of us don't recognize it, though. Maybe God's tired of me pestering Him to put me in whatever high place He has."

After some more quiet conversation, she said, "I'd better go check on your father."

"All right. I'll go see what we'll be having for dinner tonight."

★ ★ ★

Kat stayed busy all day. She took Gregory's supper to him and at his request sat down and talked with him for half an hour. He did not feel well, but he did seem eager to have company. He asked her to tell him about America, and he listened attentively. "I'd love to go there someday," he whispered hoarsely.

"You should. You and my father would get along well. You're alike in many ways."

"Oh, he's a handsome man, is he?"

"You're full of vanity, Lord Braden! Yes, he is a handsome man, and I think he's the most honest and decent and loving man I've ever known."

"What a wonderful thing to say of anyone!"

"Well, it's true. Promise me when you get well and this war is over you'll come and see us."

"I will," Gregory said firmly. "Grace and I will come, and maybe we can get Parker and the twins to come too. We'll descend on you like the Assyrians came down on the fold, as the poem says."

"You like Byron?"

"I like that one."

"I'll read it to you sometime. I read it once and won a competition back when I was in school. Oh, I did love all the swashbuckling and roaring." She giggled and said, "But I won. Perhaps because I was the loudest."

Gregory grew sleepy, so she excused herself and spent much of the evening with the children. After she had tucked the children into bed, Kat said, "You need to go to bed too, Parker. You're trying to do too much."

"All right. I will. Sleep well, and thanks again for coming."

"I love your family," Kat said, "and I'm glad I could help."

"They love you too." He wanted to add the words "all of us" but knew that would not be right. "I'll see you in the morning."

★　★　★

Parker's condition improved considerably over the next few days, and so did that of the twins. Parker was talking about returning to duty, and the rest of the family was trying to convince him that it was too soon. He finally agreed to stay home for another day or two.

As for Kat, she had never felt so much at home with a family as she did with Lord and Lady Braden. She had not imagined that nobility could be so warm and genuine. She had imagined they might be cold and very formal.

Another surprise had been Parker's aunt Edith, who had always disliked Americans. She had returned two days ago from her visit to Oxford, where she had been doing research. She had been spending a considerable amount of time with Kat, and one day she commented to Grace that she would have to revise her opinion of Americans if Kat was a good sample.

Kat knew she had to get back to the mission, however, and Parker made up his mind to go back to the base at the same time.

"I'll just do office work," he said defensively. "No going up until the doctor clears me. I couldn't anyway."

On the final afternoon of Kat's stay, Parker and Kat were walking outside and Parker was showing her his vegetable garden. His pride was evident as he pointed out the various plants and even picked a few vegetables. "We have to have a man come in and tend it now, but I used to love doing the gardening."

"I've always loved gardening too. We had such a big one in Georgia. There were hard days when I was growing up—

the Depression and all—so we grew everything we possibly could."

They walked for a time, and finally he stopped and looked back at the house and sighed. "I hate to leave. I wish I didn't ever have to go back."

Kat was surprised. It was the first time he had ever said anything like this. She knew he loved to fly but hated the part of his job that included killing other men.

"I hate to leave too."

"Wouldn't it be wonderful if we could just stay like this always?"

"Yes, it would, but as we've said before, things change."

"That's not always true."

"What do you mean, Parker?"

"*You* don't change, Katherine. You're always the same."

"Why, I'm as changeable as a weather vane! Crying one day and laughing the next. You know that."

"In essentials you're always the same."

Kat saw the warmth of his eyes, and something came to her in that still moment. She could not face him, afraid that he might read her true emotions. "Look at that," she said, trying to change the subject. She pointed to a chipmunk that was streaking across the ground. The animal froze and tucked its front legs tightly together against its chest.

"It looks like an alderman come to beg for a donation of some sort," Parker said with a grin.

Kat had no interest in the chipmunk at the moment. She knew she loved Parker and had loved him for years. Indeed, looking back at her life she saw that she had never been able to put away the love she'd had for him when he'd been in Georgia. She suddenly felt nervous. "I think I'd better go in. It's getting chilly."

As they moved toward the house, he reached out and took her arm. "I guess I'm like the apostle Paul. I see through a glass darkly," Parker said, "but I want you to know how much it's meant having you here. More than just the help. You have such a sweet spirit."

Kat suddenly realized the loneliness that lay in this man.

She longed to put her arms around him but knew that it was not her place to do such a thing. She quickly said, "Thank you, Parker."

He followed her up the walk, and as they entered the house, both of them felt they had let a special moment slip by unheeded. Neither of them, however, felt bold enough to remedy the situation, so each went his own way and the opportunity was lost.

CHAPTER TWENTY-ONE

MEREDITH

★ ★ ★

The weariness and near despair of the RAF pilots had descended upon Brodie Lee. As he walked down the streets of London, he was depressed even more by the sights that met his eyes. A bomber raid had taken place only six hours earlier, and flames still raged in some of the buildings, although firefighters struggled valiantly to contain them. The walls left standing were being knocked down as soon as possible to remove the danger of them crashing to the ground. The acrid smell of explosives and burning buildings filled the city, the smoke hovering over it in an ugly cloud.

Brodie passed a group of repairmen taping up the ends of electrical cables that had been severed by the bombs, while a family was loading what was left of their household—a sofa, several chairs, and a few boxes of housewares—onto a horse-drawn cart. Farther on he walked around a pair of men who had rolled a rack containing women's clothes out of a bombed building and looked as if they were trying to decide what to do with it.

Brodie's deep depression also stemmed from his visit to the hospital in East Grinstead, where he had gone to visit one of the men who had been terribly burned. What made his visit even more difficult was that the pilot had been Trevor Park, the ex–movie star, the most handsome man in the entire squadron or, perhaps, in the RAF. A shiver ran over Brodie at the memory of Trevor's face burned almost beyond recognition and the look of despair in his remaining eye. Brodie had visited only for ten minutes and was glad when the nurse had come to get Trevor for further surgery.

"You'll be back with us soon, Trevor," Brodie had said.

"No I won't." The man's voice had been flat, a whisper tinged with despair and hopelessness.

Brodie passed by a restaurant with all the windows blown out. Broken glass lay strewn all over the sidewalk, but peering inside, Brodie was shocked to see that it was business as usual. The patrons were sitting next to the window, some of them laughing, and a waitress moved around, delivering food from the depths of the restaurant.

Brodie could not help but marvel at the endurance of these people. The English had proven themselves to be far tougher than Hitler and his henchmen had predicted. Even now with their beloved London being taken apart by bombers on a daily basis, they still had not given up.

Walking aimlessly along the streets, Brodie wondered at himself. He had always considered himself a rather tough individual, but what he was seeing in this leveling of one of the great cities of the world shocked him. He had heard all of his life about the treasures of London, buildings ancient and meaningful in the history of the world—and now they were nothing but heaps of rubble and broken glass and charred wood. He walked by the Tower Bridge at the edge of Central London and glanced up at the barrage balloons that were meant to stop low-flying aircraft. They looked like fat sausages pulling at their cables as if anxious to be off somewhere.

Brodie walked through the heart of London until he came to stand beneath the tall pillar in Trafalgar Square with the statue of Nelson perched atop it. He stared up at the statue for a long time. Brodie was not a great reader of books, but somehow Horatio Nelson had always fascinated him. He had once read a biography of the diminutive English admiral who had held the power of Napoleon at bay and defeated him time after time.

"Good job, old boy. I hope we can do the same thing to Adolf."

Turning, he walked past the office workers who were scurrying along the sidewalks and streets as if there had been no raid. It occurred to Brodie that thirty minutes from now this part of London might be as devastated as the part he had just gone through, and the thought troubled him. He made up his mind to go to the mission, and a fear tugged at him that it might have been leveled too, so he hastened his pace.

As he continued his walk, he passed a huge group of young people, perhaps a hundred, near an Underground station. All of them wore identification tags pinned to their clothing and had boxes that contained gas masks. He stopped a uniformed bobby who was ambling by. "Where are these children going?"

"They're being taken to homes and places of safety outside the city, don't you see?"

"That's a good thing."

"Yes, it is. Families have volunteered to take them in. I have a brother ten miles outside of London. He took two of them, and he enjoyed having them so much that he's taking in four more."

"You must be proud of him."

"Well, of course I am. But it's the sort of thing we have to do."

Brodie watched as the children were taken down to the Underground before he hurried on. He kept scanning the skies for bombers, but none appeared. As he walked, he thought suddenly of Bernie Cox. He had never gotten over the death of the young airman who had been his friend. When Bernie had died, Brodie had lost some of his own life as well, and he couldn't get over it. He still dreamed about the nightmarish incident when he had let his friend get killed. This in turn had opened him up to thoughts that he had seldom had before—thoughts of God and of eternity.

Now he came within sight of the mission building and gave a sigh of relief as he saw it still standing. "Thank God," he muttered, and somehow it shocked him that he had said such a thing. *I've kept God out of my life, and now I come expecting Him to take care of things for me. That's a rotten way to be!*

He entered the mission and asked a man he had met before about Meredith.

"She'll be leaving in a few minutes. She's taking some children out to meet up with foster parents who will take them to the country."

"Where is she, do you know?" He listened to the directions carefully and then went off to find her. He succeeded with some difficulty, and when he saw her, he was relieved. He had not realized he was so worried about her.

"Hello, little lady. Need some help with these young'uns?"

Meredith was surprised. "Yes, I could use some help," she said, giving him a smile. "Here. You take Jeffrey, and then I can handle the other two."

Jeffrey was no more than two or three, and his eyes were huge as he looked up at the tall man who stood before him. "All right if I pick you up, Jeff?"

"Yeth."

Brodie picked the boy up, and soon he and Meredith and two little girls with braids down their backs had found their way out to the street. "Where are you going with them?"

"Only to the Underground. The couple that are taking them will be meeting us there."

"That's a decent thing to do, isn't it?"

"Yes. I'm very proud of our people for helping like this."

Brodie observed how good Meredith was with the children. They were nervous and upset, but her ready smile and her encouraging words and ways helped calm them down.

"The entrance to the Underground is right over there. Oh, and there they are."

Mr. and Mrs. Williams proved to be a couple in their fifties. He was red-faced with a bushy mustache and a pair of bright eyes. His wife was a small woman with determination written on her face.

"Here they are," Meredith said and then introduced each child. "Take good care of them, now."

"We'll do that," Mr. Williams said. He reached out and took Jeffrey from Brodie and asked, "RAF, is it?"

"Yes, sir."

"Well, I wish you'd go back and shoot down a few of those nasty bombers."

"I'll do just that, with your love," Brodie said with a grin.

The children left, herded by the Williamses, and Brodie asked, "What now?"

"I've got to go make a call on an invalid—two of them, as a matter of fact. A man and his wife. They're in their late eighties. They were doing fine until she was hurt in one of the raids. His health hadn't been the best, and she was taking care of *him*. Now he's resurrected himself. A lovely couple."

"Is it all right if I go along?"

"Of course, Brodie." As they walked, she said, "You look—" She started to say "tired," but that didn't seem exactly right, although fatigue did show on him, as she had noticed it did on all the fighter pilots.

"I look what?"

"You look troubled."

"I guess I am, Meredith."

She said nothing as they continued walking, and finally she said, "Let's sit down over there on that bench. The Thompsons aren't expecting me for a while yet."

"All right."

"Would you like to talk about it? What's troubling you, I mean?" she asked.

As a rule, Brodie Lee did not choose to talk about his troubles. He believed that a strong American man should be able to carry his own load. But Meredith had a way of getting him to talk, and almost without realizing it, he began to tell her how the death of Bernie Cox had practically destroyed him. "He was a good friend, and I let him get killed. It was my fault."

Meredith listened without saying anything. He spoke haltingly at first but then the words began to pour out of him, and it soon became evident that the loss of his friend was not his only problem.

"I don't know what's the matter with me, Meredith." Despair tinged Brodie's voice, and he clasped his hands together tightly as if to keep them steady. "I was always a pretty happy-go-lucky guy, but lately it's like I've got this big weight on my shoulders. I can't shake it off, and it gets heavier every day. It makes it hard to do my work." He turned to look at her, and she saw the bleak despair in his face. "I'm afraid I'm going to get somebody else hurt or hurt myself. I can't fly carrying this weight."

"Have you ever read *Pilgrim's Progress*?"

"Read what?"

"*Pilgrim's Progress*. A book by John Bunyon."

"No, but I've heard of it."

"It's a wonderful story. You ought to read it. It's about a man who is in exactly your condition. He has a huge load on his back, and he's staggering under it and about to fall."

"Well, that's about the way I feel. What happened to him?"

"He struggled with the load and tried everything he could to get rid of it, but he finally got someone that told him to go on ahead to a certain gate. And he went, and he kept being guided, and suddenly he looked up and he saw a cross, and Jesus on the cross. And the moment that he looked, the load fell off his back and rolled away into a big hole in the ground that was the tomb of Jesus."

Brodie sat very still. "I wish that could happen to me."

Meredith knew that the time had come for her to speak plainly. "Brodie, it's not very difficult to become a Christian. It can be very difficult to *be* the Christian that you become."

"Kinda like gettin' married, ain't it?"

She looked at him and tilted her head to one side. "What do you mean?"

"Well, I reckon it's pretty easy to get to be a husband. It takes about two minutes, doesn't it, before a J.P. or a preacher? And then a fella has to learn how to act like a husband. Some fellas never do learn it, I reckon."

"It is a bit like that, Brodie. Listen, I know something about what your burden is like. I had it before I became a Christian."

"Well, it must have been easy for you. You didn't have a big bunch of horrible stuff to get rid of like I do."

"It wasn't easy at all because I was proud. I didn't want to ask God for anything, so I stumbled along, and the load got bigger and bigger. I couldn't sleep. I even cried at night sometimes, and then one day I was out in the flower garden picking flowers to dry. I'd just picked a large yellow-and-white daisy, and I was admiring it. And suddenly as I stood there I remembered a verse my mother had embroidered onto a pillow. It said, 'Come unto me all ye that labor and are heavy laden and I will give you rest.'"

Brodie turned to look into her eyes and saw the tears there. "And that was it?"

"I gave up everything I could think of and told God I was sorry for the pride I'd had, and I asked Him to come into my heart. And He did. He's been there ever since that day, Brodie."

"It sounds too easy."

"It wasn't easy for Jesus. He left the throne on high where He had all the angels worshiping Him, and He came down to live like a man. He was hungry and tired, and people insulted Him. The very people He had created ridiculed Him and hated Him, and then He came to die, Brodie. You've read the story."

"Yes, I have. Terrible thing."

"There He was, the son of God, nailed to a cross bleeding and dying and yet that was why He came to this earth. For me and for you and for all sinners. It doesn't matter how much or how little you've sinned. We're all sinners and need to come to the cross."

Passersby stopped to look curiously at the young couple, wondering what they were talking about. The pilot was bent forward, looking down at the concrete beneath his feet, and the young woman was watching him and speaking earnestly.

Neither Brodie nor Meredith was conscious of the passage of time, but Brodie was aware of one thing. The load that was weighing him down was getting heavier—and the more Meredith talked about Jesus, the more miserable he felt. He reflected on his life, but he saw nothing to be proud of. Finally he said, "I'm pretty tired, Meredith. I feel like I've been runnin' all my life."

"I think you're right. You've been running from God. I'd give anything in the world to see you get rid of that load."

He looked up and said, "Don't you have to be in a church or somethin'?"

"Brodie, weren't you listening? I told you I was in the flower garden. God takes people wherever He finds them. If a pilot fell out of his airplane and called on God with all of his heart and meant it, he'd be saved before he hit the ground."

The conversation went on, Brodie avoiding the issue, and more than once he nearly got up and left. But he found he could not. He had been sorry for wrong things before, but now as Meredith began to quote Scriptures to him all about the Lamb of God dying for his sins, he knew he could no longer bear it. "Tell me what to do, Meredith," he pleaded in a voice filled with despair. "I can't live the rest of my life like this."

"I think you know what to do, Brodie. You have to repent. That simply means to turn around and go the other way—God's way. You need to call upon God in the name of Jesus."

"That's all?"

"That's all—if you mean it. It can't be just words. You have to be willing to follow Jesus. There was this rich young ruler who came to Jesus once. Do you know the story?"

"I sure do. Kat told it to me once. Jesus told him to sell everything and come and follow Him."

"That was his problem, but yours isn't money. You don't care any more about money than I do. But you care about doing exactly what you want to do. You want to run your own life, and I think Jesus would say to you, 'Give up your life and let me live my life in you. Become my disciple.'"

Meredith knew when to stop talking and let the Holy Spirit work. She sat there tense and saw the emotions moving across Brodie's face. He was perspiring now, and his hands were trembling. She longed to say something else but felt restrained.

"All right," he said hoarsely, "do I need to get on my knees?"

"No, I don't think so. Let's just pray. I'll pray for you and ask God to receive you, and you, in your own heart, ask God to forgive your sins and tell Him you want to be His. And He'll hear you, Brodie."

He bowed his head and closed his eyes. He heard Meredith's soft voice as she prayed for him, but he was not conscious of her words. His lips began to move, and he began, perhaps for the first time in his life, to really pray. He began to confess to God the things he had done years ago. This went on for some time, and finally he hesitated and then said loudly enough for Meredith to hear him, "God, I ask you to forgive me of every sin, and I ask you to make me a Christian. I want to follow you, Lord Jesus, if you'll show me how. So I give my whole life to you."

Tears ran down Meredith's face, but she did not move. She put her hand on Brodie's shoulder and felt that he was trembling, and then she opened her eyes. Tears were running down his cheeks as well. "That was the right thing to pray, Brodie. I know God has heard you."

"I don't feel a lot different. Well . . . maybe I do."

"How do you feel?"

He straightened up, unaware of the tears that were staining his cheeks. "I feel . . . sorta light."

"You mean that load's gone?"

"You know, Meredith, it is!" He took out a handkerchief and began to wipe his face. "Here, you need this too," he said. "We're a couple of babies, aren't we?"

"No we're not. Welcome to the family of God, Brodie."

He took the handkerchief back. "What do I do now?"

"How did you learn to fly?"

"Why, I studied books and found out everything I could about flyin' and then went up on flights."

"That's what you do. You study the Bible. You pray. You talk with me and other believers. Oh, how happy Kat will be to hear about this tonight!" she exclaimed, and her eyes danced.

The two got up and started down the street toward the Thompsons' place, and Meredith reached out and took his hand. She squeezed it and said, "I'm so proud of you, Brodie! So happy."

"Me too."

They hadn't gone far when suddenly Brodie stopped dead-still and pulled her to a halt. "There's an air-raid siren," he said. "We've gotta find shelter."

"There's a shelter two blocks down. Come on."

The two started running, but it was Brodie who heard the scream of the Stuka bomber. He had never heard one before, but when he looked up, he saw the airplane coming straight down, and the siren was screaming like a banshee. "We won't make it!" he cried.

"We've got to try!"

But there was no time. The bomb from the Stuka exploded somewhere to their right with a tremendous explosion. The Stuka carried only one bomb, but it could be accurately placed.

Brodie looked up and saw another plane, this time on their left. "Run!" he yelled. "We gotta get away from him!"

But they did not get away. The bomb exploded, and suddenly broken glass filled the air. The windows had blown out of all the businesses over to their left, and the force of the explosion threw both Brodie and Meredith down. The air was filled with flying bricks, one of which struck Brodie on the shoulder as he tried to get up.

"Meredith!" he cried and blinked his eyes against the swirl of dust. He turned her over and saw that she had been struck by the flying glass. Her chest was covered with blood, but it appeared the wound was in her upper arm. He tore the fabric from her sleeve and exposed a deep cut. Quickly he yanked his necktie off and tied it above the wound. As he leaned forward to secure the tie, he realized she had another cut on her scalp, which was also bleeding freely.

He picked her up and staggered down the street, looking for an ambulance or anyone who could help. There were screams all around him, and the echoes of walls falling seemed very near.

He stopped when he heard Meredith call his name.

He looked down and saw blood on her lips, and he was horrified that she might have some internal injuries. "What is it?" he cried out.

She whispered something, and he could not hear. He put his ear to her lips. "What is it, sweetheart?"

"If I die . . . I want you to know . . . that I love you."

Brodie uttered a short cry and then held her tight. He ran down the street and flagged down an ambulance that was driving slowly down the street. When a man dressed in white jumped out, Brodie said, "She's hurt bad!"

"Here. Put her in the back. Let me check those wounds."

Brodie helped put Meredith in the back, and her eyes were closed. "I'm going with you," he said.

"All right, Lieutenant. Let's go, Harry, and make it fast!"

★ ★ ★

She seemed to be in a deep, dark pit, for everything was black and there was only muffled sound. From time to time, she would recognize faraway voices. One of them sounded vaguely familiar.

There was a faint light in the distance, and she tried desperately to find her way to it. It was as if she were trying to climb out of a deep well. Gradually the light became brighter, and the voices clearer. She began to feel pain in her arm and in her leg and then in her head. It was not terribly bad, but she moaned slightly and as soon as she did, she heard a voice.

"Meredith—can you hear me?"

Meredith opened her eyes and everything swam for a moment, and then the features of Brodie Lee settled into place. "Brodie."

"Thank God you're all right!"

Meredith was trying to understand what was happening. She was lying on a bed between sheets. She tried to raise her right arm and found that it was bound, somehow, so that she could not lift it.

"Don't try to move," he said.

He put his hand on her forehead very lightly. "Do you remember what happened?"

"No—yes! It was a bomb. I remember the bombs falling."

"That's right, but you're gonna be all right."

"How long have I been here?"

"The bombing was yesterday. They had to do some patchin' up on you." She saw Brodie's face loom over her and felt his kiss on her cheek. She lifted her free hand, and he caught it and held it. "You had me scared," he said, shaking his head.

Meredith was remembering things clearly now, and she smiled. "I remember you asked God to save you."

"That's right, I did. I don't guess I'll ever have any trouble rememberin' where I got saved."

"I won't forget it either."

"Do you remember what you said to me after the bomb went off?"

"No, not really. It's all sort of mixed up."

"You told me you loved me. I'll never forget that either.

Look, Meredith, we talked about this once. Do you remember?"

"Yes, I do."

"You said you'd never marry a man who wasn't a Christian. Well, I'll never be as good a Christian as you are, but I intend to serve God the rest of my life. And one of these days, I'm gonna talk to you about marriage some more. I don't think we've exhausted the subject. It's different now."

Meredith reached up and put her hand on his cheek, and he covered it with his own. "Yes," she whispered, "it is different now!"

CHAPTER TWENTY-TWO

SKIRMISH OVER FRANCE

★ ★ ★

"Come in, Brodie." Parker stood up from where he had been working at his desk. "I've been hearing some good things about you." The squadron had been out on a sortie when Parker had returned to take up his duties early that morning. He motioned toward the chair. "Have a seat. I want to hear all about it."

Brodie grinned broadly as he sat down. "Well, I guess you heard. I hit the Glory Road."

Parker laughed. "Well, I didn't hear it put exactly like that, but some of the men told me you'd become a Christian. I think that's wonderful, Brodie."

"I've got a long way to go, Skipper. I don't want to make a pest of myself, but to tell you the truth, I feel like catchin' guys who are just walkin' around and tellin' 'em what it's like to be saved. I never knew it could be like this."

"Tell me all about it," Parker said. He sat down and listened as Brodie spoke of his experience. When he had finished, Parker said, "So Meredith is all right?"

"Just has to do a little healin' up."

Parker looked at the American with a question in his

eyes. "You know, I always thought that you might have wound up marrying Katherine."

"I tried hard enough, as you well remember, but she had the good sense to send me packin'. But Meredith is different. She's gonna marry me one of these days, even if I have to hog-tie her."

Parker laughed. "I don't think that'll be necessary."

"How are you feelin'? Your eyes okay?"

"They're fine. That rest did me a lot of good." He hesitated, then said, "We've got an unusual mission coming up, Brodie."

"You mean somethin' besides shootin' down Germans?"

"No, we'll be doing that but in a different way. We'll be flying cover for a bomber group that'll be going to hit the Luftwaffe airfield in France."

"That'll be different."

"That's right. Always before we've had the advantage in range. When the 109s come over here, they only have ten or fifteen minutes' fighting time before they have to scoot back. This time we'll be doing about the same. I want to talk to every man in the squadron about conserving fuel. I don't want anybody running out over Germany or over the Channel coming back."

"I've been wonderin' when we're gonna get equipped with auxiliary gas tanks. That way we could go deep into Germany as escorts."

"They're not perfected yet, but they will be someday."

The two men sat talking quietly, and finally Brodie got up and said, "Well, I'm goin' back to see if I can get a bunch up to go to church Sunday mornin'. They're already startin' to run when they see me comin'. I heard Al Tobin say, 'Look out! Here comes that religious nut!'"

"You just live the life and they'll respect you, Brodie."

★ ★ ★

The mission turned out to be more difficult than any of the pilots had imagined. They joined a group of thirty Lancaster bombers and did some maneuvering to confuse the Germans. When they were over the target, Parker called, "Look out! Here they come dead ahead!" Enemy planes were rising to meet them. "We've got to keep 'em off of the bomber boys until they drop their loads, so heads up!"

The fight that ensued was as fierce as anything Parker had ever seen. The 109s kept coming into the fight, their engines snarling and guns firing, and Parker and the others had to continually keep an eye on their fuel gauges.

Brodie found himself on the tail of a 109 and gave it three short bursts. It caught fire at once, but just as Brodie broke away, he ran into three 109s that had made him their target. It took all of his skills and acrobatic flying to get away from them. *I'm lucky these Spits have a much shorter turning radius than the 109,* he thought. He glanced over and saw that Sailor Darley and David Deere were fighting for their lives against a swarm of 109s. *We'd better get out of here quick!* He joined in the fray, conserving ammunition as much as possible, but finally he saw that they were overwhelmed.

"Red Leader, Red Leader, I'm about out of ammo, and fuel too!"

No reply came over the radio, which was unusual. Parker was always quick to answer when he was called.

"Has anybody seen Red One?" Brodie demanded.

Archie Kent-Wilkins spoke up. "He got hit, I think."

"Did you see him go down? Where is he?" Brodie demanded.

"I don't know. I think he might've been hit, but I was in a fight and I couldn't keep my eye on him. But you know Parker. He'd call back if he could."

There was no time to delay. No one except Kent-Wilkins had seen anything of Parker, and Brodie had a sinking sensation as the Spitfires started herding the bombers back over the Channel.

"Didn't anyone see anything?" Brodie asked on the radio.

"I didn't see any parachutes," Sailor said. "We'd best go back to the base before we get bounced by some more 109s."

Brodie was half tempted to go back and look, but he knew that was hopeless. He would be instantly gobbled up by the 109s.

★ ★ ★

The hospital was busy, and when Brodie went to Meredith's room, he found her sitting up in bed, with Kat in the chair beside the bed.

"Brodie, it's good to see you," Kat said.

"Hello, Kat." Brodie went over and took Meredith's hand. "How do you feel?" he asked stiffly.

"Oh, I'm fine." She could sense immediately that something had happened. "What's wrong, Brodie?"

He pulled off his hat and twisted it around in his hands. "I've got some news that's not good."

Kat straightened up. "What is it?" she asked quietly.

"It's . . . it's Parker. He didn't make it back from a sortie over France." He stumbled as he gave them the bad news and finally said almost angrily, "None of us really saw anything. We were outnumbered about five to one, so we were all pretty busy."

"No one saw him go down?"

"Archie did, but he didn't see the plane crash," he said quickly. "And none of us saw any parachutes."

Kat went numb. She started to stand up, but her knees felt too weak to hold her. She wanted to ask Brodie so many questions, but she instinctively understood that he had no solid answers to give. Finally she found the strength to collect her thoughts and get to her feet. "I'll leave you two alone. I have to get back to the mission. I'm glad you're all right, Brodie. And it's wonderful news about your becoming a Christian."

"Don't give up, Kat," he said. "He most likely crash-landed the Spit. He's probably been taken prisoner by this time. It'll take a while to find out where he is."

Kat tried to smile, but it was with an effort. "I wonder if

they'll send someone to tell his family."

"I suppose they will. They always do."

Kat turned to leave, but Brodie stopped her. "You know, I haven't read much of the Bible, but I remember hearin' that somewhere in there it says if two or three people agree on somethin', it'll be done."

"That's right," Meredith said quickly. "It's in the Gospel of Matthew, the eighteenth chapter. Let me see." She took her Bible off her bedside table and opened it. "Here it is in verse nineteen. 'Again I say unto you, that if two of you shall agree on earth as touching any thing that they shall ask, it shall be done for them of my Father which is in heaven. For where two or three are gathered together in my name, there am I in the midst of them.'"

When she had finished reading, he said, "Well, I reckon we'd better do just that. Come on. Let's get to prayin'. God can do anythin'."

The three joined hands and prayed for Parker, each one of them in turn, and when they said amen, Kat's eyes were moist. "It's times like these when you need faith. When the sun is shining it's easy, but doubt comes when things don't look too good."

"Well, I'm believin' God's gonna take care of our boy," Brodie said.

Meredith reached up and took his hand. "We'll all remember that."

Kat turned to leave, but Brodie stopped her once more. "Oh, I guess you'd better hear this too." He took Meredith's hand and held it. "Meredith and I are kind of tentatively engaged."

"Tentatively engaged? What kind of engagement is that?" Kat asked as she smiled at the two.

"It means we're goin' until we get a red light, but for me right now it's green as grass."

"Congratulations. I know you two will be very happy." She went over and kissed Meredith and then Brodie on the cheek. "You see? If you'd had your own way, you would've married me long ago and I would've nagged you to death by this time. I'm happy for you both. I'll see you later. I've got to go."

★ ★ ★

Kat had not known whether to go talk to Parker's parents or not. She thought perhaps it would be better to wait for the official news. But finally she called the station and an officer there told her that someone had gone out in person to give the news.

She could think of nothing but Parker, and finally she felt strongly that she needed to be with the family. She left the mission and hired a cab to take her to Benleigh. It was expensive, but she felt it was the right thing to do.

She paid the driver and walked up the front steps. She rang the doorbell, and Parker's mother answered it.

"Come in, my dear," Grace said, her face frozen in misery.

Kat stepped inside and put her arms around the older woman. "It's going to be all right," she said. "God's going to watch over him."

Grace began to tremble, but she got control of herself. "Gregory's in the parlor with the twins."

"You haven't told them anything, have you?"

"No."

"That's good. They don't need to be in on this."

The two of them walked back into the parlor, and the twins ran to her, their faces happy and their eyes dancing. "Story! Give us a story!"

"I will before I leave, but right now I need to talk to your grandparents."

"You two go play in the playroom, and Miss Katherine will tell you a story pretty soon," Gregory said.

As soon as the children were gone, Gregory said, "I'm glad you came, Katherine."

"I didn't want to intrude."

"How could you do that?" Lord Braden got to his feet

and came over and embraced her. The gesture touched Kat, and she squeezed him and whispered, "It's going to be all right. God's going to take care of us. I just know He is."

The three sat down before the fire, and there was little to say. They all knew the details that were available, and it was Grace who said, "I'm so glad you came, Katherine. We've missed you."

A lump came to Kat's throat. She was shocked to find out how much she had come to care for these two. Clearing her throat, she said, "Would you like for me to stay for a day or two?"

"Oh, that would be wonderful! Can you get the time off?"

"I'm not scheduled at the hospital until Thursday. I think this is something I really need to do. Let me go call my supervisor at the mission."

Five minutes later Kat came back and said, "It's all right. I can stay."

Relief washed across Grace's face. "You are so good with the children," she said.

"Well, I'll go tell them that story I promised them."

When Kat had left the room, Gregory said, "There's a young woman with a very compassionate heart."

"She's in love with Parker, of course."

"Do you think so? After all this time? I knew he was attracted to her, but I didn't know how she felt."

"It's written all over her face." She glanced toward the door and whispered, "I'm so glad she's come."

CHAPTER TWENTY-THREE

EJECT!

★ ★ ★

As soon as the engine stopped, Parker knew he was not going to make it. The big Merlin engine had taken a short burst from a 109. At first Parker thought it would be all right, but then the engine coughed and the propeller began to windmill.

"Got to get away from this fight." He had little control over the plane, but as it descended, he held on to the stick and managed to keep the plane in a controlled glide. He glanced in his mirror and saw that the squadron was engaged in a fierce fight, but apparently none of the enemy saw him slip away. He searched the earth below, trying to find a grassy field where he could land.

As his descent grew more erratic, he realized he wasn't going to be able to land the plane. He released his seat belt and slid the canopy back, the wind roaring in his ears. He managed to turn the plane over, and he fell out as it did. He had heard of men getting caught by the tail, so he was careful to be well clear of the plane before pulling the rip cord. The chute opened, jerking Parker upward.

He could hear the snarl of the guns in the distance, but

he was already several miles from where the action was taking place. As he floated down, he scanned the area for enemy activity. He was heading for an open field, which was always dangerous.

I've got to hide the chute and get away as fast as I can. I'm not about to spend the rest of this war in a German prison camp.

He tried to recollect everything he had learned about making parachute jumps, but all he could remember was to land with the knees slightly bent to take the shock. The ground came up very quickly, and he hit with enough force to drive him to the ground. Rolling over, he was dragged along with the parachute as it bellowed out in the wind. He got up and pulled at the cord to collapse the chute, then gathered it up as best he could and ran for the nearby woods.

He was almost there when a voice rang out, "Halt!"

Parker groaned bitterly but did as he was told. Two German soldiers were coming out of the woods to his left. He put his hands up when he saw the bigger German aiming a Luger at him.

"Englishman, you have killed your last soldier of the fatherland!" the man declared in heavily accented English.

Parker nodded wearily. "It looks like you've got me. I guess I'll sit out the war in one of your camps."

The big man sneered. "Nein, not in a camp. Your war is over right now. My two brothers were killed by the RAF, so now I do something for them."

The smaller soldier spoke to his comrade in German, and Parker could only hope he was arguing against shooting him.

"Nein, Hans. I will shoot him myself. Why should he live when my brothers are dead? Say your prayers, Englishman."

Parker looked at the muzzle of the Luger. It seemed to grow larger, and a great weariness overcame him. *So it ends here*. Strangely enough, though, he felt no fear.

The second soldier evidently made another plea, this

time gesticulating wildly and seeming to get angry, but the other shook his head sharply.

"No. I kill him now."

Scarcely were the words out of the big soldier's mouth when a black spot appeared over his left eyebrow just as a gunshot rang out. The big man's eyes rolled up and he slumped backward, falling limply to the ground.

The smaller soldier immediately began to fire his own weapon, but then he doubled up and fell to the ground as well.

Parker whirled to see three people coming out of the woods—two men and a woman, all of them armed. One of them spoke to him in French, but when Parker shook his head, the man said in rather bad English, "Your lucky day, pilot."

"Yes, it is. Who are you?"

"Who do you think?" the woman said. "We're partisans."

"Well, you saved me for sure. He was going to kill me."

"The pig!" spat the other man, who wore the rough clothes of a peasant. "We've got to get rid of them, Jacques."

"You two do that," the woman said, "and I'll get this soldier out of sight."

"You come with me!" the woman snapped and started running toward the woods. Parker ran after her, scanning the area for the enemy.

When they reached the cover of the woods, she asked, "What's your name?"

"Parker Braden."

"My name is Marie. The smaller man is Jacques, my husband. Victor is our friend."

"How did you happen to be looking for me? You got here so quick."

"We always patrol the land under a battle. We were watching the fight in the sky."

Parker looked up and saw the distant air trails left by his squadron as they had escorted the bombers back.

"Is there any chance of my getting back to England?"

"You're alive."

"And I'm grateful for it."

Marie led him to a very old little house with smoke coming from the chimney. "We'll wait here for Jacques and Victor."

"Is this your house?"

"It belongs to a couple who are friends of ours, but they're dead now." Her lips twisted. "They were shot by the Germans. They accused them of being partisans, but they weren't."

She stepped into the house and Parker followed her. It was a typical French farmhouse, but it was sparsely furnished and quite run down.

"Sometimes the English will fly a plane in here after dark. They tell us about it on the radio that we all share. They land and take pilots like yourself back."

"Can you contact them?" he asked.

"We'll have to find out where the radio is right now. In the meantime you're going to have to stay hidden."

Parker was curious. "This is very dangerous work you're doing," he said. "Why are you helping us?"

"The Nazis killed my parents," she said bitterly, "so I do what I can to get the swine out of my country! We'll have to get you some different clothes. There should be something that fits well enough in the back bedroom. You can't wear that uniform."

★ ★ ★

Marie and Jacques watched out for Parker for two days, shuffling him from one house to another anytime they got word that Germans were nearby. Parker spent most of his time alone, praying fervently for a way to get home to his children. Even though he knew his parents were looking after the twins, it just didn't seem fair for his children to lose both their mother and father in such a short period of time. Much to the French couple's dismay, he fasted on his second day with them, spending much time on his knees pleading for a way to get out of France.

On the third morning, Parker woke up to the sound of the wind howling against the windowpanes in the attic where he had slept. He looked out the small window and couldn't see any blue above the dense trees.

He washed up quickly and joined Jacques and Marie in the kitchen for bread and cheese, asking them for any information they had about the war in the immediate area. In turn Parker shared what he knew about the British effort.

"The Germans are thick around here," Jacques said.

"Have you been able to set up any sort of rendezvous with a plane coming in?"

"No. We only have the one radio in our group, and the man who had it last was taken and shot the same day. They don't waste time with us," Jacques said bitterly. "There's no such thing as a trial or other little things like that."

After they had finished eating, Jacques said, "I'm going to take a look around—see if there's any activity nearby."

Marie called after him, "Be careful, Jacques."

"I always am."

Marie went to the stove and poured herself a cup of coffee. "Do you want some?"

"Please."

"This is the last of the coffee. It's hard to get coffee—and everything else, for that matter." Marie sat down opposite him. She was a small, plain women with no claims to beauty, but there was an intensity about her that set her apart from most women.

"Are you married, Englishman?"

"My wife was recently killed in an air raid."

"Ah." She turned her head to one side. "You have children?"

"Twins. A boy and a girl. They're three years old now."

"Who is taking care of them?"

"My parents—at our family home outside of London." Parker soon found himself telling Marie about his visit to

America and how he had fallen in love with an American woman.

"But you didn't marry her?"

"I wanted to, but she felt that God had something better for her to do. She had a bigger destiny than just being a wife of an ordinary Englishman."

"So she would not marry you?"

"No." He hesitated, then said, "Just recently she came to England."

"Oh, I smell a romance," she said teasingly. She sipped her coffee. "Are you dating her again?"

"No, not really."

"But your wife is dead. Now you can be together."

"I don't think so, Marie."

"I will never understand you English."

"It's probably best not even to try," he said with a grin. "I'm going to spend some more time in prayer today. Let me know if Jacques learns anything."

"I will."

Parker climbed the stairs to the attic and settled onto his knees beside the mattress on the floor. "O Lord," he began, "I am so glad to be alive and in this relatively safe place. Thank you for Jacques and Marie and the others who are looking out for my safety. I thank you that even now you know how this is all going to work out. I believe that you have a plan for getting me to safety, and I am so grateful that you are in charge of this whole situation."

He paused, listening to the wind howl outside the window. "Thank you for the sun and the moon, the wind and the calm." His eyes popped open. "The wind! That's it!" He closed his eyes again. "That's it, isn't it? That's the answer." He calmed himself down and listened patiently for God's voice.

After a few moments he stood up and ran down to the kitchen, where Marie was peering out the window. "Marie," he started, "there must be a number of small boats up along the coast."

"Small boats. Ah, you are thinking of going across the

Channel. That would be nice, but the coast is patrolled very well. German patrol boats go back and forth constantly. In the daytime, of course, planes watch every move."

"I'm pretty good with a sailboat. If I could borrow a boat, I could sail across the Channel and be home."

"I'm telling you, the enemy watches very carefully," she insisted. "I think it's best to wait until a British plane lands."

"Marie, when I was upstairs praying just now, God impressed upon me that I was to find a sailboat. I know it sounds risky, but I have to believe the idea came from God. And if the idea came from God, it has to succeed!"

She looked skeptical, but she tilted her head and furrowed her brow in thought. "There is one big house on the coast, built by a wealthy Swiss man. He was a stockbroker, but he's now back in Switzerland."

"Did he have a boat?" Parker asked quickly.

"Yes. Two or three boats, in fact."

"Are any of them sailboats?"

"Yes, one of them is a small sailboat." She looked at him seriously. "It would be very dangerous."

"No more dangerous than what I've been doing every day."

"You're convinced this idea is from God?"

"Yes, I'm sure of it. I'm a danger to you anyway."

"Come, we will ask Jacques what he thinks."

★　★　★

Jacques was not hard to persuade. He was a rather pragmatic fellow, and when Parker told him what he wanted to do, he shrugged. "We can try it. We'll help you get to the coast, but I'll warn you again that they patrol these waters very closely."

"With these clouds covering the moon, that'll help."

"Do you want to try it tonight?"

"Yes, definitely. If the wind keeps up into the night, it'll take me no time to get across the Channel."

"All right. After supper we'll make our way to the coast—it's only about four kilometers from here. Then when it gets dark, we'll break into the boathouse and get the sailboat."

"Thank you so much. I'll never forget the kind French people who saved my life."

★   ★   ★

"Don't make so much noise," Marie whispered. She handed the crowbar to Jacques, and he began to pull the hasp off the doors to the boathouse.

"It's impossible to do without making a little noise," he whispered. "Besides, we know there's nobody in the house right now."

"Yes, but we need to be quiet anyway," Marie insisted. "Don't be any louder than you have to."

Parker had a pistol in his hand, the Luger Jacques had taken from the dead German who had wanted to kill Parker. His nerves were at a fine pitch, but he was excited. This was better than sitting and waiting for someone to come and get him. "Can you get it off?"

"Yes." The hasp came free, and Jacque flung the doors open.

The three entered the boathouse, and Marie lit the torch she had brought.

"There! That's what I want!" Parker said.

"Are you sure you want that little boat?" Marie asked. "I'd be afraid it would swamp."

"It won't if he knows how to handle it," Jacques said. "I've seen our Swiss friend take it out many times."

"It looks like everything is here," Parker said as he checked the boat over. "I used to spend a fair amount of time sailing back before the war started."

They hauled the sailboat out of the boathouse and slid it onto the beach.

"I can't thank you two enough for what you've done."

"You can do us a favor, then. Kill more Germans," Jacques said with a grin.

"That American woman we talked about," Marie said. "Don't let her get away again like you did the first time."

"Thank you for that advice, Marie. When I get back to England, I'm going to have a plane come back and bring you what you need. I've got the list you gave me. You'll have radios and all the other things you said you could use."

"We'll be waiting for the drop," Jacques said. "Now be on your way. You need to get far away from here as fast as possible."

"God go with you," Marie said.

"And God be with you both." Parker shook hands with Jacques and then pushed the boat into the water, climbing in as he did so. He ran the sail up and began to paddle. The wind caught the sail immediately and he felt the boat surge forward; then the darkness closed around him.

It was the best of all nights, he thought as he cut through the dark water. He thought of the many times he had sailed merely for pleasure. *I'm sailing for my life now.* He could hear nothing but the slapping of the waves against the hull, and the wind among the sails was like the rustling of silk.

Get me home, God, he prayed and then settled down. There was nothing he could do except pray and steer the boat. The best of all outcomes would be if he managed to elude the Germans long enough to be picked up by an English boat. He looked up into the skies and saw a solitary star shining out from a break in the thick clouds. He remembered a nursery rhyme that his nanny had taught him, and he whispered it:

"Star light, star bright
First star I've seen tonight.
Wish I may, wish I might
Have the wish I wish tonight."

He laughed. He was overcome with gratitude that he was close to freedom and hadn't ended up in a German POW camp. Whatever happened now would be up to God.

CHAPTER TWENTY-FOUR

No Higher Calling

★ ★ ★

"... And so the big black bear and the little white bear laughed, and they ran away so that the hunters were never able to catch them. And they lived happily ever after."

"Another story!"

"No, Heather. That's all the stories for right now. I'll tell you another story this afternoon." Kat had gotten into the habit of telling the children a story to begin the day as well as one before their nap and one at bedtime.

"Come on, children," Mrs. Henderson said as she came into the bedroom. "Let's get you dressed."

Kat went downstairs and found her way to the kitchen. She sat down at the table with Gregory and Grace. "That is absolutely the worst-looking robe I have ever seen, Lord Braden," she said with a grin.

"I'm going to have to steal it from him and get rid of it," Grace said. "It's his security blanket."

"Let me get you some coffee, my dear," Gregory said and started to get up.

"No. I'll get it." She went to the stove and poured some coffee into one of the china cups. The three of them sat and talked about the children. She had been there for four days, and there had been no news at all about Parker. His parents had tiptoed around mentioning his name, Kat had noticed, but she herself spoke about him as if he were just away on a short visit.

"After the war is over," she asked, "what have you and Parker planned to do about the cattle?"

"We haven't made any specific plans," Gregory said. "Parker has always liked the farm better than the factory. He always talks about getting more land."

"Yes, that's right," Grace said with a nod. She started to say something else, then apparently changed her mind. "What about your friend Meredith?"

"Oh, she's going to marry Brodie."

"That was rather sudden, wasn't it?" Grace asked.

"I think it was, but Brodie's a different man since he found the Lord."

"From what you've told us about him, he must have been a rather wild young fellow," Gregory commented.

"Yes, he was, but he'll have a good wife to keep him straight now."

The morning sun was streaming through the windows, and Grace suddenly said, "I don't know what we would have done without you, my dear."

"That's right," Gregory agreed. He reached over and patted her hand. "The children are so good with you. They don't listen to a thing I say."

"That's because you spoil them," Grace teased.

Kat was feeling restless. "I think I'll go over to the pastures and see the new calf."

"And Hercules?" Gregory grinned. "You love that animal still."

"Well, I guess I do." She took Gregory's hand and held it in both of hers. "He's going to come home, Gregory," she said quietly. She looked into his eyes and then turned to Grace. "We mustn't give up on God."

The couple sat there as Kat left the room; then they watched her out the window as she headed for the pastures.

"If only Parker had married her," Gregory said with a sigh.

"It would have been different, wouldn't it?" The two sat there for a time and finally Gregory got up and said, "Well, I'm going to get dressed. I can't wear this ratty old robe all day."

Grace shook her head. "You've got two more robes practically new."

"Well, I like this one," Gregory said firmly and left the room on that note.

★　★　★

The sun was warm on her face as Kat stood beside Hercules, stroking his back. From time to time he lowered his head to pull mouthfuls of fresh grass and chew them slowly. She put her hand out, and he licked her palm. "You always did do that, Hercules."

The buzz of engines caught her attention, and she looked up. A flight of bombers was making its way northward across the sky, and she watched until it disappeared over the horizon. She leaned against the huge bulk of Hercules and prayed as she had been doing almost constantly. First her prayers had been frantic, demanding God's attention, but that had changed. For the past two days she had continued to pray, but somehow in her spirit she knew God was with her in a special way. Even now her prayer was not an insistent begging for God to bring Parker back but rather a time of thanksgiving.

One of the Scriptures she had long treasured was the verse in First Thessalonians that said simply, "In every thing give thanks." It had taken her some time to puzzle that out. At one time she had struggled with the concept of how to give thanks for something that seemed to be all bad. But the Lord had gradually revealed to her that the verse did not say, "*For* every thing give thanks" but "*In* every thing give thanks." And now she knew that was what she was doing.

She was thanking God not only for His blessings but simply for who He was.

She had learned to praise Him silently at times. At other times she would sing hymns under her breath or even aloud. Now she began to sing her favorite hymn, "When I Survey the Wondrous Cross." She knew all of the verses and was singing "love so amazing, so divine" when she heard a voice calling her name.

It was Parker!

Turning, she saw him running toward her and with a glad cry she flew to greet him. He picked her up in his arms, swung her around, and then began showering her with kisses.

He put her down and pulled away to look at her face. "Please don't cry, my darling."

"Parker, I knew you were alive. I just knew it!"

"It's a miracle that I'm back here at all."

"Did you stop in the house and see your parents?"

"Yes. I thought Father was going to pick me up and carry me around the room." He laughed and shook his head. "They're still shouting, I think, but Mum made me come out and tell you."

"Come along," she said. "Let's go back inside."

But Parker took her arm and turned her around. "You must know I love you. I've loved you since I first met you. I can't lose you, Katherine."

She looked up and smiled. "You're not going to lose me." She pulled his head down and kissed him. "I found out something about myself over these past few days, Parker. Being with Paul and Heather and with your parents touched something deep in my heart. And I've been praying as I never have before."

"Praying for what?"

"To know what to do. That's always been a problem for me, hasn't it? But this time I know. The Lord let me pray for a long time, but now I know what He wants me to do with my life."

"The high calling?"

"Yes. I've been searching my heart and searching the Bible, and during this time, which has been so hard, Parker, one verse jumped up at me out of the Scripture. It's in the forty-fifth chapter of Jeremiah, the last verse. It's just one little phrase. It's something that Jeremiah said to a man called Baruch."

"What did he say?"

"He said, 'Seeketh thou great things for thyself? Seek them not.'" She smiled tremulously. "And then it was all so simple, Parker! It was like God opened a window in my soul and poured light into me! I'd been looking all my life, it seemed, for some great high calling. I always thought it would be something *big*, something that would be in all the newspapers. But during these last days here with your family and seeking God, I know what my high calling is."

"And what is it, then?" Parker asked quietly.

"The high calling is serving in whatever place God puts you in. Serving Him with all your heart no matter how small or insignificant the place may seem to you. And now I have a question for you."

"Ask me anything."

Kat smiled and put her arms around his neck. "Will you marry me, Parker?" She laughed aloud as she saw the shock in his eyes. "Because I know now that God wants me to be a wife and mother. There is no higher calling than that."

He put his arms around her and held her tight. Her cheek was pressed against his chest, and they stood there holding on to each other. Finally he whispered, "I've never stopped loving you deep in my heart."

They started walking toward the house. "When will we marry, then?" Parker asked.

"Oh, we'll have to wait long enough for it to be acceptable."

"We've wasted too much time. I want to marry you now."

"Well, you can't. You'll have to wait a little longer—but maybe not too long."

"Do you know what Father said to me when I was back at the house?"

"No. What did he say?"

"He slapped me on the shoulder and said, 'Don't be a dunce, Parker. Go down and propose to that woman at once.'"

"And I beat you to it."

She took his arm and turned him around, her eyes dancing. "I'll have to practice my English accent."

"No, you don't have to practice anything, Katherine. You just stay exactly as you are."

And then she broke into a run.

"Don't run off and leave me!" he called as he caught up to her.

"Don't worry. I'll never leave you—and you will never leave me."

As they ran they saw Parker's parents waiting for them, and Parker cried out, "I did just as you said, Father!"

As Kat was embraced by her in-laws-to-be, she knew with a deep and joyous certainty that she had at last found her high calling.

A Poignant Novel Based on the Captivating Story Behind

"It Is Well With My Soul"

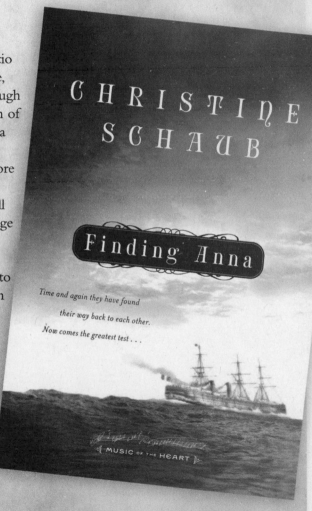

Finding Anna follows Horatio Gates Spafford and his wife, Anna, as they struggle through their losses in the aftermath of the Chicago fire. He plans a European holiday with his family to get away, but before he can board the ship, he receives a telegram that will delay his crossing and change his life forever.

When tragedy brings him to his knees, he writes a poem on the back of a telegram—words that have become a hymn of hope for millions facing sorrow.

Finding Anna by Christine Schaub
www.christineschaub.com

DAKOTAH TREASURES

HISTORICAL FICTION
FROM THE HEART OF THE WEST

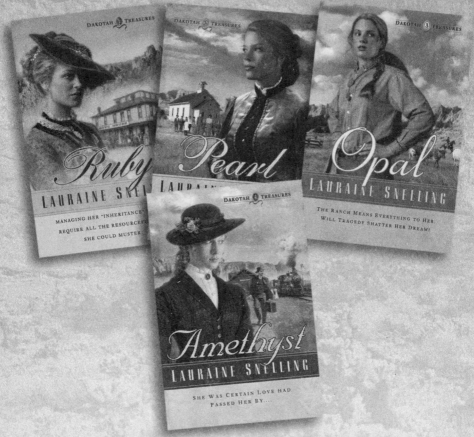

Ruby and Opal Torvald's estranged father has left them an inheritance. Leaving the comfort of New York for the unknown wilds of Dakotah Territory, the sisters soon discover what he left is something quite different from a gold claim. The girls will have to weather the storm of scandal to keep Dove House. As the series continues, Ruby and Opal are joined by a schoolteacher from Chicago with a secret in her past and a newcomer hoping to find her future on the frontier. Lauraine Snelling's bestselling series DAKOTAH TREASURES tells the stories of four women surviving and flourishing in Dakotah Territory. Courage, endurance, and love are at the heart of these wonderful stories.

DAKOTAH TREASURES
by Lauraine Snelling

Ruby • *Pearl* •
Opal • *Amethyst*

◆ BETHANYHOUSE